The past never sleeps.
The truth never dies.
Only Harlan MacKenzie can sense the troubled history of the Big Purple House. When he's hired to restore the historical mansion, he doesn't foresee the secrets—secrets that entangle his family in deceit and murder.

Phaedra is selling the house that has been in her family for decades. As her friends-to-lovers relationship with Harlan escalates, she puts her values on the line and chances losing him.

After a stranger comes to town, weaving her web of deception, hell-bent on correcting an old grievance connected to the house, dark revelations of the past implode the present. Harlan and Phaedra are thrown on a dangerous path, not only risking love but possibly their lives.

D1738566

OTHER BOOKS IN THE MACKENZIE CHRONICLES
Secrets of The Ravine (The MacKenzie Chronicles, book1)

Praise for Secrets of The Ravine

Readers:
Secrets of The Ravine is a mystery gift in a romance box tied with a paranormal ribbon. I loved every minute of it.

What if the spitting image of your long-lost love walked into your place of business? I'd write a book...because it's the perfect introduction to an intriguing mystery.

Do not open this book unless you are prepared to be sucked in, lose track of time, and forget to feed your family!

Reviewers:
NN Light's Book Heaven
Brenda Whiteside is known for writing compelling contemporary romantic suspense (her Love and Murder series) but in this one, there's added depth with the historical mystery sub-plot. Once I started reading, I couldn't stop.

Long and Short Reviews
The plot was creative, interesting and unpredictable and the pace moved along in waves.

Storeybook Reviews
This book has a lot going for it – interesting characters, a mystery to be solved, an attraction between Magpie and Zac, family drama, and so much more. I enjoyed the back and forth in time and between the characters and their memories of the past and the history of Joshua.

For Lin Felix –
Enjoy the read!

Mystery on
Spirt Mountain
The MacKenzie Chronicles, book 2

Brenda Whiteside

The Mackenzie Chronicles, Book Two
Published in the United States

Acknowledgements

As always, my first nod of thanks goes to several women that have been in my life for years. I'd never be able to get a book from my computer to out into the world without them. I rely heavily on my critique partners (in alphabetical order): Tamara Hogan, Joyce Proell, Heidi M. Thomas, and Jody Vitek. These women are all successful authors in their own right, but they give their time willingly and freely to read every paragraph before I go to print. They are such unique individuals that my books benefit from the spectrum of their knowledge and creativity.

Mystery on Spirit Mountain had the benefit of beta readers. My thanks to Gena Anderson. Her input helped smooth out a few wrinkles. And as always, thanks to FDW, my number one beta reader, husband, and partner in all things.

Dedication

For all the kindred souls who believe there is much more than meets the eye in this universe.

CHAPTER ONE

Harlan MacKenzie shifted into park and gazed out the open window of his truck at the Big Purple House. His typical enthusiasm for tackling an historic remodel in the Copper Hills district wouldn't materialize, and he couldn't figure out why. Normally, he thrived on refurbishing the old homes in Joshua, Arizona. But this 1920's mansion seemed blanketed by a dark cloud that obstructed his artistic vision.

Lilac Lane dead-ended at the cracked sidewalk in front of the imposing structure which stood at the base of Spirit Mountain. Although christened Lilac End when built in 1923, as long as he could remember, everyone called the home the Big Purple House. He cut the engine and sat a few minutes longer. He had to overcome this reluctance. The one bright spot might be consulting with the owner, Phaedra, on a regular basis, although the tension between them lately had him doubting they could be more than friends.

Quiet cocooned him. High above the town and insulated by mountains on the backyard side, the sparse noises from main street died before they could invade the neighborhood once populated by mining barons. The homes with wide yards occupied one side of Lilac Lane while the other side sloped down the mountain creating a spectacular view of the town and valley beyond.

He opened his truck door and stepped onto the sidewalk as he dug a silver key from his jeans pocket. Two steps connected the sidewalk to the walkway across the unfenced yard of dead grass.

The walk and steps gaped with cracks and missing chunks of cement. *Dangerous footing.* Shading his eyes from the sun, he surveyed the roof. Too many loose tiles. The flat roof of the wraparound veranda couldn't be seen, but he'd bet it needed reroofing also. At the end of the walkway, seven more steps, cracked but in better shape, brought him onto the veranda, railed with a picket fence effect.

As he ascended the steps, he fingered the key without any sense of the house it would unlock. Sidelight panels displaying dust-encrusted stained glass, flanked the peeling, white, front door. The worn brass doorknob poked from the middle, unusual by today's standards but not for then. To the right, a brass mail slot with the initials JH embossed the tarnished cover. Classic and an original. John Hersey had built this house.

Surveying the exterior again, the door and windows, gave him nothing. Nothing more than it would give any onlooker. Repairs and paint needed. The original façade hadn't been altered. That much he knew from years of experience. But where was the vision he normally embraced when met with the challenge of restoration? Where was his clear feeling? What reason could he have for the roadblock sensation that came over him when he set foot on the property? He curled his fingers around the key.

While waiting for the normal surge of inspiration before entering, he strolled the veranda in one direction until it ended a third of the way around at a long window where the wall jutted out farther. He couldn't see through the heavy curtains, as opaque as the shroud over the house obscuring his perception. Retracing his steps to the front of the house, he tested the varnished wood planks of the floor by pushing his foot down hard with each measured footfall. Not much work would be required on the floor of the veranda, other than refinishing. Better condition than a couple of other houses he'd refurbished in this neighborhood. He stopped to listen, waited for the house to speak to him, but moved on when no clear communication came. *Odd.*

Past the front door, he continued around the other corner to the back of the house. Steps led down to the rear with a view of the mountains. He contemplated the sizeable property. The location at the end of the cul-de-sac allotted more yard than the other homes on this block. From this angle, he could see the tip of the J for Joshua painted on the side of Spirit Mountain. Instead of ruggedly beautiful as the Black Hills normally appeared, today the mountains hemmed in the yard like a barrier, making the property oppressive. He had no desire to investigate the rear of the house in that atmosphere.

He scratched the back of his neck, crossed his arms, and swiveled on his sandal heel to face the front and the view below. On the opposite of Lilac Lane, the land sloped downward to Clark Street where the historic Sacred Heart Catholic Church stood on the corner of the intersection of the two streets. Below Clark, Main Street embodied the heart of Joshua—restaurants, a couple of museums, several wine tasting establishments, gift shops, and historic sites. Beyond, he could see some of the town as it cascaded down the side of Spirit Mountain.

Old man Hersey knew how to pick a view.

The Verde Valley, green as the name implied, spread across the horizon. Only wisps of clouds littered the bright blue sky that met the red, sunbaked mesas beyond the green valley. He took a deep breath of clean mountain air. The air was clear, but the energy residing around this house still felt murky.

He jiggled the key in his hand. Maybe the fog surrounding inspiration would lift if he went inside.

Phaedra counted on him to make restorations before the new owner took possession. Whatever gnawed at his creative core had to be put to rest. Back at the front, he faced the door and decades-old paint. He admired the stained glass. A work of art. Surely the soul of such an old house could speak to him through the craftmanship of the fine details. He closed his eyes a moment but opened them and snorted. *Not giving me anything, are you?* When he finally touched the key to the lock, he took a deep breath to quell his reluctance to enter.

"Are you the owner?"

The voice jarred him, and he dropped the key. He whirled around and met the largest, violet eyes he'd ever seen. Then again, he'd *never* seen violet eyes.

"I'm sorry." She laughed an apology. "I didn't mean to startle you."

"That's okay." He stooped to retrieve the key. His mind must really have been occupied to not hear the green Chevy Cavalier pull up and park behind his truck. "Can I help you with something?"

"I'm not sure. You seem to have a key to the house, although it looks vacant." She squinted at the windows. "Are you the owner?" Her husky voice contrasted with the petiteness of her features.

"No. I'm the renovator. What's your interest, if I might ask?"

"I'm an author. Nora Cook." She offered her hand. "I'm writing a book on unknown historical homes of Arizona."

"Harlan MacKenzie." He shook her hand. "An author? Sounds interesting. How did you find the Big Purple House?"

The corner of her mouth twitched. "The Big Purple House. Appropriate. I saw it as I drove around. There's no way to find these treasures other than hitting the road. Small towns or historical cities like Joshua are the best." Her gaze swept his face. "And I meet the most intriguing people." Thick lashes, a deeper shade of red than the full bangs and chin-length hair framing her face, blinked slowly.

Her obvious flirtatious gesture puffed his chest. *You're an easy mark, MacKenzie.*

"Have you started work on this house yet?"

"No, as a matter of fact—" The white Jeep stopping next to the curb behind Nora's car drew his attention. "Here's the owner, for now anyway." He waved to Phaedra when she hopped from the Jeep.

"For now?"

"Yep. She's selling."

The redhead's eyes widened.

His lifelong friend traversed the cracked sidewalk in strappy, leather sandals, her tight jeans hugging long legs making her appear taller than her five-four height. Her appearance made the sunny day sunnier. When they were kids, golden braids bobbed on her shoulders. At forty-three, silvery-white hair fell to the middle of her back. She wore a flimsy, long-sleeved white blouse tucked in and belted. The swing of her hips caused a stirring he'd recently recognized as a whole lot more than friendship.

"Hey, there." Phaedra greeted him, stepped past Nora, and smiled a question.

"This is Nora Cook. An author. Nora, this is Phaedra Halloway, the owner of the Big Purple House."

The two women shook hands. If the writer hadn't been in heels, he judged she would be the same height as his friend. But their physical appearances were as different as autumn and winter.

"Nora is interested in historical homes. She's writing a book."

"How interesting, but the house hasn't been designated historical."

"I'm not writing about designated homes." The writer waved a hand in the air, pushing that point aside. "Anyone can find those."

"Ah, so an off-the-beaten-path kind of tour book?" Phaedra tilted her head.

"Something like that. I'm particularly interested in homes that are in the original condition. Do you think this house has had any changes over the decades, like additions or, well, structural changes?"

"Doesn't appear to." Harlan answered as Phaedra shook her head.

Nora smiled all the way through her eyes as if that answer pleased her. "Harlan tells me you're selling." She didn't speak directly to Phaedra but scanned the yard as if looking for a realtor sign.

Phaedra shot him a sideways glance, an apparent communication he couldn't decipher. "I haven't listed it. Someone made me an offer, and I decided the time is right to sell."

"An offer. So, they haven't actually purchased it yet."

"No." Phaedra crossed her arms over her chest. "I'm having Harlan restore the property first."

"And no one's living here now." She slid her gaze, the purple glint fastened on him. "How long do you think your work will take?"

Phaedra's brow wrinkled ever so slightly. Harlan guessed she wondered why this woman was so interested in the sale.

He opened his mouth to answer, but Phaedra jumped in first. "The buyer won't be back for a couple of months, so we're not in a huge hurry. Why do you ask?"

"I would just *love* to include Lilac End in my book." She smiled at Phaedra and then dipped her chin in his direction. "I'm hoping you might be able to show me around. Give me some insight before the new owners move in."

"Well, I—"

"How did you know the original name of my property was Lilac End?" Phaedra's stance changed into a wide-leg planted posture. Her lips thinned.

Something bothered her.

"What? Oh, research. That's what we writers do. John Hersey, the original owner, named it that in 1923. All of the mining moguls lived in this neighborhood." She gestured with a sweep of her hand.

Harlan knew some of the house's history, and some old-timers might remember. But Phaedra's wrinkled brow and hesitation in responding told him she found this stranger's knowledge odd.

"Are you going to be around for a few days, Nora? Right now isn't a good time." She sidestepped closer to him.

"As a matter of fact, I am."

"Then maybe we can get back to you." Her dismissive tone came through loud and clear. "Where are you staying?"

"At the Copper Line Hotel for the next few days. It's on Bennett Street."

"I know it." Phaedra flashed her a quick smile that didn't reach her eyes. "Harlan, are you ready for the early lunch I promised?" She looped her arm around his. A whiff of roses floated over him.

They hadn't made lunch plans. For some reason, she wanted to dismiss Nora Cook, and he wasn't about to dispute her. He'd known her long enough to know she had something on her mind. Besides, he always enjoyed time with Phaedra. "Sure am."

Nora's mouth briefly tugged in a pout, but she recovered with a flat smile. "That sounds great. I'll continue my sleuthing around Joshua this afternoon." She slipped a hand into a small pocket on her hip and pulled out a white card. When she turned her attention on him, she raised one brow and batted those thick auburn lashes over the intriguing violet eyes. "I'm in room five, but in case I'm not in, here is my cell number." She tucked the card in his free hand. "So nice meeting you both, and I look forward to seeing you again." With that, she carefully maneuvered the veranda steps in her heels. Only then did he notice the nicely rounded bottom and narrow waist displayed in a fitted blue dress.

"Oh, puh-lease." Phaedra hip-bumped him. "Put your tongue back in your mouth."

He choked on his own saliva. "What? I wasn't." But he had to laugh. "And what is this about lunch? I wasn't even expecting you today."

"I got hungry, that's all." She narrowed her eyes as she watched the writer close her car door.

Jealousy? Friends don't get jealous, do they? "Yeah, well, I'm up for a break. Kind of hungry myself." He pocketed the key. Walking into the Big Purple House could gladly be put off awhile longer.

****

A redhead? Really? Phaedra buckled her seatbelt as Nora Cook's car disappeared around the corner in her rearview mirror. She didn't know Harlan was a sucker for redheads. "She was a peculiar one."

"You mean the violet eyes?" Harlan secured his seatbelt with a snap.

"What? No. And they were dark blue."

"Blue?" He frowned. "Then what was peculiar about her?"

"You didn't feel it? Her curiosity about when the new owner planned to move in for one thing. And how would she know the original name of the house?"

"She said research. She knew who originally owned the house— John Carl Hersey, millionaire gone missing. One of Joshua's more famous mysteries. And I would think curiosity is part of being a writer."

She darted a glance at him before she pulled onto Clark Street. She'd never wondered about his attraction to women. His neutral expression told her nothing. "There was something about her. Sneaky or hiding something." *And flirty, damn it.*

"She seemed nice enough to me."

"Nice enough ass anyway, huh?" It slipped out. Went right from thought to words. Her neck heated.

"What's with you today, Phae? I've never known you to be jealous."

"Why on earth would I be jealous?"

"I don't know. How about you tell me."

A tiny green-eyed monster did a happy dance on her shoulder. "I've had a shitty morning, that's all." But that wasn't quite the whole reason. Why would he understand when she couldn't get her own thoughts around her feelings? He was one of her two best childhood friends, but now a strange sort of chemistry brewed between them. And the round little butt he'd gawked at had her sorry about her recent addition of a few damn pounds.

"What's wrong, Phae?"

"You wouldn't understand. These jeans are a bit too snug and— and—oh never mind." What in Hades was wrong with her? She needed a dam between her thoughts and her mouth.

"Too tight?" His chin dipped as if scrutinizing her legs. "Is this one of those is-my-butt-too-big moments?"

Close friend, yeah, but still a clueless man. I mention snug pants, and you mention big butt. "Do you remember the time in the third grade when I beat the tar out of you for making fun of my braids?" She pulled into a parking space in Upper Park and killed the engine.

"Remember it well."

His deadpan response made her want to laugh, but she swallowed it and flashed him a glare.

"Got it." He opened the door and met her on the sidewalk.

She wasn't really mad at her friend—especially when he stood there, his chin tilted down and the slightest hint of a smirk, giving her his classic Harlan gaze. She couldn't resist a truce in the form of a wink. Taking his arm for the half-block walk to Ghostly Goulash, she appreciated his solid, warm bicep under the cream-colored Henley with the sleeves pushed to the elbows. They trudged the slight incline in silence. Lately, the banter that had always been part of their friendship didn't come as easily as it used to. Maybe because being just his friend no longer satisfied her. She wasn't sure when she'd transitioned to thinking of him as an interesting man instead of a childhood friend. At times, an awkward schoolgirl with a crush took over her body, and she couldn't figure out how to act toward him.

He edged in front of her to get the door and waited for her to enter.

When did he start with the differential actions like opening doors for her? And what in Hades was the tickle in her gut when he did? Not to mention noticing how great his legs looked in cargo shorts.

"You good with sitting on the covered patio?"

She brushed aside her musings. "You bet."

After they ordered their burgers, Harlan frowned and cleared his throat. "Are you sure you want to sell? You wouldn't want to move into the house yourself?"

Shrugging, she shook her head. "I like my bungalow in The Ravine. I don't need a big house." The overhead fans whirled, sending a couple of strands of hair across her face. She tucked then behind an ear.

"Wasn't it your first home in Joshua?"

"Yeah, but I don't remember much about living there. When my folks and I moved here, right after I was born, the Big Purple House was the only thing available and cheap as hell back then. The out of state owners had grown weary of keeping it rented out to hippies."

She spread her napkin in her lap. "Not sure you know the story." She glanced beyond his shoulder as she spoke. From their perch on the side of the mountain, green shrubbery framed the three-foot high patio wall and posts with only blue sky beyond.

"Probably did at one time."

His iced tea and her diet cola arrived. The waitress deposited them on the table without comment.

She called upon memories but also the explanations her mother gave her about the first few years of her life. "My father is the one who uprooted us to Joshua with some get rich quick scheme. When it didn't pan out, he split. Left us high and dry as they say. Which really does describe being deserted in Joshua, doesn't it?" She quirked a smile. Her mother always followed the men in her life, which never proved fruitful. "Mom eventually realized she'd make more money renting out the place, and she moved us to The Ravine." Although not an actual ravine and situated north to south while the town ran east to west, it did sit lower than the rest of the town.

When she moved to The Ravine, the MacKenzie family lived down the block. Homes of various sizes and structural components, haphazardly strung along dirt roads, made up the neighborhood tucked below the Black Hills at one end and Joshua on one side. The area remained virtually unchanged from the late 1800s. When the mines ran too dry to support the town, the residents abandoned the area, and The Ravine lay dormant until the 1960s when hippies and artists descended on Joshua. "I can still conjure memories as far back as age four when I had the run of The Ravine with my two partners in crime, you and Magpie."

Harlan chuckled.

"Here you go folks." The waitress interrupted. "Condiments on the table unless there's something else you need?"

"No, thank you."

"I'm good."

"Mom rented out the house for years." She popped a fry in her mouth. "The year I moved back to Joshua, Mom succumbed to moving away with her new husband. She always gave in to the hubby. She gave me her cottage in The Ravine. I didn't need the Big Purple House."

"But with two girls, didn't you want a bigger place?"

How bizarre they'd been lifelong friends, and yet he had so many

9

questions. They'd lost touch during their college and baby years. When he returned to Joshua, years after her migration back, their friendship rekindled, yet they'd never visited those lost years. She'd have thought his sister, Magpie, would've kept him informed of her life happenings. Magpie kept *her* in the know about Harlan's son and his wife's death. But the sister and brother grew apart when their mother died, so apparently Mags didn't keep Harlan updated on her. "When the last tenants moved out in 1999, I'd just had Poppy. Poppy's father and I, well, we had our issues and worrying about the house wasn't on my radar."

Talking suspended while they ate for several minutes. Subdued chatter from the closest tables whirled around as if stirred by the overhead fans.

"Lilac End," Harlan said. "Too bad the locals saw fit to rename it the Big Purple House."

She snickered. "The renters painted the house purple in the mid-sixties. The hippies liked purple better I guess." She sipped her diet cola. "I can't remember the last time I was inside. How bad is it?"

He took a sudden interest in dipping his french fry in ketchup. "We'll need a cement contractor to replace the sidewalk steps. Maybe repair or replace sections of the walk front and back." Scooping the last of the ketchup with another fry, he kept his eyes averted. "The floor of the wraparound veranda is in decent condition. I might replace a board here and there, but refinishing will spruce it up. I haven't been on the roof yet, but my guess is you need a new one. Of course, the whole house needs painting—"

"Tell me what I don't know."

"I, uh, haven't been inside yet."

She stopped chewing. His discomfort was obvious. "Why not? I gave you the key two days ago."

"I went by that day, but I got a phone call and had to divert to the remodel below the switchback." He washed down the fry with his last swallow of iced tea. "I'd only had time to walk about the outside this morning when you pulled up."

"Morning?" She'd known this man all her life and could certainly tell when he fudged the truth. "The day's half gone." She wasn't irritated. He'd get the job done on time, but her interest piqued at the reason for his hesitancy to begin the work. "Why the stall?"

He grimaced. "I'm not stalling."

The waitress stopped at their table. "Anything more I can get you two?"

He shook his head and fussed with his empty iced tea glass, leaving her to answer. "We're fine."

"Then here's the bill, but no hurry. Thanks for coming in."

Once the waitress turned away, Phaedra thumped the table. "Harlan!"

He jerked his head up. "What?"

"If you're too busy, say so. I can hire someone else."

"Well, if you'd really rather hire—"

"Hell no, I'd not *rather* hire someone—"

"Shh. I'm right here. You don't have to yell." He snatched the bill and pulled out his wallet. "Got it this time." He stood as he tucked two twenties under his knife then shoved the chair under the table. "Ready?"

She followed him out, perplexed by his behavior. This man loved his work. An old house like hers, with origins dating back nearly a hundred years, should have him salivating. They'd have to see each other more often, outside the weekly hikes with Magpie or twice-a-month dinners at his dad's. Most weekends, they met at the Apparition Room when Magpie sang. The outings were never one on one. Now they'd collaborate on the restorations. Just the two of them. She fell into step next to him. The decades of easy friendship they'd shared seemed anything but easy over the last year. Could that be her fault? Could she be forcing some sort of evolution in their relationship he didn't feel? Her stomach churned her burger. She didn't want to lose what they had…but she found herself so *attracted* to him lately.

They reached the car in silence. Standing on the passenger side, he studied her across the hood. "I'm sorry I've dragged my feet, Phae. The house holds challenges for me, and I want to get it right for you."

"You've got time, but as I've heard, time is money. The work's not really for me anyway. Annette just wants the property restored and livable. It's been empty over twenty years. Could be creatures living in there. Who knows what condition the plumbing is in? She'll be in Puerto Rico for at least two more months taking care of whatever wealthy people take care of before they make a major move. Didn't she say once she moves to Joshua, she'll know more about what changes she wants?"

"Yeah." He moved to open the door.

She slid onto her seat and buckled before starting the engine. "Then schedule the work as you need to." She backed out of the parking space. "What challenges, anyway? You haven't even been inside."

"I'll let you know when I get it figured out." He stared straight ahead, his voice firm, ending that line of conversation.

It's not seeing me more, then, that has you in a foul mood? The house is the culprit? Curiosity tickled.

What aren't you saying, Harlan MacKenzie?

****

Nora plumped the pillows against the headboard on the hotel bed, relaxed her back with her legs straight out, and set her glass of wine on the bedside table. She removed the wrapper from the sandwich she bought at the deli and took a bite. With a delicate touch, she lifted the nearly one hundred-year-old journal which had belonged to her great grandmother, Genevieve Jenkins, onto her lap. She'd read it cover to cover while lolling in jail for check fraud.

After her mother died, she had needed a few months of her mother's social security checks to get on her feet. Having your husband dump you and steal your daughter away should count for some leniency. She would've paid it back eventually, once she found a job. Well, hell, she did draw a cracker jack public defender, or she'd have been locked away longer.

The old trunk she'd found in her mother's garage contained bits of the lives of her grandmother and great grandmother. She had only vague memories of her great grandmother, GG, who died when Nora was seven. The journal proved to be a treasure. Gingerly, she lifted the cover and opened the book several pages into the book.

> *February 24, 1924*
>
> *I like most of the girls I work with. Ma Betsy (she insists we call her Ma) takes care of us but won't tolerate no shenanigans from her girls. I want to laugh every time she says that, but I'm not sure what her lack of tolerance might bring me. Today, Ma took us all to the visiting doctor at the Copper Line Hotel. He comes to town once a month. He checked us out*

real good. He was nice. Respectful like. But I get that pretty much from everyone, except from the bible ladies. And maybe some of the rich wives who live high up on Spirit Mountain. They won't even set foot down on our street. Snobby witches. If only they knew about their husbands! But maybe they do. I don't care.

Ma and the girls are more like family than those people I ran away from in Phoenix. Blood don't always make people love you. Ruth and Margaret are going to throw me a party for my birthday next month when I turn sixteen. I can't remember ever having a birthday party—blowing out candles and eating cake! I'm so excited already. I wonder if any of the customers will be invited. I hope not. My first birthday wish is to have a party with just MY FAMILY. Ma and the girls.

There's a nice man I entertained two nights ago. I haven't liked any of the men I've had so far, but this one was different. Most of the miners don't even wash under their nails. The few rich men I've entertained have been weird with their sex requests. Not John. And he was in no hurry. He even told me to call him John. Most the men don't much care what you call them. In fact, they don't want to talk at all. John is very cultured and gentle. I heard Ma whispering to her friend Josie that she hopes John Carl Hersey tells his friends about our house. We need more of his kind of money, she said. I think he liked me too. He was very, what I am going to call, appreciative.

She closed the journal, took another bite of her hoagie then lifted her wine glass. John Hersey had stood on the veranda of Lilac End, right where she'd stood today. He'd descended the same steps on his way to meet GG. As she sipped her wine, a vision of what her relative looked like came to mind. From the back of the journal, she slipped out an ancient, cloudy, black and white photo. Young Genevieve Jenkins resembled Nora so much the image came to life, leaving her breathless as she stared at her GG's face. From entries in the journal, describing her great grandmother's hair as red and her eyes as deep blue, she could color the black and white photo in her mind. With one hand to her chest, and her gaze glued to the picture, she lifted the wine glass. Empty. She poured another. *What the hell. Why not? This was a vacation—sort of—with a mission.*

As she chewed the last bite of the sandwich, she wadded the wrapping and tossed it into the round metal can. With another thought, she set the journal and photo next to her and stood. After downing most of her drink, she slipped out of her clothes and reclined again on the bed. A nap sounded good, and she needed to think about the house, decide how to achieve her goal. Admittedly, she'd jumped off on her quest without much forethought. Now here, she had to get her bearings. With the last swallow of wine, her eyelids grew heavy. "Don't worry, GG. I'll think of something."

CHAPTER TWO

After lunch, Harlan managed to avoid more discussion about his reluctance to begin work on the Big Purple House as Phaedra drove. Maybe when he figured it out, he'd share his insight with her—as much as he could. How he approached a project, the impetus that normally spurred him forward, would be hard to explain. In fact, he'd never discussed his sensations with anyone.

He opened the passenger door but paused when Phaedra shut off the Jeep's engine. "What are you doing?"

"I think I'll check out the house. Today is the first time I've set foot on the property in at least a dozen years." She unbuckled and opened the door. "From the way you're dressed, I'd say you aren't getting any real work done today, so I won't be in your way."

"Was that a dig?"

She chuckled and got out.

Although preferring to walk a house alone the first time to get a feel for how to bring the house back to its original beauty, this house sent up a haze before he'd even gotten inside. Maybe Phaedra's presence would help clear the air since she had a history with the place.

As he came around the car and met her on the sidewalk, her earlier comment about her too snug jeans puzzled him again. She looked damn good—as always. He put his hand to her back as they avoided the missing chunks of cement by the sidewalk steps. His fingertips registered the warm skin beneath the thin blouse. "I did walk the veranda." While they strolled the path across the yard, he left his hand on her, pressing firmer, enjoying the contact. "Like I said, on first look, it's in decent shape."

How many times had he touched her in the nearly forty years they'd been friends? They'd wrestled and rolled around on the ground as kids. A vision of tackling her for the same activity now sent a surge below the belt. He slowed to regain composure as she ascended the veranda steps.

"That's good news." She regarded the rough planks of the porch.

"I'll get it sanded and refinished. If there are any weak spots, I'll find out."

"So…" She gestured, her hand beckoning as if impatient. "Open the door."

He dug the key from his pocket, and she stepped aside while he unlocked and pushed the door open. "After you."

A musty scent greeted them when they entered the foyer. He left the door open for fresh air, not that he found the odor offensive. He liked the smell of old, the smell of history and lifetimes of experience.

"I hired someone to clean the place after the last tenants moved out. Of course, that was a couple of decades ago." She scanned into the parlor to their left and dining room to the right. "A little dusty. Some cobwebs." She gestured at a door directly in front of them to the back of the foyer. "This is obviously a guest closet, but it seems like…"

"What?"

She peeked one direction into the dining room and then shuffled toward the parlor. "I have a vague memory of an office on the bottom floor in this area where Mom would let me sit at a desk and draw. But that doesn't make sense."

"Sure it does." He opened the door. Hooks hung on one of the side walls, a rod stretched across the area a couple of feet in, and a mahogany rolltop desk stood against the other side wall. "Closets did double duty in the twenties and thirties. People didn't own as many clothes back then, and they would fold and keep them in trunks or a chest of drawers. Early closets also served as private spaces. This was probably a small office. Maybe for the man of the house. And it's in the perfect area, close enough to the fireplace for comfort. The renters must have converted it into a front closet, adding hooks and a hanging rod."

She leaned against the door jam, a wistful smile on her face. "It looks like the same desk." She nudged him. "Do you think it could be?"

As if a tape stretched across the entrance with the words "no trespassing," he hesitated. His entrance into the room would be an invasion.

Phaedra sauntered past him. "Take a closer look."

He crossed the threshold with the urge to offer an apology. He squinted at the desk and touched a hand to the edge. A tingling traveled from his fingertips to his elbow. He jerked back. *Hell.* The tingling stopped.

"What do you think?" She ran her hand over the rolltop. "Is it an antique or a knock off?"

He needed air. Backing out of the small space, he rubbed his hand then his chest.

She swiveled around. "What's wrong? You look like you've seen a ghost."

"Nothing. I don't think lunch agreed with me. I'll be okay. The, uh, desk. Yeah. Real old. I'd say as old as the house."

"Really? It's the same desk?" She stood a moment longer, cocked her head, and shoved at the corner. "It isn't flush against the wall at this end." She shoved again. "I think it's bolted down or something."

"Could be why it's the only piece of furniture, on this floor anyway." He retreated farther into the foyer. Rubbing his thumb across the fingertips of his hand, he puzzled over the physical reaction he'd experienced. *Nothing like that's ever happened.*

"Well, if it's been here all along… I don't know whether to leave it go with the house or take it home." Shrugging, she joined him. "I'll think on it."

I'll think on it too. If he was getting a sense of the house, the process wasn't like any presented before. "Let's look around." He crossed the parlor to unlock a window that looked out on the side yard of the house. The heavy curtains sent dust motes flying as he shoved them apart and secured them in brass holdbacks. "Why didn't you rent out the house all these years?"

"I don't know. I didn't need the money." She followed him, stopping in the middle of the room. "I had two little girls and a man I couldn't be sure of."

"Hmph." With a grunt, he muscled the window to slide upwards.

"Crusty in the track." He dusted his hands on his shorts and took a deep breath before he faced into the room. The air inside wasn't too warm—old houses were insulated well—yet the stuffiness, closed-in atmosphere, needed airing out. "Couldn't be sure of?"

"He wanted to change me. I didn't want to marry him."

He didn't say anything, but marriage didn't appear to be something Phaedra much cared about with anyone. She'd never married her first daughter's father either.

"We struggled to figure out what we were for three years then gave up." She wandered to the fireplace next to the window he'd opened. "The house wasn't of any concern. I never got up this high on the hill, never *saw* it, so out of sight out of mind." She shrugged.

The chandelier overhead tinkled as a light breeze blew through the window, disturbing a crisscross of webs on the dusty crystals. A hum tripped along his spine as if the sound vibrated his skin. The webs swayed. *The original chandelier. Beautiful.* Finely crafted like a piece of art, practically wasted on this house. He stared until the webs settled.

"This is some fireplace, isn't it?"

He lowered his gaze with effort and joined her. "Yeah, back in the day fireplaces, more important than now, provided heat for the house. The one in the parlor would have been the focal point of family gatherings or when the owners entertained."

"Parlor?"

"Living room nowadays."

When Phaedra touched the carved red mahogany on one side, he ran his hand over the matching pillar on the other side. Emptiness filled his gut as if what should've been the center of family enjoyment never existed.

"I have no recollection of Mom entertaining here. But I bet the Herseys did back in the1920s. They were wealthy."

"There was a time..." Although the emptiness he sensed ran deep, a smattering of camaraderie made tiny fissures in the vacant atmosphere surrounding the fireplace. The good times were few in this house. He turned his attention to the green inlaid stone running vertically between the wood and the black iron composing the middle of the fireplace. *More beauty of craftsmanship.* Hersey hadn't spared any expense bringing handcrafted structural furnishings for the house. But the warmth that should accompany the designs was missing. The chandelier and the fireplace cried out for attention. *This* presented more like how a grand old house should. Yet in this case, the intensity and clarity came from features of the house instead of the overall structure. *Odd.*

"Earth to Harlan." Phaedra's voice pulled him back to the present.

"Yeah?"

"I asked what time are you talking about?"

"Eh, lost my train of thought." Partially true. Enough explanation for Phaedra, now anyway. This house stirred his thoughts like a dust devil wreaking havoc down the center of The Ravine.

She swished her mouth to the side, studying him with those crystal blue eyes. Her stare had grown deadly over the last few months, seeming to upend him whenever her gaze fell on him. He had the strongest urge to kiss her, and not like a sister, whenever the connection lasted too long. One of these days, he'd give away his thoughts and then what?

It isn't nice to lust after a childhood friend...especially one who might consider me more like a brother.

He cleared his throat and moved out of her range toward the back of the room. An air conditioner filled the bottom half of a window looking out on the backyard.

"Central air never installed." He glanced upward looking for vents.

"I'm not a lot of help on what's been done. I doubt there have been many updates like AC."

A door on the adjoining wall caught his attention. "The stairs must be through here."

"They are."

Opening the door, he peered into an area about four by four with stairs going to the second story, an open doorway into the kitchen, and another to a room at the back of the house behind the kitchen. He strolled into the area.

"This brings back a memory. Mom loved to bake, and she'd sit me on the kitchen floor with my dolls." She slipped around to the counter, skimming her fingers over the surface. "Mmm, warm snickerdoodles." She pivoted in a circle. "A sewing machine sat on a table. There. Her sewing, cooking, and ironing paid the bills."

Harlan listened intently, letting Phaedra's joyful memory wash over and around him, yet her reminiscing did nothing to dispel the barrier protecting the house. *Protecting the house? Or the memory of who lived here long before Phaedra?*

"Oh, gosh. I just had another recollection." She rushed past him to the back room off the kitchen.

He joined her in an area about five-foot square. A gold refrigerator, vintage 1970s, sat against one wall, and on the adjoining wall a door with a window looked out on the backyard. Annette would want to replace the appliance which most likely didn't work.

"See this?" She pointed to a small, closed compartment about waist high and painted pale yellow, the same as the walls.

"For milk and grocery deliveries."

"Oh, of course you'd know." She levered the handle down and opened the metal compartment.

A door on the outside opened for the milkman to leave milk and butter in the box. The richer segment of Joshua residents in the twenties and thirties had delivery compartments on their homes. The poor folk, if they had delivery, would get their milk on the front stoop.

"One day, I climbed in and got myself locked inside. At first, I giggled, hiding from Mom, but after a while, when no one came to find me, I panicked and screamed." She grimaced. "Might have something to do with my fear of tight spaces now."

"That would do it." He half-listened to this story while he faced back toward the kitchen, his mind more involved with plumbing, new fixtures, and the work that needed to be done.

"I think I'll leave. You seem to finally be paying more attention to the house than me."

"You don't have to." He appreciated her connection to the house, but he enjoyed her connection to him. "Don't you want to go upstairs?"

"Nothing but the four bedrooms and the bathroom up there. Besides, I'm supposed to meet the owner of a Copperdale shop at the mercantile at four. I need to pull a few of my purses, vests, and blouses to show her. Might be a new account."

Phaedra made unique women's accessories, supplying his sister's store, Magpie's Mercantile, as well as others with her handcrafted creations. One of many things he loved about her was her creative nature. *Loved?* He physically jerked at his thought. *Sure, love is the right word for a lifelong friend.* He'd given up on any other kind of love a long time ago.

"Did you hear me, Harlan?"

"What?"

"You're in the ozone today, aren't you? I said this door over here leads back to the dining room and front stairs, which connect to the same upstairs landing as the ones from the back."

He didn't bother responding to her ozone remark. How could he argue the point? Between figuring out how to approach this house and how to react to her, yeah, his feet were anywhere but planted on mother earth. "Let's look." He held his hand out in a you-go-first motion. He didn't mind following her self-proclaimed too tight jeans, although watching her walk didn't do anything to clear his head.

Inside, a tiny landing with narrow stairs ascended to the right. Another door straight ahead, which she opened, revealed the dining room with a clear view of the foyer. "You can go upstairs from here. I'd say don't work too hard, but I doubt there's any chance of that today."

"You're a slave driver, you know that, Phae?"

She rubbed the scar along her chin, her nervous gesture, then rose on tiptoes to give him a kiss on the cheek. "I'm out of here." With that, she sashayed across the dining room and went out the front door, leaving him with her scent of rose oil. He touched his face. Her lips registered warm and soft on his cheek. A quick kiss shouldn't leave such an impression.

"Hmph." Over the years, there'd been spontaneous hugs between old friends. Today, the kiss seemed different—thought out, with her hesitation and rub to her chin. Why did she appear nervous? Could she be adding mind reader to her talents, or was his wondrous new attraction for her obvious? Could the kiss on the cheek be her way of saying, "Hey we're just friends?"

He could analyze that to death.

With a shake of his head, he put those thoughts to rest and ascended the narrow, curved stairway. They ended in a hallway. Directly across, the slightly wider staircase he'd seen off the kitchen led down to the back of the house. Standing in the hall, he pivoted, glancing into each room, one larger than the others. The layout appeared original. Nothing he could see had been added or altered. Peering into the smallest, nondescript room, an uneasiness crept over his shoulders. He had no desire to cross the threshold. *Odd.* "Why does that word keep coming to mind?" His voice echoed in the empty space.

He wandered back to the largest bedroom, presumably the master. Seventies-vintage wallpaper would have to be removed, and the doors needed refinishing. No sign of water damage or critter infestation. Standing at the window overlooking the backyard, he thought about how many others had stood in the same spot over the decades. He doubted the mountains or the view out the window had changed much, yet lives had come and gone. This house held those memories, and he'd be damned if anything but a mixture of unease, emptiness, and peculiar vibrations came forth. The desk tingling his fingers was more than peculiar.

The chandelier provoked a strong desire to refurbish it to the original shine, make it a center piece to the house along with the fireplace. Give them purpose to entice new owners to enjoy their beauty. But the house as a whole structure closed off to him. Although not an artist, could he be experiencing something akin to artistic block? Did his dad ever draw a blank when he looked at a piece of wood to carve? Did he ever feel the wood wrong or not authentic in some way? He'd have to ask him.

A quick glimpse of the bathroom revealed fixtures that needed updating, but the floor and ceiling looked good. He guessed the biggest renovation Annette might want to make would be another bathroom. Unless she intended on keeping the place to its original floorplan.

While descending the main stairs at the back of the house, he tested the footing, pleased they were in sturdy condition. Old houses were built to last. Halfway down, as he glided his hands along the railing, briefly wondering how many hands had touched the wood, his head spun as if two quick shots of whiskey had hit his bloodstream. He stopped, clutching the railing for steadiness. His stomach heaved sending a wave of nausea. Swallowing the threat of retasting his lunch, he pounded down the last few steps. *Get the hell off these stairs.*

He didn't stop until he reached the doorway between the kitchen and the small room with the refrigerator. The doorjamb supported him as he took three deep breaths. The dizziness and nausea vanished as quickly as it had come. Was it lunch? Maybe he had a touch of food poisoning. Glancing up the stairwell, a tinge of sadness engulfed him. He retreated farther to the back door while the sadness floated just out of reach. He needed air.

On the back porch, he breathed deeply and puzzled over his reactions. Whatever had come over him as he'd descended the stairwell, left just as quickly. Never in all his life had he encountered such strong sensations when faced with objects or the scores of houses he'd remodeled. How could he figure out what these physical reactions to areas of the house meant? His mom, an intuitive mystic, would probably have had an explanation or at least a theory. The best he could do was to visit his artist father.

Lingering a few moments longer, relaxing, he surveyed the yard. In the far corner, remnants of scraggly bushes indicated what might have been a garden at one time. The dead grass appeared golden in the sunlight, except for splotchy pale green areas under what he recognized as a dead apricot tree just off the porch. "Huh." He squinted, wondering if the color was an optical illusion from the shadows. *Must be.* No evidence of consistent water leakage from the eaves could explain accidental watering. Yet... "Huh. As if this house isn't peculiar enough, am I fabricating mysteries now?"

Back inside, he locked the back entrance, closed the window in the parlor, and left through the front door. Climbing into his truck, he one-handed his cellphone, clicked on his father's number, and cranked the engine. Frank MacKenzie answered on the second ring.

"Hi, Harlan."

"Hey, Dad. You busy right now?"

"I'm making iced tea is all. You need something?"

"I thought I'd come by, if you're not in the middle of anything."

"I'm not. Come on. I'll have a glass iced for you."

Only one route led from the Copper Hills district to the area known as The Ravine where Frank had lived for over fifty years and where Harlan and his sisters were raised. The bulk of Joshua could be reached from the four main roads running horizontal, stacked one above the other across Spirit Mountain, and overlooking a mishmash of houses and ruins farther down the mountain. Getting to his father's house required taking at least part of three of the roads. In the distance, the Verde Valley glistened green. Harlan drove east on the lowest of the three roads, Bennett Avenue, named for one of the founders and mining financiers in the late 1800s. Frederick Bennett had named the city after his first-born son, Joshua.

When he passed the Copper Line Hotel, his thoughts carried him to Nora, the woman writing a book about little known historical homes. That described nearly every house in Joshua. Long ago the city council had ruled no new buildings could be constructed within the city limits. There had to be at least an original foundation from which to build. The town residents, either old original hippies or the type of people who wished they had been, cherished Joshua being left as the town looked in its heyday of the early 1900s. Nora would find more than a few old stately houses to include in her book. He'd remodeled a fair share of them.

He slowed around the switchback and then turned onto the so-called road leading into The Ravine. Dodging small boulders and kicking up dust, he passed several homes that varied from one-story wood or stone structures to two-story stucco and clapboard. He left the main road, drove past his dad's friend, Snuff's place and onto the narrow, equally rough road fronting his childhood home. He stopped behind Frank's twenty-year-old black Ford truck and cut his engine. Even now, at age forty-four, his body relaxed with coming-home contentment when he saw the pinkish-tan clapboard house. A few spots on the white trim looked dingy. *Might need a new coat of paint next year.* He breathed in what he always thought of as The Ravine smell. The residents tended to plant fragrant flowering bushes in this part of town. His dad threw seeds of wildflowers around the edge of the wraparound porch. Oranges and purples were abundant this year.

The door opened, and Frank waved. He wore a blue, button-down cotton shirt rolled to his elbows and tucked into worn jeans. Even in summer, he preferred jeans and boots.

"Hey, Dad."

"I'm taking a break from a metal project. Thought I'd sit on the porch unless you'd rather go inside."

"Outside is good." With temps in the mid-eighties and the breeze, the shady porch offered a cool spot. Harlan claimed the bench. "What's the metal project?"

Frank settled onto the chair after placing a pitcher of tea on a side table. "A wall decoration." He took a drink and swiped the back of a hand across his mouth. "A couple up from Phoenix came into Magpie's last week. Saw my metal work. The wife is an artist, so she rendered me a sketch of a flower arrangement."

"Metal flowers?" He sipped his sweet tea and glanced down the hill. Snuff walked from in front of his house, waved, and disappeared again. "Did it present any…challenges?"

"Nah. I've done similar."

"Have you ever approached a job, say, wood or other medium, and couldn't find the inspiration?"

"Some pieces speak to me more than others, if that's what you mean."

"Yeah, it is." Harlan hitched a breath. Maybe his dad could explain his odd feelings. "The wood or metal *speaks* to you?"

"Of a sort. I study the texture, the colors. Have to know what I'm working with. There's no forcing a piece into something it's not."

He sighed. His dad meant "speaks" metaphorically. "Do you ever draw a blank?"

"Can't say I have." Frank quirked a brow. "What's the interest in sculpting, Harlan? You thinking of tackling a piece?"

"No." He drew circles in the condensation on the glass. "When I refurbish an old house, I get a *feel* for what needs to be done. I'm not inspired by the Big Purple House."

"Inspiration's the problem?" His father dipped his head ever so slightly and peered directly into his eyes. "Not something else?"

How did he do that? His mother had been the one everyone called mystical—the woman who seemed to see into your soul and knew how you felt before you knew yourself.

"Want to talk about it?"

"All of my life you could tell when I didn't quite tell you the truth. That was Mom's thing, but you? How?" Harlan drained the rest of his tea and set the glass on the floor.

"You wiggle a foot."

"What?"

"It's your tell. You wiggle your right foot." Frank laughed.

Harlan chuckled. "That's how you knew I took the car to visit my girlfriend after you went to bed?"

"Yeah, and got into my stash when you were seventeen." He chortled. "More than once. I couldn't see inside you like Susie Muse could. But if I made mention of Marsha or my stash looked low, your foot went to wiggling."

"You know I'll now be able to hide anything I want from you." He smirked.

"Doubt it. Even without the tell, you're a damn poor liar."

Harlan picked up his glass, jiggled the ice cubes, and drank the water from their melt. He'd never before put into words what happened when he touched certain objects or entered an old house. Why would he? Didn't everyone have the same experiences? At some point, he realized what seemed natural to him, wasn't natural for others. And with Elidor talking about voices in her head, he certainly didn't want to be an oddball like his sister. He'd kept his intuitions to himself.

Frank stayed silent, sipping his tea. His father could be a patient sort.

"When you said your raw material speaks to you…houses speak to me. Sometimes objects."

"You hear voices?"

He puffed his cheeks with a held exhale, then blew the air as if forcing the words to come. "Not voices, per se. But they do open themselves. Usually."

"What is it you expect the house to reveal that isn't coming to you?"

The answer was about as clear as Goldwater Creek after a two-day storm. "Hard to put into words."

"Clairsentience."

"Like Elidor?" How could his father compare him to Dory?

"Susie Muse said Dory's gift was larger than most."

"My sister wouldn't use the word gift." Dory fought her own nature most of her life. "And I don't eavesdrop on other people's thoughts like she does."

"Dory is an empath to the extreme. It's a form of clairsentience, but her gift is connected to the present." Frank set his glass on the table. "Let me think." He rubbed a hand across his face. His hazel eyes grew green as he stared into the air.

His mother always said his dad had chameleon eyes.

"She can't help but tune into human emotions, which is what an empath does. If I remember what your mom told me, your ability comes down to being sensitive to energy changes. Clairsentience means clear feelings. Your mom said your gift—"

"What? Mom knew?" His breath caught. "I never told her."

"Susie Muse had her own set of talents, now didn't she?" His father, like everyone else in Joshua who knew his mother, called her by her maiden name. Susie Muse's reputation loomed as large as the love she engendered.

Harlan poured himself another glass of tea. "Okay. So, what did she say about me?"

"At the time, oh, maybe thirty-five years or so ago, she said you appeared to discern energy left behind. Like on objects or, as you say, from houses." Frank cocked a brow. "I mostly believed your mom, but mostly I let her believe herself."

"Dad—"

"Now, Harlan, I've had a lot of years to think about my time with Susie Muse, and I'm inclined now to be less of a skeptic. She certainly understood your sister. Apparently, she saw something in you too."

As a teenager, he didn't remember confiding in her much. And then they lost her. His chest tightened and his lids grew hot. He'd like to confide in her now.

"The Big Purple House causing you problems?"

"I get a sense of the need to bring certain parts of the house back to the original beauty and purpose. But for the overall house, I see the craftsmanship, the basics of what I need to do, yet no clear feeling…" Huh, that's what Mom called it. "Conflicting vibes at best. The essence of the house stays hidden. I had a sick feeling at one point. Not sure if it was lunch or what. Probably."

"What does that mean for the refurbish?"

"Technically, nothing. I can still do the work. Go through the construction or upgrades, whatever."

"But you're bothered? Kind of like if I'm sculpting wood and forcing the shapes to take form without a vision. A piece of art flows *through* me, not *from* me."

"Sounds right." His dad's summation perfectly described how he'd always approached his evaluation of a new project.

"Maybe you should learn the history of the house."

"I know a little. One of the mining moguls built the house. He disappeared, but I don't know the whole story. He named his home Lilac End in the twenties."

"Lilac End?"

"Yeah."

The faraway look in his dad's eyes accompanied another rub across his face.

"What, Dad?"

"Susie Muse mentioned Lilac End. I mean," he rubbed a temple, "she said something about a house called Lilac End. Hmmm."

Harlan waited. Frank seemed to be struggling to call up some memory.

"Hells bells. Been so many years. I guess I didn't know the Big Purple House used to be Lilac End. Or I forgot. There was something…" He shook his head. "All I can recall is Susie had visited someone living there and said she didn't like the feel of the place."

If his mother had sensed a disturbance, he could validate the peculiar vibrations he sensed. And he had to find a way to deal.

CHAPTER THREE

"Thank you." Phaedra waved to the owner of a fashionable Copperdale clothing store as the woman inched her car from the curb and onto the street. Stepping back inside Magpie's Mercantile, she locked the door behind her. "That was a reasonably profitable meeting."

"Talking to yourself?" Magpie descended the stairs inside the shop that led to her apartment upstairs.

"Ha. No, I heard you clomping down the stairs."

"I don't clomp." Magpie sat on the bottom step.

"Thanks for letting me use your store and my rack of clothes. I don't have enough inventory at home to give her a good sample of what I make."

"Mi casa su casa. And besides, you sort of manned the store so I could go upstairs early." The shop owner patted the step next to her. "She's going to handle your clothing?"

"Yep." She eased down. "We're starting off with six jackets, three capes, eight blouses, six skirts, and five bags."

Her friend's eyes widened with congratulations. "But do you have that much in inventory?"

"No." She cringed. "I'm going to be busy. I told her two weeks." This was a good problem she could weather.

"Well, if you run short, I suppose I could let you take a few things off my rack."

She squeezed her arm. "Thanks, Mags."

"But you'd still have to bust butt to replace them."

"I can do that." Her stomach grumbled. "I can't believe I'm hungry after having lunch out. Time to head home." She grabbed the banister and levered herself to stand.

Magpie tugged on her sleeve as she got to her feet. "I'm warming last night's lasagna, and I have plenty of kale salad. Come on up."

"Okay, but I'll pass on the kale." That got her a smirk. She followed her friend up the stairs. "When is Zac coming up from Copperdale?"

"Right after he closes his law office on Friday. Should be here in time for dinner."

Inside, she sat in a chair at the table as Magpie pulled plates from the cupboard. "Have you set a definite date for the wedding?"

"We decided to have an outside ceremony in the spring. I'm leaning toward April." She opened the oven and peeked at the lasagna.

"Next year? Why wait so long? You could've gotten married last April."

When she righted, her face told the story of memories to bear. "Too close to all of the uproar."

In February, Magpie, Zac, and her father had been smack-dab in the middle of uncovering the truth behind a decades-old murder that had nearly gotten her killed. Magpie leaned her hips against the counter, caught a loose curl from her mass of hair, and tucked it into the messy knot on the back of her head. A few frown lines touched the outside corners of her eyes. "Nothing like a wedding on the heels of two funerals."

"Understood, but is Zac okay with waiting for spring to roll around again? He seemed anxious to put all the mess behind and get a ring on your finger."

"We're good." Magpie disappeared into the living room for a moment, reappearing with a bottle of red wine and two glasses. "Speaking of romance...what's up with you and Harlan?"

Her mouth went dry. She didn't know Magpie had any inkling of her growing desire for her brother.

"Don't give me that face." Magpie set a bowl of greens on the table and plopped into a chair. "I'm not blind. The mess with Dad and Zac distracted me, but I still sensed something going on between you two."

"How can anything be going on?" She uncorked the bottle and

poured the wine. "We've been friends forever. Harlan, Magpie, and Phaedra." Holding the glass as if toasting, Magpie followed suit and clinked her glass. "The three musketeers since pre-school."

Her friend swallowed a sip. "Yeah, but there were a lot of years sprinkled in when we weren't. College, marriage, children. About fifteen years for you and Harlan. Life happens. Things change."

I've changed.

"Well yeah, we grew up. But these last fourteen years, all of us back together, it's like we never parted, only now we hike instead of playing chase. And we rarely play pranks on unsuspecting Ravine neighbors." Phaedra swirled her wine. "Has your brother said something?" Taking a sip, she let the wine linger on her tongue and avoided saying more. She wasn't sure she wanted to confess her confusion about Harlan, even to Magpie.

"That would be the day he confided in me. Our musketeer bonding ended years ago."

As much as she loved both Harlan and Magpie, she'd never taken sides. The decades-old rift between them was more of an undercurrent than an all-out river of contention. They still hung together, just not as close as once upon a time. Magpie tended to be as critical of herself as she was of her brother, so she didn't hold him to a higher standard. But her friend held a strong view that Harlan, a year older, had let down the family twice. The first time when their mother died. Magpie, at age twelve, found herself in the position of caretaker of her brother, younger sister, and her father whose mourning slipped into an alcoholic haze. Three years later, when their father's girlfriend was murdered, Harlan again let Magpie take the helm. She might resent the way Harlan backed away from responsibility, but they both had been too young to be put in such a position.

She breathed easier, dismissing her growing lust for Harlan and addressing Magpie's relationship with him, a subject far easier to discuss than her own. "Have you really talked—"

"Forget it, Phae. It's ancient history at this point. It just irks me that now he's like a bull in a china shop at times with his macho-take-charge attitude. When it suits him, that is."

People change.

Lasagna aromas wafted from the oven. Phaedra took another sip of wine to quell her increasing hunger. Maybe talking to Mags about her brother wasn't—

"Have you slept with him?"

Her gasp succeeded in choking the last of a swallow of wine down wrong. "What in Hades, Mags?" She grabbed a napkin from the holder on the table and wiped her mouth. "No."

Magpie grinned and twined a loose lock of her caramel tresses around a finger. A single strand of silver glittered and disappeared as she wound.

"That would definitely be the shortest route to ending a friendship. And anyway, he may not have the slightest notion of me as anything more than the friends we've been for decades." She confronted her friend's gold speckled eyes. "I don't know *what's* going on in my head. Why on earth, after all these years, am I lusting…having…feelings for him?" Her fuzzy thoughts didn't gain clarity with confessing about one friend to another—about the brother to the sister.

"He's been looking at you differently too." Magpie peeked over the top of the wine glass when she sipped.

As if she'd just sped through a dip in the road, her stomach lurched. "He has?"

Her friend twirled the stem of her wine glass. "After all these years." She appeared as baffled as Phaedra. The neutral slant to her mouth and crease in her forehead might mean she wasn't too pleased. Did Magpie think she might hurt her brother? She shouldn't have confessed. This could blow over or end badly, and now she'd opened the can of worms. The lid couldn't be replaced.

"Forget I said anything. Please. Can you? Maybe I'm just going through a thing and—"

"Why don't you address your feelings with him?" Her friend slid her hand across the table and patted her fingers.

"Is it feelings? Or have I been too long without a man in my bed?"

Magpie chuckled. "Love or lust. Whatever. Address it."

"You wouldn't mind?"

"Why would I?"

She'd read her friend's facial expressions wrong. "If it all falls down—"

Magpic nailed her with her golden gaze. "If this last year has taught me anything, it's you can't let uncertainty rule you."

"I wouldn't even know where to begin. And I really am afraid of ruining a lifelong friendship. You two are my people." She twined her fingers through Magpie's. "If I screw it up with him, I could screw it up with you."

"Never."

"He's your *brother*."

"You're my sister. By choice."

Untangling her fingers, she patted Magpie's hand and sipped more wine. "Yeah, but I don't know." Taking a deep breath, she sighed in frustration. "My history with men isn't the best. I'm pretty happy on my own, not too involved with any one man. And Harlan is a wounded dove. I'd hate to—"

"Wounded dove?"

"Yes, don't look so incredulous. After eleven years of marriage, losing Allison in the car accident devastated him. He hasn't had a serious relationship in the thirteen years since, has he?" Magpie hadn't ever mentioned Harlan involved with anyone. "I'm not sure I've even seen him with anyone more than once. And not many at that. But then I wasn't paying attention—until recently."

"He's had his share. I might take issue with my brother's personality, but there's something about him that sure as hell attracts the women. Hmm…maybe not in the last year or so."

"I said *relationship* as in one and for a length of time."

"Good grief, Phae. Sounds like you've given this some thought. Is that what you want? A till death do you part relationship with Harlan?"

"I've *got* that right now—a close friend until death do us part. Which is what I'm afraid I'll destroy if I pursue these crazy, physical cravings."

****

"Appreciate the dinner, Dad." Harlan finished loading the dishwasher while Frank wiped the counter. Even with the smells of food still hanging in the air, the aroma of wood shavings and metal sculpting permeated the house. A relaxing ambiance of being at home.

"I'm glad I could talk you into staying. Doesn't take much to make a hamburger. I enjoyed the company." He draped the wet cloth over the sink divider. "Isn't that grandson of mine coming home this summer?"

"Doesn't look like it. I think *home* is Minneapolis for Garrett now, anyway. He's taking classes right through the summer to finish his masters. Already has a couple of companies looking at him."

"Smart kid. Want a cup of coffee?"

"I don't think so." Harlan peeked between the wooden slats on the kitchen window at the glowing pink dusk. A cozy evening with his dad tempted him. "Phaedra is already accusing me of stalling on the job. I need to run into town for bread and butter at the Little Market before I head home and get a plan hatched."

"What are you going to do?" Frank reclined against the counter, arms folded across his chest.

"Tackle the basics. I'll have a crew cut loose from another job by Monday. I'll work alone tomorrow doing some prep work." Plucking the truck keys from his pocket, he considered what Frank suggested earlier. "Maybe I'll go by the Historical Society in a day or two and see what history they have, if any, on the house. Just for the hell of it. Like I said, I can do the work, but I'd rather have the frame of mind I'm accustomed to possessing when I'm on a job."

"Makes the work a sight more enjoyable when inspiration is your guide."

He gave his dad a quick bear hug. "If you talk to Annette, don't let on the contractor isn't inspired."

Frank waved off the worry. "The work will still be top notch. But I won't make mention."

He strode to the front door, opened it, and paused with one foot on the porch. "So, you two do talk now and then."

"She's…an old friend." With a shrug, Frank jammed his fingers into the pockets of his jeans.

"Yeah? That all? You seem happier since she made the decision to move to Joshua."

"I, uh, now you, uh, I—"

"Forget it, Dad." He clapped him on the shoulder and laughed. "You don't have to talk about your love life to me."

"Love life?" His dad's eyes grew wide.

"Or whatever you two have going on." And for sure there was *something* going on. He'd never seen his father so flustered. "Thanks again for dinner."

"Okay, yeah. Good luck with the house."

Crossing the porch then descending the stairs, he couldn't wipe the smile off his face. After all these years of loneliness, his dad deserved a woman in his life who put the light back in his eyes.

As he bumped along The Ravine road, a fleeting thought of Allison skittered across his vision. His wife had died more than thirteen years ago, and no one had come close to filling the void. When Phaedra's bungalow on the edge of The Ravine came into sight, his thought flitted to another memory—the first time he'd seen his childhood friend after losing Allison. He'd decided to move back to Joshua. The first week had been tough on Garrett, only ten at the time. Treating him to a break from unpacking, he'd taken his son for ice cream and ran into Phaedra and her two girls. His chest had expanded with joy when she'd hugged him. Her friendship meant so much. Gripping the steering wheel, he dodged a pothole and pulled onto the asphalt road. And he'd better keep that friendship in mind and stop thinking about how she filled out her jeans. Over the last year, his mind had gone there far too often. His usual standard of not looking below the surface of a woman, only fulfilling a mutual sexual need, and then moving on the moment she formed an attachment wouldn't do for Phaedra. She was above all else, a good friend. He wouldn't want to—

A woman on the sidewalk waved, and he slowed. The writer.

Now, wearing a white button-down shirt tucked into blue knee pants he thought were called capris, Nora Cook looked more casual than earlier. She waved again as he pulled alongside her. Her red hair caught the last rays of sun, and a breeze lifted the full bangs from her forehead. When she leaned in the open passenger window, her violet gaze raked over his face. How Phaedra saw them as blue he didn't understand.

"Hi, Harlan. What a pleasure running into you." Her husky voice added another layer to the word pleasure.

"Are you out for an evening walkabout?"

"I'm on my way back to the hotel from dinner. I walked up Main Street and ate at a restaurant called Rose's Cantina. Wonderful food. Now I'm headed back to my *lonely* room." Her pouty lips invited.

"Rose's has great food." He chose to ignore her flirting. The woman, pretty enough, had a figure to stare at, but there was something hardened about her.

"So, what are you up to?"

"Had dinner at my dad's and heading home after I make a

stop at the Little Market."

"Oh, would you mind if I tag along? I wondered if there might be a market where I could get a couple of things for my hotel room while I'm here."

"Um, sure, hop in." He stretched across the console and opened the door as she grabbed the handle. Once she buckled up, he asked, "Planning on being here awhile?" He eased behind a passing car.

"I'm not sure. I haven't gotten a chance to make a plan for my snooping yet."

"No?" He wondered if all writers were so unorganized. "I would think you'd have covered all of Joshua this afternoon. The main part of town is only about a square mile. The other neighborhoods bring it to about four-square miles. Not much ground to cover."

"Oh, I did a quick drive around, but I was pretty tired from the trip here, so I took a nap. Tomorrow, I'll start fresh. Any suggestions?"

"I might be able to point you to a few homes."

"Where do *you* live?"

He darted a glance then back to the road. Her chin dipped in the way some women used, and she batted her lashes.

"My house is at the west end of Miners' Mile."

"Miners' Mile?"

Her research hadn't covered much historical data if she hadn't heard of the area where most of the Hispanic and Asian mine workers lived between the late 1800s and 1920s. "Yeah, down the hill. Street name is North Avenue now. Lots of small homes, although there are a few larger ones. What kind of houses are you looking for? Do they need to be upscale, maybe remodeled and occupied, or in the original shape?"

"What kind?" She ran a manicured finger along her neck. "I haven't really decided." Her words trailed off as she stared out the passenger window.

He wondered how she ever got anything written without a plan.

At the far end of Main Street, he parked along the curb in front of the Little Market. "This is it. Hope you're not after anything too specific."

"Do they have any wine?"

"Of course. You're in Joshua. We have wineries, and I think the market stocks a couple of bottles from each one."

He waited for her on the sidewalk. The day's heat disappeared with the sun behind the mountains. Overhead, the first star twinkled as the turquoise horizon morphed into deep navy. "They don't carry much in the way of fresh food. They're more of a boutique market. Beyond a few basics, they have high-end deli stuff." He opened the door and stood back as she entered.

"I don't need much. There's a tiny fridge in the room so thought I'd throw in a couple of things."

After picking up a loaf of bread and a two-stick carton of butter, he reached the check-out just ahead of her.

"Hey, Harlan." The cashier, a brunette with a toothy smile and a turned-up nose, greeted him. "Have you heard from Garrett lately?" She scanned his two items. Mary Jo Byerson and his son had been an item in high school.

"I know he's not coming home this summer. Says he's cramming in a few summer classes." He plucked a ten-dollar bill from his wallet.

"That's too bad." She frowned. "I mean, sounds good for him, but I bet you miss him." Handing him his change without counting it out, she managed another toothy grin.

"Yeah, well, he's driven, and I can't complain about that. I just might go see him if my work ever slows."

She tucked his bread and butter into a paper bag. "Well, you tell him I said hello. Maybe we'll see him at Christmas."

"Will do." Sliding the sack off the counter, he moved aside for Nora to set her items on the counter.

"Will that be all for you?" Mary Jo rang Nora's purchase of two bottles of Sauvignon Blanc, a box of wheat crackers, and a package of two-inch round cheeses coated in wax. The kind he loved.

"Looks like a good hotel room snack." When he drank wine, he preferred a dry white like she had.

Out on the sidewalk, the writer paused and gazed down Main Street. The streetlights flickered on. Her expression held a faraway contemplation.

"Wondering about something?"

"Oh." She blinked. "Trying to picture this street back in the day."

"The day?"

"The 1920s, when Lilac End was a grand home high on the hill. And the sidewalks were crowded with miners, wealthy owners, and ladies of the night." Shrugging off some distant thought, she strolled around the pickup bed to the passenger side.

He moved to follow, but she peeked over her shoulder and gave a light laugh. "I can open my own door."

"You seem to be enamored with the Big Purple House." He buckled his seat belt then started the engine. "There are a couple of grander homes that might really intrigue you."

"Hmm. Maybe you could break free for a while tomorrow and show me around?" She cocked a brow that played at her bangs.

"I can't tomorrow. I won't have a crew for a couple of days to work on the house. Unfortunately, I'll be tied up there, working on my own. Pretty busy." He'd welcome the solitary work for once. Steeping himself in the vibes of the Big Purple House, alone, might be what he needed to feel the creativity surge.

He maneuvered a U-turn on Main, took a left on Joshua Avenue, passing Magpie's Mercantile, and cut over to Bennett.

"I guess I'll crack the reference books I brought to do more research on the town."

Although not knowing anything about writing, he might've done his research prior to landing in town. And on a laptop. Joshua was a renowned ghost/tourist town, yet there might not be homes worth writing about if you hadn't done the research. But then she did seem to know some history on Phaedra's house. "How did you say you came to learn about the Big, er, Lilac End?" He stopped across from the Copper Line Hotel.

"I, uh, found an old book in my mother's things after she died. She, uh, loved western history. The book had a chapter about Joshua and mentioned a few of the mining moguls like John Hersey. Something, I really don't remember what, caught my eye so I researched him. Joshua called to me." Her deep-throated chuckle filled the cab as she batted thick lashes. "Kind of glad it did."

Her violet stare tugged his attention. "You have very unusual eyes."

"I do?" Canting slightly toward him, the corner of her mouth quirked upward.

He wished he hadn't given her an opening to what could only lead to more flirting. He broke eye contact and glanced at the street, now vacant on a weeknight. Tourists were either tucked inside their rooms or lounging in the Apparition Room with beers in hand. "Would you like me to see you inside?" *Hope not.* He really wanted to go home and plan.

"Such a gentleman." Her husky voice teased. "No. I can find my way. Unless you'd like to see me all the way to my room." She touched his arm.

"Nora, I—"

She laughed. "I'm joking. I know you're a working man who needs his sleep. If you can't break free to show me around town tomorrow, could I stop by Lilac End?"

He required a full day without distractions. Although not in his nature to be rude, brushing her off was exactly what he needed to do. "I've got a really busy day tomorrow and—"

"Then Friday. I won't take much time. I'd really like to get a look-see around to gauge if it's photographically suited for the book before I settle on including it."

"Well—"

Her touch increased as warm fingertips tickled the hair on his forearm. "I promise not to get in the way, and I won't stay long."

God, those eyes. "Sure. I think I could spare a little time on Friday."

"Oh, thank you." Her fingers trailed over his skin before gripping her grocery bag. With a click, the door opened, and she stepped out. She leaned in the window. "See you on Friday, Harlan." After looking both ways, she crossed the street.

He waited until she'd opened the door and waved before driving away.

Damn. Something about the woman. He wasn't attracted to her in a traditional man/woman sense. Yet, he wanted to know her better. And he *needed* to know why he cared.

****

Nora stored the wine and cheese in the hotel room refrigerator. Tempted to open one of the bottles, she gauged the impulse would be weaker if she couldn't see the bottle. After two strong Margaritas at dinner and all the spicy food, wine might not sit well. Besides, an idea had come to her when Harlan complimented her on her choice of a hotel room snack. With his determination to get home, she'd dropped the notion of luring him back to her room. But with his agreement to let her tour Lilac End Friday, why not take some refreshments with her? Get him relaxed and cozy, just the two of them. She wanted to know everything he knew about the house in addition to what his renovation schedule would be and just how deep the renovations would go as far as the structure.

After hanging up her blouse and folding her pants into a drawer, she stretched out on her stomach on the bed in her bra and panties. She scooped the journal from the bedside table, propped a pillow under her breasts, and then opened the crinkly pages. She never grew tired of reading GG's words.

> *February 28, 1924*
> *John came early this evening and told Ma he would be back and to make sure I was available. God, I was so excited! Not for the sex, but because it's like I'm special. I got to skip laying with any of the miners who came in while I waited for him. He's so clean and smells spicy. Word spread through the other girls and judging from their reaction, having a client of his stature in the mining industry ask for me in advance is quite particular. I got to bathe in FRESH water, and Ma let me use her special perfume. At least, special to me. Helen helped me ready my room. She said she felt like a lady-in-waiting. We giggled until Ma told us to shut up.*
> *Then I was alone, waiting, and so nervous— like my first time all over again, only more so because I knew who would walk through the door. He'd ASKED for me! I couldn't eat. My stomach was a tangle of nerves. Then he knocked. KNOCKED! Like he was making a call on a lady friend. What was I supposed to say? Come in? I just sat on the bed with my hands all sweaty. When he opened the door and stood there just looking at me, my heart galloped. I could only stare back and wait for him to DO*

SOMETHING. He doesn't have the most perfect face. His nose is crooked, and his lips are thin beneath his mustache, but his eyes are bright and kind. His shoulders are broad. His waist slim. He dresses fine. Always smells so clean. I love clean!

So he just stood there. All of a sudden, I figured out he was waiting for me to do something. I motioned him forward. The scent of sweet tobacco and his spicy aftershave floated in with him. He kissed my hand. Like I'm some lady or something. Like we'd just met. He asked me how I was. I almost couldn't speak with his kindness. I don't know where I got the courage, but I decided to treat him like he really was my guest, and I really was a lady. I took his hat, helped him out of his suit coat, and stored them in my armoire. I asked him to please have a seat. I felt rather stupid, worrying he'd think I tried to be something I'm not. But he didn't look like he thought that, and he sat in the chair, NOT ON THE BED! He told me he'd had a busy day and was quite tired. I knelt at his feet and removed his shoes. I stayed kneeling and asked what I could do for him. Some of the other men like that sort of thing. But what he said to me nearly sat me on my butt. He told me I could continue to be his beautiful Genevieve. He cupped my chin with his large hand and stared so hard into my eyes I wanted to look away. He told me I had the most beautiful eyes. He called them the deepest blue he'd ever seen. And then his hands were on me, and I wanted that.

With a sigh, she gently turned the page.

March 1, 1924
Today has been so unusual and so filled with joy, I don't know where to begin. I want to write it all down to remember later. Early in the day, Ma sent Helen, Ruth, and me to Main Street for supplies. Two men tipped their hats to us as we passed on the

41

sidewalk. Helen says it's because of John Hersey. And me! Sara said she'd entertained one of them last night. She didn't know for sure if he knows John, but he dresses like him and must be with the mining management. You don't see any of the wives of these fine men on Main Street. They have their food and other goods delivered to their door. It's not proper for so-called reputable ladies to be walking around the business district where we live and work. POOH ON THEM. Their loss.

Before we left to shop, Ma gave me money to buy a length of blue voile and an equal part of linen. She said I needed a new dress, and she would pay for it. I didn't know why, but I didn't protest. Then she hurried back to her business closet, and I swore I saw the back of John in there, but Ruth pushed me out the front door before I could get a sharp look.

After dinner, Ma took me into her closet. She told me Mr. Hersey has reserved me. I didn't know whatever she meant. And then she told me the most wonderful thing! I would not be lying with anyone but HIM from now on. I almost started clapping, but Ma doesn't like silliness. She'd already arranged the financial part of it. I have no say in any of that, but what Ma procured made me happy. My share is sizable! She said tomorrow we would sew my new dress. It's going to be the newest fashion of voile over linen with a drop waist and hemline falling just below my knees. I've seen them in some magazines. I can't believe this is happening to me. It's her gift to me for raising the status of our house. MA IS GIVING ME A GIFT! John will visit me Monday evening, and he has requested I be clothed. That's why I get the new dress. I floated out of her closet. My feet didn't touch the floor, I swear. Up the stairs and every girl in sight stared at me like I was a princess among them.

"You should've been a princess, GG." But what GG missed out

on, Nora could at least profit.

CHAPTER FOUR

Harlan spread the 1960s architectural drawing of the Big Purple House across his drafting table. He could almost date this drawing by the smell alone. The scent of old paper and the familiar aroma of the weed his dad still partook of occasionally, met his nostrils. Too bad the original blueprints were long ago lost, most likely destroyed in one of the many fires in the early days of Joshua. Phaedra came across this first-floor rendition by accident when sorting through boxes of her mother's. The owners prior to her mother considered dividing the house into apartments. The reason the conversion didn't happen would never be known. At this point in time, it was a good thing. Annette fell in love with the house on first sighting.

Zeroing in on the kitchen, he noted where the lines ran for the sink and water heater. That helped. The upstairs bathroom was right above the kitchen, which—

His cellphone rang. The vibration danced it toward him on the tilted drafting table. Surprised to see the face of his youngest sister, Elidor, pleasure and irritation mixed with curiosity. "Hey, Dory."

"Hey back. What are you up to?" Her quiet response took him back to his childhood. She didn't spend many of her adult years with the family.

"Working. What else? Looking at some plans for a renovation. How are you?"

"I'm good." Hesitation colored her words.

"Yeah? Where are you?" She was always somewhere— anywhere but Joshua.

"I'm still in Corydon."

"That's Ohio, right?"

"No. Indiana." Her tinkling laugh sounded tiny and matched his image of the petite, youngest sibling,

"Sorry. You get around. Who can keep up?"

"I've been here for a while. Well, here and gone and back and... Maybe long enough."

"What's wrong, Dory?" In spite of his dissonant feelings about his youngest sister, he worried about her apparent inability to find peace with herself.

"Oh, just work stuff. And I'm feeling...homesick."

"Homesick as in Joshua and family homesick?" He didn't even try to keep the astonishment out of his voice. She hadn't been home in close to five years. Leaving Joshua more than twenty years ago, she'd been back only three times, never staying for more than a couple of months. "Are you coming home for a visit?" In spite of not really knowing her, his chest tightened with the desire to see her. He had a few good memories of little Dory from the years before their mother died.

"I don't know. Right now, I just needed to hear your voice."

"You didn't call Dad?" He normally clued them in on her life. She rarely called Harlan or Magpie.

"Yeah." A dry chuckle came through the phone. "You were my second choice. I think he was talking on his cellphone. I heard the funny blip that comes through when someone is on their cell. I tried a couple of times but gave up. He must be on one heck of a phone call. Tell me something. Anything. About all of you."

"I'm renovating the Big Purple House and—"

"Are you enjoying that?" She practically whispered. He found himself plastering the phone to his ear to hear her.

"Yeah, well, it's work."

"Lots of energy. Some dark."

"What?"

"Sorry." She sighed. "Heard it in your voice. Forget it."

"You don't have to be sorry." There was so much he wished he could ask her, but only his conflicted interpretations would translate to her. She read people not inanimate objects. Maybe if she was here... "Phaedra is having me refurbish—"

"Phaedra? You and Phaedra."

"What? No. She's selling it. I'm doing the work."

"Hmm…"

He let it go. Even hundreds of miles apart and on the phone, his sister could divine his inner emotions. He changed the subject. "Magpie and Zac are, well, whatever they are. He's still lawyering in Copperdale and spending weekends here. Magpie is still the family merchant and singing some weekends at the Apparition Room. There's talk of a wedding. Dad continues selling his art pieces at Magpie's, and he has a girlfriend."

"Really?"

"Yep, her name is Annette Russo. She's a friend from the sixties who's moving to Joshua in the next couple of months. Do you remember Lolly?"

"Who can forget Lolly?"

"Annette is Lolly's sister, but they're as different as diamonds and rubies according to Dad—although both gems and the real thing. She's buying the Big Purple House."

"That's great. Dad needs the company. The joy." Silence followed a gentle sigh.

"Agreed."

The quiet stretched out. *She must be alone.*

"You still there, Dory?"

"Yeah. I need to get going."

"Come visit." He thought of the little wide-eyed child, only ten when they lost their mother. With her keen senses, she couldn't help but ache for all of them on top of her own hurt. Between her words he heard something more than a checking-in call. "Are you okay?"

"I'm fine. I'll visit. Soon. Love you, bye."

Clutching the phone in his palm, he thought about calling her back. She wanted a rundown on her Joshua family but offered up nothing about herself. Dory's life remained a mystery to him. He didn't really *know* her, yet he sensed something bothered her. But if she'd wanted to confide in him, she would've. He wondered if the voices in his sister's head had quieted over the years; if being away from Joshua diminished her clairsentience. She'd stayed away because she claimed Joshua heightened her abilities to tune into others' feelings, so overpowering when here, driving her to distraction.

Driven to distraction described his current situation, only not by *too many* voices. The Big Purple House clammed up, keeping its essence a secret. One more look at the drawing and he stood with a huff.

He'd make his own diagram and plans tomorrow. In three strides, he reached the bed in his office/bedroom. His gaze fell on the sun/moon pendant on the thick silver chain. Not one to wear jewelry, he kept the necklace his mother had given him over three decades ago always visible on the bedside table. He sat on the edge of the bed, lifted the pendant, and opened it. On one side, his younger face stared back. His wife smiled from the other. Underneath those photos were his mom and dad. He brought the two sides together with a noiseless click and rubbed his thumb over the blue and yellow sun/moon faces. "I bet you'd have some advice for me, wouldn't you, Mom?" The love she exuded touched his soul every time he held the necklace.

He toed off his sandals and slipped out of his clothes. Sidling beneath the covers, he stowed the pendant under his pillow then switched off the lamp. On his back, he tucked his hands in his pits and stared at the ceiling. *Dad's right. I need to know more history about the house.* Dory was right too. There was something about Phaedra. And him. *Phaedra and me.*

His bemused feelings for Phaedra were as big a mystery as his befuddled attitude about the house.

****

The next morning, Harlan did a visual check on the crew working at the east end of Main Street. The conversion of a three-story house into a bed and breakfast proceeded smoothly. The phone call to his two-man crew at a remodel in Copperdale satisfied him, so he drove to the Big Purple House. After unloading his telescoping ladder, he clipped a metal tape measure to his belt. With a large drawing pad and pencil in hand for making his notes, he first surveyed the outside of the house. Once done, he positioned the ladder and walked the roof. Clouds hung on the horizon, but sun beat on his neck and forehead, making him wish he'd put on the ballcap he carried in his truck. He found curled, missing, and discolored shingles. This could be the one major expense, next to his bill, for Phaedra. New roof. Back on the ground, lunchtime drew near as he unlocked the front door then stepped inside.

With a deep breath, he scanned the dining room to his right and then the parlor to his left. He smelled the past, one of his favorite things about decades-old houses. Unfortunately, this house wouldn't quite reveal exactly what went into the scent.

Traversing the edge of the parlor, he inspected the baseboards—jointed with a decorative cap on a wider base. He'd seen the style before in other upper crust homes of Joshua. The wood appeared to be in good condition, but the paint was marred and scratched. A light sanding and new coat would fix that. Standing in front of the fireplace, he again admired the workmanship, sensed the generations of those who'd sat before it…in the beginning a joy and then loneliness. "Hmm."

He pivoted, glanced at the chandelier, and experienced the same sense of need as yesterday. A hollow spot in his chest. Loneliness. He had the urge to talk to the crystals, tell the ceiling light he planned on shining it up, and Annette would enjoy this room. "You're getting batty, MacKenzie."

Areas of the house left him cold, while others imparted physical manifestations he'd not experienced before—why? No wonder he was off his game.

"I need to know more." With the tape measure and notepad in hand, he stepped outside, locked the door, and strode back to his truck. He'd take his lunchbreak at the Joshua Historical Society. The urge to get some history on this house overwhelmed the need to stay on schedule. He'd never be able to concentrate if he didn't discover the mystery behind the Big Purple House. Or rather, Lilac End. He needed to dive deeper into the history.

Luckily, as he approached the JHS on Main Street, a parking spot opened directly in front. He didn't notice the closed sign in the window until his hand pulled down on the locked door lever. "Damn." He looked at the hours. Nine to one, Monday through Friday. He just missed them. Peering through the door glass, he saw Wanda Byerson. They'd worked together on the library committee for the high school when her daughter and his son were school mates. She knew more about Joshua than most people of his or his father's generation.

Wanda waved, came from behind the counter, and unlocked the door. "Why, hi, Harlan.

"I didn't know the office closed at one."

She peeked around him in both directions. "I'll let *you* in."

Locking the door behind him, she nudged him forward. "Come away from the window before we attract anymore late-comers. Not that we're ever flooded with customers." She tightened her gray ponytail as she led him deeper into the office. "What can I do for you?"

"I need to do some research and don't know where to begin. But I can come back. I don't want to trouble you."

"Nonsense." Bright gray eyes sparkled in her round face. "I'll at least see if we can be of any help, so you know if you need to come back. What are you researching?"

"The Big Purple House."

"I heard Lolly's sister is buying it from Phaedra. Isn't that super?" She clapped once, and a toothy smile like her daughter's, whom he saw only yesterday at the Little Market, lit her face. "I've always thought that house should come to life again." Her remark reminded him of what he liked about living in Joshua: close knit community, concern for the history and the city.

"I'm wondering about the original owners, the Herseys."

"Ah, yes. The disappearing millionaire. Probably a billionaire by today's standards." As she talked, she climbed onto a stepping stool and stretched to take a book from a shelf behind her. "Probably something in here for starters." She plopped it onto the counter.

"What's that?"

"It's a registry of sorts. Dates back to the late 1800s as to who owned what residential properties. There're ones for the mines too, but they're much more complicated. Mr. Hersey'd be sure to show up in those. But let's check the Big Purple House. Maybe there will be something interesting on a personal side." She opened the book and flipped a few pages then peered over black framed reading glasses. "What's the address? And do you know the exact year the house was built?"

"1923." He gave her the address and moved behind her to look over her shoulder.

She ran her finger down the print then flipped another page. "Here it is. Lilac End. Completed in June of 1923. Built and owned by John Carl Hersey."

"Is there any more—"

"Oh, wait. Looks like ownership changed later in the year."

He waited, anxious for her to find the section in the back of the book cross-referencing the change.

"Well, that's unusual."

"What?"

"Apparently, he added his wife to the deed as full owner in October of 1923."

"Unusual?" He stepped aside as she turned toward him.

"Yep. For the times. Men were men and women were, well, not quite equal partners. I'm not saying it wasn't done, but especially in the testosterone history of Joshua, these mining moguls gave new meaning to macho. Did you know at one time women couldn't own property unless a male relative was on the deed with them? And it wasn't until the seventies that a woman could access a line of credit without a man cosigning?"

Wanda was always a wealth of little-known facts. "No, I didn't." No doubt she had more women's rights details to impart, but he needed to keep her on track. "And so he added Lilac Hersey?"

She found the entry on the page again. "Yep. Lilac Louise Lambert Hersey."

Lambert? "L-a-m-b-e-r-t?"

"Yes. That's how it's spelled. Does the name mean something to you?"

A curious twitch in his chest. "My mother's middle name was Lambert."

****

Nora stepped out of the Bordello Bakery and caught a glimpse of Harlan's truck pulling away from the curb. *Damn. Just missed him.* She folded down the top tighter on her sandwich bag and strolled around the corner to the vacant lot next to Magpie's Mercantile where she'd left her car.

An hour spent in the Mining Museum on street level and the Bordello Bakery in the basement did little to give her any insight on what used to be Ma Betsy's establishment, "The House of Pleasure." A plaque on the outside wall imparted some of the infamous crib's history, but GG's journal revealed more than the historic designation. A few items in a glass cabinet and one faded photo were all that was left of Ma Betsy's. GG didn't appear in the photo. She might've combed her hair with the pearl-handled comb or drank from the porcelain cup, but Nora had no way of knowing. They were thought to be items owned by the madam, Betsy.

She tossed her sandwich on the passenger seat then started the car. An urge to reread some of her great grandmother's journal entries gnawed at her stomach more than hunger.

Inside her room, she slipped out of her shoes and then opened the small refrigerator. She removed one of the bottles of wine, uncorked it, and filled the plastic hotel room cup. With the book in her lap, she ate her lunch and read.

> *March 3, 1924*
> *It's all through the crib now that I am John's and ONLY John's!!!! When Ma made my new dress yesterday, the rest of the girls kept peeking in to see what we were doing. I've never felt so special! While I got dressed today, Ruth tried her best to get me to cut my hair, but I refused. I know it's all the rage with society ladies to have a short style, but John complimented me on my hair the first time he came to Ma's. None of the men EVER complimented me. I twisted and tucked it up, and Ruth took a strip of the voile and tied it around my head so I looked stylish. Ma moved a small, round table and two chairs into my room. All she told me was I'd be having dinner in my room. Did that get a look from Ruth! Ha! I dressed in my new clothes and felt totally silly standing around my bedroom all dressed up. I couldn't sit or think straight. No one but John will ever be in my bed again!!!!*
> *When John knocked, I went to the door and let him in like he was calling on me at my home. Which it is, I guess. I took his hat and coat again and asked him to sit. This time he said I should sit with him. We sat at the table (at the table, not on the bed!), and before I had time to say two words, there was another knock. He told me to stay seated, and HE answered MY door. I was speechless. In walked a boy with a large wicker basket. John spread our meal on the table. We ate. We talked. We laughed. I could've been in Paris with the Eiffel Tower out my window.*
> *After dinner, he directed we should "adjourn to the bedroom." His words, which got a giggle from*

me. All we did was step away from the table. When I started to take off my clothes, he stopped me. He insisted on doing it. I was sort of embarrassed but touched too and excited. And the sex was good as always, but the best part, the saddest part, the happiest part was what he told me as we lay afterwards. He had one hand behind his head, and he held his cigarette with the other blowing smoke circles in the air. It's what he does and I LOVE it. The other men just do their business and off they go. Anyway, I like to lay my head on his chest while he smokes. I can hear his heart and when he talks his words rumble in my ear. This time, he got so personal. My God, I must be special if he tells me these things.

His wife, Lilac, is pregnant. Their baby is due next month. But he's not a happy man. Lilac doesn't allow him to touch her. I can't believe he told me this. She hasn't let him have her since she found out she was pregnant. There is NO LOVE in his house. He told me even when they did have sex, before the pregnancy, she was colorless. She didn't do for him what I do!!! At once, my heart ached and it soared. Although sorry for him, I was glad he was unhappy. Isn't that awful of me? I don't care. I am. I climbed onto him, took the last drag of his cigarette and then asked what pleasure did he want from me. And he said, and I have to think about it over and over, he said HE WANTED TO PLEASURE ME. I don't care about Lilac or the baby. John Hersey is MINE.

March 27, 1924
Sometimes, after John and I make love, he lies next to me and is silent. I like it better when he talks. I don't know what to do when he's silent. He's there but isn't. I mean his body is with me, but he seems to concentrate on the ceiling or something he sees in the air. Tonight, I asked him why. He drew me close, kissed each cheek and my nose and pulled me into

him. His breath warmed the top of my head as he spoke. He told me lying by my side is the only time he feels peace and comfort. The time allows him to think clearly. What would he be thinking after making love, lying in my bed with the scent of me on him? Is he thinking about me? I wanted to know, but he grew silent again.

While he was thinking, I did my own thinking. I never ask him about Lilac. She must be an awful woman to be married to. But I thought about how much time he is with me and how much more time he spends with her. The thought of how much of his life he's unhappy angered me. I told him so. He scooped me up and sat me on top of him. He was rough, and his face got pink like he was angry. He clutched my shoulders so hard, it scared me. He told me she's his wife, and he wouldn't have me speak poorly of her. She's with child and has a proper attitude about sex. She's a proper lady.

He may as well have slapped me across the face. What does that make me? He can't enjoy her, touch her, and croon to her like he does to me. She won't do for him what I do! My whole insides crumbled. I hurt. My eyes burned so bad that I couldn't stop the tears. I'm nothing more than his whore, nothing more than an outlet for his sexual appetite. I knew I'd never be anything more than that to him. I couldn't stop crying.

He started huffing. I was sitting on him and felt his anger. His cheeks got really red, and his thin lips grew thinner. Maybe I should've been scared, but all I could feel was pain. I shut my eyes to his disdain. He held my shoulders so tight, I couldn't move. We stayed like that for several moments. I suppose. It felt like forever. Then his grip on my shoulders went soft. His hips shuddered where I sat and his hardness formed. I wanted to leap off his belly. But I couldn't. He'd paid for me. Ma depends on his money.

When his hands slid down to my breasts, and he

fondled me ever so gentle, God help me I was happy with his touch. He whispered my name twice. This was the John I'm happy to be with. I stopped crying, but I couldn't look at him. I still hurt. He told me to look at him. I just couldn't. Then he whispered Genny, Genny, Genny. He'd never shortened my name like that. And his voice sounded jerky. I opened my eyes and saw him. Crying!!! He told me he was sorry. And I knew he meant it. And I knew whatever Lilac is to him, I AM MORE. He gripped my thighs with his large hands and lifted me and entered. He told me he'll love me forever. HE LOVES ME!!!

Nora wiped the tear off her cheek. "What a sap you were, GG." She tipped her glass for another swallow and found it empty. Lifting the bottle from the nightstand, she poured another glass. *Love can do that to you.* "I guess." If she'd felt that way about Ed—if he'd felt that way about her—maybe things would've turned out differently. Oh hell, who was she kidding? Her great grandmother had loved someone madly who professed endless love, and look where that got her.

Yeah, what's love got to do with it? She raised her glass in a toast. "I'm with you, Tina Turner."

****

Halfway back to the house, Harlan did a U-turn. He could've called Magpie, but if she had customers she wouldn't answer. Hanging around her store to catch her in a free moment would be better. He didn't know if he should drill his dad on Susie Muse's family history. Sometimes his father loved to talk about his mother, and other times he grew sad.

He parked beside her store. Inside, as expected, Magpie stood behind the counter taking money from a customer. He nodded at his sister then pretended to be interested in the music boxes on the shelf next to the counter.

"I put my card in the bag. If you decide you'd like another piece, give me a call. Frank MacKenzie does special orders too."

The bell on the door jangled as the smiling customer opened and then closed it behind her.

He straightened the music box he toyed with then faced her.

"Hey, Mags."

"Aren't you supposed to be working on the Big Purple House?" She lifted a water bottle from under the counter, unscrewed the lid, and took a swallow.

"I am, in a way. And maybe you can help."

"What's up?"

"Mom's middle name, Lambert. You know anything about it? Kind of different for a woman's middle name."

"Hmm." Magpie set aside her water and then leaned on the counter, chin in hand and eyes squinted. "I never thought much about it. I assumed Lambert was a family name on Mom's mother's side."

"I never thought about it either." He tucked fingers into his pockets. "I have only a vague memory of her father. But I do remember his mom and dad, our great grandparents. The Muses."

"Yeah, they more or less raised Mom." His sister fingered the sun/moon pendant on the chain around her neck. "Her dad wasn't very involved. Seems like I remember something about him being a record producer or something in San Francisco. Died before Mom."

He scanned memories but nothing popped. "I remember the great grands and visiting some of the Muse relatives but have no memory of her mother's side."

"Nope. We never saw them. I do know Mom's mother's name was Monica Lambert Biddington before she married Jacque Muse. Mom said her mother contracted pneumonia when she went to the hospital to have a baby. She died in the hospital, and the baby died a month later." She straightened and crossed her arms. "Mom wasn't quite two. But I have no memory of anything about the Biddingtons, which would've been her grandparents. They must've been out of Mom's life after her mother died." She came from behind the counter and leaned her jean clad hip against it. "Why all this sudden interest in the family tree?"

"When I went to the Historical Society to do some research on the Big Purple House, the name Lambert came up."

"Research? What kind of research?"

"I wanted to know more about the history of the house." An engine raced on the street outside. He gazed out the window. "To help me get a feel for the renovations."

"Do you always do that?"

55

"No."

"Why now?" She cocked her head, inquisitive as ever. His sister always had a million questions about everything. The pesky bird whose name she bore fit her.

"It's hard to explain." He'd made a giant leap confessing to his dad about the clear feelings he absorbed from inanimate objects and houses. He'd never been able to confide in Magpie. Her self-assuredness battered his.

"Try me."

"I'm not real inspired." *And I'll leave it at that.* "Dad thought it would help if I knew more history on the house. I found out Lilac Hersey's maiden name was Lambert."

"*Sacrebleu!*"

"Yeah, I thought so too. Dad might know something, but I wasn't sure I should ask him about Mom's relatives. Wanda volunteered to do some more digging for me. Said to check back with her."

"She's great with historical research. But ask Dad."

"You think?" The bell on the door jangled, and he glanced over his shoulder to see Phaedra enter the shop.

"Hey, looks like the gang's all here." She strolled closer.

He took in a heady whiff of her rose oil. "You following me? Checking up on my progress?"

"You're so suspicious." She bumped him with her hip. "Actually, I did see your truck and decided to stop. Maybe I should start paying you by the hour."

"Oh man. Another stab. You're full of them." He returned her bump, squatting to make it hip to hip. Her blue eyes twinkled like crystals. A strand of white hair hung along her cheek, threatening to stick to her glossy pink lips. He caught it with a finger, trailing his knuckle along her cheek. And he was lost in her gaze.

Until Magpie cleared her throat.

Phaedra blinked, and a noise somewhere between a gasp and a sigh parted her lips. "Oh, uh, Mags, I wanted to see if I could get the blue jacket for the store in Copperdale. I'll replace it next week." She sidestepped, then riffled through the rack of her clothes.

"Sure." Magpie answered her friend, but her scrutiny, cocked brow, and half smile, addressed him.

With Phaedra's back to them, he frowned and narrowed his eyes at his sister with a keep-your-questions-to-yourself expression. She hadn't missed whatever just happened and smirked.

"I better get back to work." Mags made him uncomfortable and the physical effect their friend had on him caused reactions he didn't want his nosy sister to notice. "I'll call you later, Phae, with a progress report."

She whirled around, blue jacket in hand, clanking against the rack of clothes. "Oh. Okay. Or why don't you come to dinner tonight? I've got two steaks in the freezer I need to cook. You could fill me in while you grill the steaks and I make salad."

"Invite me to dinner and make me work for the meal?"

"Got to get some kind of work out of you."

He smothered a laugh and feigned a frown. "It really isn't wise to antagonize the contractor. But I'll be there with a full report. I missed lunch, so how about an early dinner. Five-ish?"

"Sounds good."

On the sidewalk, he strode to his truck, feeling far more anticipation for the evening than a conference with a homeowner and old friend should bring. He breathed deep. A light scent of rose oil lingered in his head. The puffs of clouds on the northern horizon billowed higher in the late afternoon sun. He leaned against his truck fender. The sun-heated metal penetrated his jeans as he dug his cell out of a pocket and checked the time. After three. Not enough time to get anything done at the house. He called his crews for updates then slid onto the truck seat. A stop for a good bottle of cabernet he knew she'd like with steak and then a slow shower was all he could wrap his mind around right now anyway. A steak, a glass of wine, and an evening in The Ravine with an old friend who happened to be the sexiest lady in Joshua had his engine revved higher than his truck.

CHAPTER FIVE

Harlan parked his truck in the driveway behind Phaedra's Jeep at a quarter to five. The double-eave, one-story, yellow bungalow with brick pillars and a covered porch across the front embodied the essence of The Ravine of the 1930s. Small boulders formed a two-foot-high retaining wall, separating a dinky front yard from the street. A walk cut through the mishmash of flowers and plants filling the yard. The brightest house in The Ravine in his book.

She opened the door when his foot hit the top step. "Right on time." Her head nodded, appraising him head to toe. "You didn't come straight from work."

"No, you hardnose, I didn't." He handed her the bottle of wine when he stopped in the doorway, his hand brushing hers, and smiled. "I thought you might appreciate dining with my cleaned-up version."

She visibly swallowed. "I appreciate your thoughtfulness."

An impulse to put his arms around her and plant a hello kiss on her lips rocked him. Giving himself a mental shake, he moved out of kissing range and into the matchbox sized entry. "Lead me to the grill."

Following her through the living room, he stopped in the kitchen when she halted and pointed to the Dutch door. "The grill is on the brick patio out back. It's small but roomy enough for a table."

"And *who* did you have build it?"

"Don't get your hackles up. It was years ago before you opened your own business." She handed him seasoned steaks on a platter and a long-handled fork. "It's already heated and ready to go.

"Well, hell, you've done half the work."

"With the way you've been—"

"Don't." He poked the air with the grilling fork and made a squint-eyed, mad face. "Just pour me a glass of something, and chill, lady."

She laughed. "You got it. I'll bring you a glass of the wine you so graciously brought. I see you were smart enough to buy red to go with the steak."

Outside and down two steps, he found the grill on a patio made of red brick that matched the pillars out front. The propane grill and a table for two filled the space. Tiny white lights rimming the bricks and the roof of the house, would throw just enough light onto the area once the sun went down. The backyard was no larger than the front. Juniper, cedar, and honeysuckle rimmed the perimeter, creating a private sanctuary. Flagstone paths crisscrossed between other native plants and vines. He breathed deep of the last remnants of honeysuckle and clear mountain air. Although The Ravine spanned an area lower than the town, the elevation was still at about five-thousand feet. After the steaks hit the grill, sizzling and sending up a delicious scent, he scanned the blue sky. He'd just stepped into a little piece of heaven.

"Here you go, Chef." Phaedra came beside him with two glasses and handed him one.

"This is gorgeous, Phae." He swept a hand through the air. "I didn't know you had a green thumb."

"Yeah, I love digging in the dirt. But about all I have to do now is a little maintenance." She gazed across the yard, an obviously proud grin on her face.

"Why haven't I been here before now?" The tendency seemed to be to gather at Frank's, which always felt like "home," Magpie's because she liked to cook, or outdoors in the mountains or parks.

"You have." She chuckled. "We used to play chase through this yard."

"Sure didn't look like this." Only grass adorned the property back then. A fleeting memory of rolling in it after tackling Phaedra in a game of chase made him smile.

"No, I've made a few changes."

And we've changed too. He studied her profile as she regarded her sanctuary and sipped wine. Like skirting around a sink hole in the ruins below Miners' Mile, he'd made wide circles around the issue of their evolving friendship. In his mind. The only reason he'd not given in to his newfound attraction was fear of losing his friend. But each moment spent with her, he slipped farther into the sink hole.

"You're staring. Flip the steaks."

Her words jarred him, and he laughed. "You're kind of bossy for a boss. We're on social time now."

"Social, huh? Thought you came over for a free meal while filling me in on the house. You have other issues to report?"

He flicked a glance at her. Did she refer to a report on the house or did she have something else in mind? Because he thought he might want to tell her what he thought of the way she filled out her jeans. How her shiny pink lips invited him. Or the admiration he held for her creative nature, biting sense of humor, and independent streak. How he treasured her friendship, but realized he wanted more.

"Harlan? You're staring, again."

"There *is* something about the house." Talking to her about his sensitivities regarding the house would be simpler than broaching the subject of his...feelings for her. "First, how do you take your steak?"

"Pink."

Like your lips. "Then I think we're about there."

"Great. I'll get the baked potatoes from the oven and the salad. Unless you'd rather eat inside."

"Out here is fine."

She moved away then paused. "Want to tell me about the house first?"

"Let's talk while we eat. I'm starving."

Once the food covered the round wooden table and their wine refreshed, Phaedra resumed the conversation where they'd left off. "Now, what's the problem with the house?"

"I don't know."

She chewed slowly and fixed him with a puzzled expression.

He poured blue cheese dressing on his salad. "The house is structurally sound. No worry there. You need a new roof, but it's not to the leaking stage yet. I'm experiencing...odd sentiments. Like the

60

house is hiding something or protecting someone."

Her forehead smoothed, and her puzzlement vanished. "Why am I not surprised?"

"You get what I'm talking about?"

She cut her steak "Probably not."

"Then—"

"You're a MacKenzie. You're all a little odd." She spoke around chewing her food.

The wine in his mouth went down roughly, and he laughed. "That's a glowing assessment."

"It's not a bad odd. Like Magpie is fond of saying the universe *talks* to you. Or her anyway. Elidor has other voices in her head. I'm guessing houses communicate with you." Shrugging, she scooped potato onto her fork. "I love you guys. You're...colorful." She tilted her head, popped the healthy bite into her mouth, and chewed through a beguiling smile.

He should've known the roadblocks the house threw up wouldn't surprise her. She'd known his mother, had been damn near part of their family for decades. Cutting his steak, he avoided her gaze. Yeah, part of the family. But she didn't give off family vibes any longer. Dory intuited his passion over the phone. How did Phaedra feel?

"Is the house telling you to get the hell out and leave it alone? Threatening you?"

Chuckling, he wiped his mouth and leaned on the table. "No, it doesn't work like that. I'm feeling sadness and...something disguised or hidden." He still wasn't sure about the dizzy episode on the stairs—Dory's dark energy comment?

"Hmm." She kept eating, nodding to encourage him to explain further.

"Do you know anything about the original owners, the Herseys?"

"A little, I guess. Like what?"

"I found out today Lilac Hersey's maiden name was Lambert. My mother's middle name was Lambert. Seems like a freakish coincidence. And with the vibrations I'm getting..."

"You think you could be related to the Herseys?"

"No idea. We know next to nothing about my grandmother's side of the family, the Biddingtons. Mom's mother, whose middle name was also Lambert, died when she was two. Her father's parents, the

Muses, raised her. We had contact with that side some, but not the Biddington side."

"Time to do some family tree research."

"But how quirky is it my mom, Susie Muse, would end up in Joshua, decades after one of her relatives lived here? And mining moguls to boot. You'd think that kind of family history would be talked about." He pushed his plate back. "More than a strange coincidence."

"The universe *does* work in *strange* ways."

"Or so Susie Muse told me many times." He quirked a smile.

Phaedra clasped her hands under her chin and sighed, her crystal blue gaze going dreamy.

"What?"

"What?" She dropped her hands to the table then diverted her attention to the lush backyard.

"You were looking at me like…"

"Like what?"

Like you'd like to kiss me. Like I'm not just your buddy. Standing, he rounded the table and gripped her arms, bringing her to stand.

She didn't resist. In fact, her chin came up, and her shoulders relaxed into his grip. "So, are you going to…can you still work on the house or—"

"I don't want to talk about the house. I want to talk about you, me, the way you look at me—like just then."

For a moment, only their breathing filled his ears. The quiet of The Ravine settled around them, muffled further by fauna and flora enclosing Phaedra's paradise. Her thighs brushing at his sent a beam of heat to his groin.

She peered from under dark lashes in total contrast to her white hair. "It's that look of yours. Do you know you do it? Chin tilted down and the slightest hint of a smirk. It's classic Harlan. And you've had a light shadow beard lately which adds a touch of bad boy."

A laugh stuck in his throat. She looked way too serious for him to find her assessment amusing. "And?"

"And what?"

Further relaxing, her breasts sent a caress over his chest. He waited. He wanted to kiss her, run his hands all over her, but he waited. This would send them over the line. He needed to know she was of the same mind as he.

"And it's sexy." Her chest expanded with a deep breath, pressing into him. "And all I want to do is this." She broke free of his grasp, clasped him around the neck, and brought his mouth to hers.

Her lips feathered against his, tentative.

Pressing his mouth firmly on hers, he wanted her to know he was all in on this. When he tasted her, she moaned and responded like she didn't get enough to eat and wanted his kiss to satisfy her hunger. He drank the wine and sweetness of her, yet he wanted more. While she massaged his neck, he slid his hands down her sides and then cupped her butt to press her harder against his building ache.

She broke the kiss with a gasp. "What are we doing?"

Not realizing how lost in the fog of passion he was until she spoke, her words came as if spinning from the depths of a mining shaft in Spirit Mountain. When they echoed in his brain, he took a ragged breath. "I think it's kind of obvious."

"Yes. But no. It's not."

He didn't want to let go of her or her heat pulsing against his groin. Her hands splayed his chest. When did she slide them from around his neck? "I thought—"

"I don't think we *are* thinking, Harlan."

"Do we need to analyze this?"

"Maybe?"

Gliding his hands from her butt, he brought his fingers to the small of her back and fingered the tips of her hair. "Okay. What do you want to talk about?" As if he didn't know—as if he didn't have concerns about going from friends to lovers. *Before.* Before he'd kissed her, before his hands caressed the woman, before he sensed the passion and pleasure she possessed. And before he knew he wanted to please her in every way he could.

"We've been friends for so long. I treasure our friendship."

"Your friendship means the world to me, Phae. I don't want to change that."

"But what if..."

What could he say to convince her when he didn't have the answer? He'd sure as hell like to try it out though. As long as he touched her, looked into those angel blue eyes, felt her heat from breasts to hips, he couldn't think about anything else. He let his hands fall to his sides, and he backed away from her fire. With a deep breath, he said what he figured he needed to say. "Let's think on it. I've been imagining kissing you for weeks, maybe months now. I just didn't know if you would hate me or kiss back. You kissed back. Hell, you kissed me first."

"Oh, Harlan, I—"

"No, no, that's fine. But you're right—what if? So, we'll just let this simmer for now." *Simmer is exactly what's happening. A slow burn.*

"Harlan…" She touched his cheek, scruffed her fingertips along his jawline.

He bent and kissed her nose, then lightly on her mouth, swollen and soft from the kiss. "Let's do the dishes—"

"No. I'll take care of them. Better we say goodnight now."

No. "Yeah."

Following the flagstone path, he walked to the side of the house toward his truck out front.

"Talk tomorrow?" She called.

With a glance over his shoulder, he answered, "Of course."

Was she really afraid of spoiling a good friendship, or had kissing him convinced her they should remain plutonic friends? In his truck, he thumped the steering wheel. He'd been so hot and bothered, had he missed her lack of enthusiasm? No. His own desire wouldn't have escalated if there had been no heat of desire coming from her. He started the truck. Okay. Just let her simmer for a while. When the time was right…

****

Phaedra. The first thing on his mind when Harlan woke, and a damned good reason for an early morning arousal. Pushing pleasant thoughts and sensations aside, he swung his feet to the floor. *Work, MacKenzie.* Phone calls to his crews in the field ate up the better part of two hours. A tepid shower and cold cereal breakfast later, he grabbed his to-go coffee mug to make the drive into the Copper Hills district to work on the Big Purple House, the uppermost home in the shadow of Spirit Mountain. *A house that might have a few spirits of its own.*

On Lilac Lane, he eased his truck along the curb then cut the engine. After clipping on his tape measure and lifting his pad from the seat, he stepped out into the bright sunshine of midmorning. As he walked the sidewalk, Nora's violet eyes flashed across his mind when he glimpsed the house. Phaedra called them blue. Did he have purple on the brain? Did they appear purple next to her low-hanging red bangs? He paused on the porch. Did his curiosity about her, her curiosity about the house, and the mystery he sensed surrounding the house have anything to do with how he saw her? *What the hell does that even mean, Mackenzie?* Yeah, he had purple on the brain.

He unlocked the front door, ready to resume where he'd left off yesterday inspecting walls and baseboards. The closet in front of him needed a closer inspection. The door stood ajar. With a light touch, the door eased open to reveal the once-upon-a-time office. A walk-in sized closet by today's standards, but not big enough for a modern office. Standing in the doorway, he again experienced the perception that his presence would be an intrusion. He crossed the threshold, eyeing the desk. "Here goes." He brushed his fingertips over the wood surface. This time the tingling brought a distinct sense of joy to his gut. The quivers traveled from his hand to his elbow and ceased as soon as he lost contact with the desk. Where it startled him yesterday, today the experience was pleasant.

"Hell. This place is a real mixed bag." He switched on the overhead fixture, which provided only dim lighting, then pulled a small flashlight from his pocket and ran the beam along the bottom of the walls. The baseboard, a single edge, ornate style, horribly gouged and scraped, needed to be replaced. With the metal tape, he measured and recorded the dimensions of the space, righted, and regarded the desk. *The master's closet.* The man had his secrets, good and bad. He knew that as sure as if he'd been there. He lifted his hand, his fingers close to the desk, when a creak jarred him.

****

"I startled you again." Nora laughed. "I seem to be good at that." When she'd seen the front door open, she hadn't bothered knocking. She would've liked to slip unseen into the closet with him, press against his back, and wrap her arms around to caress his chest, but the wood floor gave her away. *The closet.* Curiosity flooded her with excitement. "The door was open. Hope you don't mind I came on in unannounced. I thought you might need a break." Clutching the uncorked bottle of wine to her breast with one hand, she held out the bag containing cheese, crackers, and two plastic cups from the hotel.

"That's fine. I wasn't sure what time you were coming by." He moved out of the closet, coming deliciously closer. "You didn't need to bring…food."

"I saw you eyeing my wine and cheese when we left the Little Market."

"Did you?" He took the bag from her hand. His half-smile was hard to read, but he wasn't turning her away.

"Shall we roam around a little? Give me a tour while we find the perfect spot for wine and cheese?" She sidled closer. "Or are you ready for a break now?"

"There isn't any furniture, so let's put your refreshments in the kitchen."

"Looks like a desk behind you." Nudging by him, she made sure her leg grazed his. "And it's so cozy in here." She set the wine on the desktop then held out her hand for the bag. "Gimmie." Wiggling her fingers in his direction, she cocked a hip. His eye flicker told her he'd registered her movement.

He came back into the closet. "Kind of early for wine and cheese. You didn't need to—"

"Of course I did." She pulled the cups and food out of the bag. "I'm totally interrupting your day." She poured as she spoke, bending just enough that the gap from the top button she'd left undone hopefully gave a hint of what could be found beneath her tailored shirt. "I bet you've been up since the butt crack of dawn. Consider this an appetizer to lunch which is right around the corner." She took his drawing pad out of his hand and set it on the desk. He stuck his pencil in a shirt pocket. Handing him a glass, she held hers in a toast. "Here's to new friendship and collaboration on my book."

He laughed then drank. "I don't know about taking any credit on your book."

She peeled two mini Babybel cheeses, the wax the same bright shade of red as her fitted capris, and handed him one. He shook his head when she offered the box of crackers. "But you're my source, my own private source in Joshua. I can't really do this without you." How much he'd help her remained to be seen. If the way he stared into her eyes indicated anything, they could at least have a little fun.

After refreshing their wine before needed, she slowly peeled another cheese. "I just love these, don't you?" She stepped closer to put it in his hand.

"As a matter of fact, I do. Awfully nice of you to share your room snack with me."

Lots more I'd like to share, sugar. She filled her mouth with wine and chastised herself. Information first. Fun second. "This is a good-sized closet. Roomy enough for an office, although the desk takes up a lot of floor space." Big, old piece of furniture. "This desk looks ancient."

"I think it's as old as the house. Closets doubled as offices or private rooms in the twenties so I'm guessing that's why the desk is in here."

Closet and *office*. Her pulse raced. She glanced around, pivoting, and purposefully bumping him in the process. "Really?" The thrum of excitement caught her breath. "So, this was John Hersey's office?"

"That might be a reasonable conclusion. Hard to say, but—"

"But of course." Words from GG's journal played in her mind. "Yes, it is."

Harlan stirred; his knee touched her, and she mentally slapped herself back to the present.

"You sound certain. Something in your research?"

"Oh, well, these old houses …well, it makes sense is all. With the desk…" She contemplated the walls. *Could this be the place?* "Do you think the room has been changed since the Herseys lived here? It's so exciting to find a house with history and still has the original…walls and such." She met his gaze with what she hoped came off as a professional, but enticing, smile. "What a writing point for my book."

"This room hasn't been changed. Someone hung a rod and some hooks, but nothing else that I see. I haven't gone through every room yet but outwardly, the house appears to be exactly as built in 1923."

Unable to contain her exhilaration, she looped her arm through Harlan's and leaned into him. "This house could be the cornerstone of my whole book." Aware of her breasts peaking against the hard muscles of his bicep combined with the headiness of her goal being within reach, her breath quickened. This man was gorgeous. His muscles tensed. In her peripheral vision, the desk invited them. Seduction on the same desk GG made love to John Hersey? Should she? Tempting.

He cleared his throat and set his glass on the desk. "Why don't I give you the tour of the house now." He gestured for her to lead the way.

"Sure. That would be super." Inwardly, she chuckled. He appeared a bit nervous, yet she knew his thoughts were the same as hers. But he was a gentleman. *God, there aren't many of those around anymore.*

"If you'll come this way, you see the parlor which would've been the center of all things social in the twenties and thirties. I suppose still could be, although a lot of entertaining goes on in the kitchen and outside nowadays. The fireplace, even the chandelier, are original."

"Beautiful." *I don't care.*

"Come back through the foyer, and this is the dining room, and this way the kitchen. There are two stairways to the second floor. Let's take this one." He gestured into the dining room then waved his hand at the stairs, directing her upward.

She used the opportunity to sway just enough as she ascended the stairs. His eyes would have to be on her butt. Stopping abruptly, she swiveled, and his face stopped inches from her breasts. She put her hands on his shoulders. "Sorry." Dipping her chin, she sighed, her fingers twitching on the muscled man beneath her touch. "I was just going to remark how steep these stairs are."

"The economy of getting from one level to the next. Not for visual appreciation for sure." He nodded as if to urge her forward, yet he didn't move. His expression conveyed an interest she'd take advantage of eventually.

"I've heard these old houses contain hidden compartments where the wealthy owners kept their valuables. Are there any stories of hidden treasures at Lilac End? Have you gone treasure hunting yet?"

"That would be a first for me. I've never run into any hidden doors or compartments in any of the houses I've remodeled. This house looks pretty straightforward from what I've seen. And considering Joshua's rep as a ghost town, with plenty of myths floating around, I've never heard any anecdotes about Lilac End."

He angled his shoulders toward their ascent, but she kept her breasts at eye level for him.

"It would've been fun to have a legend attached to the house." When he merely shrugged, she continued the climb. *Good. This is good. No treasure hunting in this house. Yet.* At the top of the stairs, she turned into him. "The bedrooms are on this level?"

He scuddled around her. "And the bathroom." Pointing out each room, he directed her into the largest with a wave of his hand. "This is the master and has a great view of the mountains and backyard below."

The closet on the first floor still occupied her mind. She eased close to him and looked out the window.

He cleared his throat. "Great view, don't you think?"

She didn't give a bat's tit about the mountains or the view. Her mind raced. "I'm more convinced than ever this house is going to be the cornerstone of the book. And I'll bet you have other houses you could show me." Pivoting her hips, she brought a thigh against his leg. "I might not even have to look any farther than Joshua for what I need…and want."

****

Phaedra parked behind Nora's car. *Again?* Not able to call Harlan earlier on her dead cellphone, she'd opted to make a surprise appearance while her phone charged on the drive. Maybe she could lure him away for an early lunch. After last night, she thought an innocuous shared meal in the middle of the day would give her some insight on what in Hades she almost did. She admired Harlan as a friend, as a father, as a man. Would adding lover expand their relationship or kill what they had?

The front door stood open. As she stood in the foyer, the sound of footsteps and voices, unintelligible words, drifted overhead. Clutching her keys to her abdomen, she ventured a step toward the staircase when the clutter on the rolltop desk in the closet caught her attention. A bottle of wine, half gone. A box of crackers and a package of cheese rounds; red wax peelings scattered on the wood surface. The footsteps ceased, quiet, and then a few more murmured words. Her heart thumped high in her chest. Her head swirled as she slunk to the bottom of the stairway off the dining room. As much as she wanted to ascend the steps and interrupt whatever they were doing, she couldn't get her feet to move.

Glued to the spot, she stared upward, emotions flared, and the blood rushing in her ears blotted out any noises from above. *I have no right to be angry or jealous.* If Harlan meant nothing more to her than a longtime friend, she would be laughing about him hooking up with the writer. But after last night… A throaty chuckle from the woman broke into her thoughts. Nora was hot, and he was a hotblooded man. Desire slapped her face with heat.

I am jealous. I want more than friendship. And she'd turned him away last night. Cautious. *Since when do I choose caution over passion?* But if an encounter was nothing more than a one-time roll in the hay, their lifelong friendship could sour, die. Maybe it would anyway. She was so physically attracted to him. How could she go back? Another giggle...

What to do? Huffing, she whirled to leave and bumped the handrail. Her keys flew from her hand and dropped to the floor with a loud thunk that echoed up the narrow passageway. Damn. Had they heard? She scooped them up, jaw clenched, and poised to vault.

"Phaedra?"

Too late.

CHAPTER SIX

Harlan jumped, disengaged from Nora, and rushed to the landing. "Phaedra?" She stood at the bottom of the stairs. "Hey, come on up."

Nora brushed against his back, her breasts making a distinct impression, as she leaned around him. "Hi, Phaedra. I'm getting the nickel tour. Harlan is a great guide."

"No, um, continue the tour. I see you've had *lunch*. I'll grab some in town and get back to work. Call later. About the house. If you want."

She waved a hand and traipsed out the door.

"I need to update her on my progress. I'll be back in a minute."

He took the steep stairs as fast as he could, catching Phaedra as she slid onto her vehicle seat. "Hey, don't rush off."

"No problem. I didn't know you had company."

He braced hands on knees to come eye to eye with her. "She's not company. She popped in on me while—"

"You didn't know she was coming by today?"

"Well, yeah, she told me when I took her to the store Wednesday night, but—"

"You spent Wednesday night with her?"

"I didn't *spend* the night with her. I ran into her on the street when I was headed to the Little Market. She asked to go along. She told me she wanted to drop by today so I could show her the house."

She shooed him back and closed the door. "You don't have to explain yourself to me."

With his forearms on the window sill, he frowned in at her. "I'm not. I'm telling you why she's here."

"With wine and cheese." She started the engine.

"It's not what you think."

"I don't think anything."

"Phaedra—"

"Really. Stop. Nothing to explain. No big deal. I need to grab some lunch and get back to work. I have a huge order so you might not see me for a while." She gestured toward the house. "If something comes up, you can call." She flashed a quick smile, cranked the steering wheel, and inched from the curb.

He had no choice but to back out of the window or be dragged along with the Jeep. "Yeah, I'll do that. I'll call."

She angled around Nora's car before the last words left his mouth, made a U-turn, and then drove away. Without a wave. Without so much as a glance.

What the hell just happened? There could be no mistaking the jealousy his best friend displayed toward another woman. His reaction came slowly until he felt for sure he looked like an idiot grinning at the now empty street. Whatever the feelings he found himself embroiled in when they were together affected her too. Last night wasn't a fluke.

Shoving his hands into his jean pockets, he pivoted on his boot heel, stepped over the chunks of sidewalk, and ambled toward the house. He strode into the foyer. Thinking of Phaedra as a friend *and* lover expanded his heart…and sent ripples southward. *Whoa, MacKenzie.* How he approached this turn of events needed to be carried out with less aplomb than he normally possessed. Let her take the lead. Phaedra was an independent—

"Oh! There you are." Until she spoke, he hadn't seen Nora inside the foyer closet; he had totally forgotten about her. Her wide eyes held a note of surprise.

"I'm sorry. I had some things to discuss with Phaedra."

Nora's interest in him, in the house, created a mystery. What was or wasn't happening between Phaedra and him posed a bigger mystery. One he'd rather tackle.

"That's okay. I decided I better let you get back to work. I was cleaning up our little mess on the desk. Would you like me to leave any of this?"

"No. I'm good. Thanks, by the way." He held out a hand. "Can I help you with that?"

"I've got it. Unless you'd like to help me finish it tonight?" She lowered her husky voice to a come-hither drawl and cocked a brow that disappeared under her bangs.

"I can't." If he did anything tonight, he'd see Phaedra. His stomach lurched wondering what to say to his lifelong friend.

"Okay then. I'll get out of your way. I'm going to hold you to showing me some more old houses."

"Yeah, sure. When I can fit it in around work." He made a wide gesture with his hand. She could find houses on her own. She could find men who were sure to respond to her flirtations. Yet he couldn't help a modicum of interest from her obvious come on—he wanted to know why—why he intuited something more than simple sexual attraction. People weren't his thing, but this woman drew him in for some reason other than the obvious.

"Surely you don't work on Sundays. Since the houses I'm interested in aren't designated historic, and they're lived in, I could sure use the help of a local to get me in. I promise to be ever so *appreciative.*" She cocked a brow, using the come-hither dip of her chin.

When he didn't answer immediately, the telltale eyelash batting eased, and she flashed him a smile. "I'll buy dinner. Or lunch. What do you say?"

The woman was persistent. Despite his resolve, a lingering curiosity persisted. "I suppose I could break loose awhile on Sunday."

"Thank you." With a squeeze to his bicep, she left. "See you then," she called over her shoulder.

As she traversed the veranda, he closed the door behind her and moved to the window. She loaded her wine and bag into the green Cavalier, threw him a wave, and drove away. She wasn't hard on the eyes, but that wasn't the reason he'd relented. Her interest in this house, her story about her book, seemed off. Her flirting didn't seem authentic. And his gut told him he needed to know why.

"Agh." He rubbed the back of his neck. This house with the secrets it hid. The veiled motives of the writer. What he should do about the evolution of his relationship with Phaedra. Confusion, indecision, mixed messages. Was the energy of the house throwing his universe out of kilter? He had no idea what he could do to right it. "Keep on working, MacKenzie."

In the foyer closet, he lifted his pad from the desk, a slight tingle traveling over his fingertips. In more than forty years of experiencing clear feelings from inanimate objects, there had never been a physical manifestation. The reoccurring wave of joy in his gut bumped him. Someone, in some time had enjoyed… *Pleasure.* He took a breath. *Gone.* Shaking his head, he backed toward the door.

Outside the closet, he rounded the corner to the dining room—a room not used often. The baseboards and floor looked fine. In the kitchen, his mind wandered to Phaedra's stories of her time in the house as a child. If he'd known her then, played here with her, he would've tuned into the house, even at the age of two or three. In fact, the vibes would've been clearer as a child. *Children are more open to their inner feelings.* But he hadn't known her, not that he could recall. Until her mother moved them to The Ravine, he had no memory of her. They'd made so many memories after. He gazed out the backdoor window to the J on Spirit Mountain. His gut told him he could make a whole new set of memories with her.

****

Nora clutched the prize in her fist, driving with her left hand and one finger of her clenched right hand. Her heart pattered like she'd hit the lottery. She angled into a parking space at the end of the building which housed the Copper Line Hotel and killed the engine. Beyond the front windshield, the Verde Valley stretched in the distance. Only when she'd stepped out of her car and stood at the railing in front of her bumper did she open her fist. The key's red imprint marred the center of her hand.

Luck had worked in her favor ever since she'd stepped foot in Joshua. First, a room in the hotel of which GG wrote. Then the sexy Harlan MacKenzie working on Lilac End…the not yet occupied house. My God, how much more perfect could it get? How about finding a key to the front door of Lilac End? She laughed out loud, pivoted, and strolled to the hotel entrance.

How convenient Phaedra arrived while she and Harlan flirted. An interruption, but it worked in her favor. From the look on the woman's face and her body language, she guessed they must be dating or something. No matter. She'd continue her pretense of needing to research other houses until she had what she came for at

74

Lilac End. When she'd asked for some time on Sunday, a flicker of a frown across the handsome construction worker's face told her she might be laying it on a little thick. As gorgeous as he was, he might just be a straight shooter. How…unusual.

She bounced up each step of the hotel stairs to her room. When Harlan chased after the current owner, and Nora found herself alone in the house, she'd done a rapid rummage through the desk drawers, empty except for one tiny drawer where the key lodged between the side and bottom. A swift check to see if the key fit the front door lock and the plan got a whole lot smoother.

She tossed the sack with cheese and crackers on the bed, then set the key and the half-full bottle of wine on the nightstand. She'd need something for dinner while she waited for nightfall this evening. With the room card and a twenty in hand, she made a quick trip to the deli attached to the hotel. She carried the sandwich and potato salad back to her room and stored them in the fridge.

Kicking off her shoes as she collapsed onto the bed, her head hit the mattress. "Life is damn righteous sometimes." The house wasn't rumored to have hidden treasure. No legends surrounding it. *This is good, very good.* If no one had ever gone treasure hunting in the house, then the house still guarded the fortune. Hersey's wife, Lilac, spoke the truth to GG. Lilac Hersey had been a stupid, vengeful woman.

Rolling onto her stomach, she slid the journal off the nightstand to the bed and randomly selected an entry.

April 20, 1924

I've been so bored and so lonely. Lilac had a baby girl. Louise. Not that John has been around to tell me. It's the talk of Joshua. I haven't seen him in almost two weeks. Will he ever come back? Ma hasn't put me on the floor yet, and I'm continuing to receive my portion, so he must still be paying. But I am sooo scared. What if having a baby with her makes him want to give me up? I'll die. I just know I will.

Margaret and I went to Main Street today to get supplies. I prayed I'd run into him. Even if I couldn't speak to him, at least I could see him. But I didn't.

God probably doesn't answer those sorts of prayers for girls like me. Margaret says I should be happy. As long as he keeps paying, I don't have to spread my legs for dirty miners anymore. She's so uncouth! They aren't dirty, anyway. Not really. Well maybe some are. And I won't do it anymore anyway, even if he doesn't come back. There's nothing Ma can do to make me. I have enough money saved to leave this place if I have to. I don't really know where I'd go or what I'd do. That scares me. I could probably get a job in Phoenix as a housekeeper or waitress. Oh, I'm so, so, so unhappy. I don't want to leave. I just want John to come back to me.

She crawled higher on the bed, stacking pillows against the headboard, bringing the journal with her. She never tired of living vicariously through GG. Rearranging into a sitting position, she lifted the bottle of wine off the nightstand she'd shared with Harlan. After pouring a plastic hotel room glass full, she gently thumbed the pages to find the entry where her great grandmother had first visited Lilac End.

May 13, 1924
JOURNAL OF GENEVIEVE JENKINS, TO BE GENEVIEVE HERSEY ONE DAY SOON!!!
This last week has been glorious. Seeing John makes life bearable, if only for brief moments. And then tonight happened, and I can't even express how I feel. I have to try. I have to be able to remember this feeling for years to come, after I'm old and can't remember the me of today.
He'd only just walked in. My face must have given away my mood. I'd been deep in thought about what my future would be like if John hadn't come into my life. I was nearly in tears, scared, and sad to think about it. Holding me, he asked what was wrong. I admitted to him I was afraid he wouldn't love me anymore, and one day he'd stay home with her and the child, and I'd never see him again. That my life

and my future would be nothing.

He laughed! He called me his silly, little Genny. And then he scooped me up and carried me down the stairs and out to his car. A couple of the girls sat in the parlor. I thought their eyes might pop out of their heads. I didn't know what to do. I couldn't talk. It's like my heart hurled itself into my throat. He set me in his car and off we went. I kept asking him what are you doing, John? What kind of madness is this? I really thought he might be mad or possessed or something. He said the time had come for me to see my future. I got dizzy and could barely breathe. I couldn't dare to imagine what he meant, but when he parked in front of the grand house, I nearly fainted. Was he going to march me in and parade me in front of his wife?

I practically screamed at him to stop. To leave, take me back to Ma's. What are you doing, I said. He was going to ruin both of us. I shook all over.

Then he told me she was gone. He laughed and grabbed my hands. He kissed my fingertips, but I still shook. He said she'd taken the child to the doctor in Copperdale and wouldn't return until the morning.

After checking the street to see no one was about, he hurried me to the front door, scooped me up, and carried me inside. I wanted to hold on to him and never let go. There was a closet. He set me down and pushed me inside. My knees still wobbled. From a drawer of the desk, he took a sheaf of papers to show me. I couldn't really tell what he wanted me to see. They looked important. I skimmed over them until I saw my name. And then he told me he changed his will. I would be the beneficiary of his estate. Once the words sank in, after he'd repeated it twice, I have to say, I had a fleeting thought about his wife and daughter. I blurted it before thinking. How stupid can I be? I said but what about Lilac and Louise. Yes, so stupid of me!!! What if he'd told me oh you're right. I better leave it all to them. But, thank God, he didn't.

He explained his current wife and child would be taken care of and not to worry. That explanation made my heart stop. Oh lord, CURRENT? And then he said he had a very special surprise coming in the next few months, a gift as beautiful as I am. Finally, a rush of excitement made me bounce on my toes. Happiness I've never, ever felt in my whole life. I threw my arms around him, and he lifted me to sit on the desk. He shoved up my skirt and took me right there on the desk, and I loved him back with all of my body and soul.

John Hersey's closet held secrets. A secret door in the floor? The desk? She hadn't had enough time to search, but she would. And she'd find the promised gift. She slid the key from the table, rubbing it between her thumb and forefinger. Having dug it from the drawer, she'd guess Harlan and the woman didn't know the key existed. Now, she wouldn't have to figure out how to break into the house tonight. The closet that doubled as an office had to hold the treasure. Her inheritance. Due her. GG would be avenged. The world would be righted. And she would be rich.

****

Harlan chose a table away from the stage near a window in the Apparition Room. Magpie would be singing tonight, and he needed some dinner anyway. He'd labored over material lists and plans of the house when he'd gotten home. Twice his mind wandered, and he'd considered calling Phaedra. Not sure what he wanted to say, and over the phone, he'd pushed the notion aside and decided not to call her. Tired eyes and hunger forced him to stop work. Phaedra often watched his sister perform on Friday nights, so dinner at the bar seemed like a no-brainer.

The window provided a view of the sidewalk and the corner on Main. The summer sun hung low, partially obscured in purple clouds. The aroma of hamburger sizzling and chili steaming floated from the open kitchen door behind the bar. His stomach growled, and as if she took her cue from the rumble, the waitress appeared with his food.

The Apparition Room, one of two bars in Joshua, added to the flavor of the mining town turned Hippie haven turned tourist destination. The building escaped the four major fires between 1894 and 1898 which destroyed most of the business district. The pressed brass ceiling and cherry wood bar were original. While he ate chili and a side salad, his sister came in with Zac, her someday husband. When they made their way toward the stage without seeing him, he called out, "Magpie." The place hadn't filled yet, so the din hummed low except for the country music playing overhead. She stopped as if she heard him but continued on. "Magpie!" This time she whirled around and waved.

When they reached him, he stood and shook hands with Zac. "Hey, you're in town again."

Magpie shot him a look, but Zac smiled and spoke. "Yep. How are you?"

He ignored her irritation. Didn't take much to get her going. She must've taken the harmless comment as a jab at the couple's living arrangement. He always seemed to say the wrong thing to her. "Great." He kept his tone light, chipper for the lawyer. "Have a seat. You don't go on for a half an hour, do you, Mags?"

"No, I can hang for a minute." She caught the waitress's attention at the next table and waved her over.

"What can I get you, Magpie?" Mary asked.

"A cola with a squeeze of lime."

"Hey, Zac. Good to see you. What can I get for you?"

The waitress had eyes for his sister's fiancé. Magpie kept her head bowed, but Harlan caught the smirk she attempted to hide.

"Nice to see you, Mary. I'll take whatever light beer is on tap tonight."

"You still good, Harlan?" Her gaze flicked to him but back to Zac.

"Yep." He tapped his nearly full bottle of beer.

When she sauntered away, Magpie nudged her fiancé and laughed.

"What? She's an attentive waitress."

"Maybe you two should set the date so the single women in this town quit hitting on you." He tipped his bottle at Zac, then took a drink.

"We have a date in sight," his sister answered. "April."

"Next year?" As soon as he blurted it, he flinched. But damn, why so far off?

Mary appeared with their drinks, more than likely saving him from a reproach from his sister. He finished his chili while the smitten waitress took her time. Magpie's mouth set in a forced smile, and he knew her attitude had everything to do with his slip and not Mary's attention to Zac.

"She's all about having a spring wedding." Zac answered once Mary had served them. "The woman knows what she wants."

The lawyer was a nice guy. From some of their conversations, he knew Zac had pushed for the wedding. His sister might've continued with the status quo if he'd not wanted to marry her. "Seems like you should have a little say in it. Give my sister an inch and she's all about taking charge." He said it with a chuckle, but again Magpie seemed to be looking for a fight. The sliver of hard feelings between them ran as deep as the purported last vein of gold in the mountains of Joshua.

"At least I know how and when to lead, Harlan."

"What the hell, Mags? You always—"

"Whoa." Zac scuffed his knuckles on Harlan's forearm. "It's a joint venture. We're good. Gives us lots of time to plan." Then he put an arm around Magpie. "I'll sit here and visit with your brother. I'll move up front when you're on."

"Okay." She stood, slung her purse over a shoulder, and lifted her cola.

Ah shit. He stood, circumvented the table, and gave her a quick hug. They faced off for a moment, her eyes reminding him of their mother. "Enjoy yourself up there. Hey, uh, you know if Phaedra's coming in tonight?"

This brought the hint of amusement that vanished with her words. "I think so, but listen Harlan, I—"

Zac cleared his throat.

"What?" What did she know about Phaedra that her fiancé interrupted? And why?

"Nothing." She kissed the lawyer and strolled toward the stage.

"It's hard enough understanding women at times, but understanding a sister is near impossible." He took a swig from his bottle and reclaimed his seat.

"I hear you."

"Is there something upsetting Mags tonight? She rarely cuts me any slack, but I seemed to have stepped into it with the wedding

80

date."

"I think she's had the question of why she's putting it off until spring a few too many times."

"Yeah? With Mags and me it's something more. She probably tells you…things. We haven't really gotten along great in years. Our sister, Elidor, called me the other night. We don't see much of her. Too bad I can't find a way to get along with the sister who's here."

"Have you told her that?"

"The subject's never come up. Exactly. She holds a grudge for those years after our mother died. Magpie is a headstrong woman. Hell, she was a headstrong girl. She's always had her feet on the ground, unlike Dory and me. Without Magpie, this family wouldn't have hung together as well as it did after Mom died. And then the whole murdered girlfriend fiasco. Dad was a mess. Dory couldn't get past the voices in her head, and I…well…I didn't give Mags much help."

"You were just a teenager."

"She was younger."

"Have you said any of this to her?"

He finished his beer, and in his head recalled a few past conversations. If you could call their dissonance conversation. With her hackles raised for so many years, any discussion of those times seemed useless. *Her* defenses? He pushed the bowls to the side. Or his. Was he avoiding a truth about himself the same way he avoided any responsibility back then?

"Magpie isn't an impenetrable force, Harlan. If you've never really talked this out, I don't see how either of you know what's going on in the other one's head." He motioned at his bottle. "Want another?"

"No, thanks. I think I'll get a little air before Mags starts singing."

"And I need to get a table closer to the stage."

"Grab that table for four. Let's assume Phaedra will show." He threw a tip on the table. "And thanks, Zac. If I haven't said it before, glad you're joining the family."

He ambled outside onto the sidewalk. A few paces from the entrance, he leaned against the green metal pole of a 1930s streetlight. The moon outshone the electric bulb. Summer nights in Joshua, in the mountains, usually filled him with contentment. Tonight, the chili formed a lump in his stomach. Unfinished business with his sister...the need to put dissonance behind them weighed heavy. But he'd been dealing with that for years. Or not dealing with it.

Right now, how to approach Phaedra's jealousy weighed on him heavier than a miner's lode. His gut told him the direct approach wouldn't work. She'd get defensive and deny it if he mentioned jealousy. Hells bells, as his dad would say. Seems he excelled at bringing out the defensiveness in the women in his life. He strolled around the corner, wasting time, hoping Phaedra would arrive soon. Maybe he wouldn't mention jealousy at all. Stop analyzing and trying to understand her and go with his gut. Dive in and take charge of their feelings. Face her head—

"Are you coming or going?" A hand on his shoulder and Phaedra's voice caught his thoughts and his breath.

"Hells bells, Phae." He spun into her.

She giggled. "You sound just like Frank."

He couldn't help laughing. "Yeah, I don't know where that came from."

Their laughter quieted, and he gazed into crystal blue eyes. "Look, about Nora today—"

"Forget it."

"No, I won't. She hadn't been there long. She asked to take a tour inside the house and promised not to get in my way and then she shows up with wine and cheese and I didn't see any way not to be rude." He rambled, not particularly smooth.

"I had a bad first impression of her, but if you find her—"

"I find her pushy. And I don't know anything about writing a book, but she doesn't seem to know enough about Joshua to write anything."

"Yeah?"

"Yeah. But I'm going to show her around on Sunday. And not because I have any...attraction to her. But I want...need... to know more about her."

"Why?"

"Because." How could he put it into words when he wasn't sure why? "Something seems off...about her interest in the Big Purple House and her claim to be a writer."

She squinted, as if considering his words while her thumb rubbed the scar along her chin. He remembered the day she fell, sliced her chin open on the sharp edge of cement in the ruins they weren't supposed to be playing in, and they all got grounded. The moonlight played in her silver-white hair, loose and long, the ends resting on her rounded breasts. Her ever-present scent of rose oil seemed to waft from the embroidered red flowers on her blouse peeking through the tresses. He stood too close to see her curvy hips, but the image was so imprinted on his memory the total vision filled his head. And how she tasted. The softness, the passion simmering. The warmth of her tongue.

"You're staring." Her low voice teased.

He lifted a strand of her hair, opened his hand, and let the silkiness fall back to her breast. "You seem to have that effect on me. You do the moonlight justice."

"Why…that's poetic."

"You didn't know I had poetry in me?"

"I'm beginning to think there might be lots of things I don't know about you." She angled closer.

He tightened his thighs yet couldn't suppress the effect her nearness caused. "What do you want to know?"

"Oh, are we going to have a tell all?"

"Is there something about you I should know?" His hands found her hips without any forethought decision. Her bottom lip trembled with a hushed gasp. He envisioned drawing her against him, letting her feel what she didn't know about him.

"Hey, boss."

Over her shoulder, two of his employees came toward them. Reluctantly, he drew his hands from her and tucked his fingers into his pockets. "Kevin, John." He nodded.

A brief frown of what he hoped signified disappointment flitted over her brow when she greeted the men. "Hi, Kevin. Long time no see, John."

John came beside her, a grin on his face. "It's good to see you too."

Harlan had the urge to tell him to get out of her space, but bit off the comment. Phaedra might be the only woman in Joshua John hadn't dated.

His employee's body language, a shoulder dipping toward her and feet shuffling closer, were easy to read. "If you're going into the Apparition Room, I'd be happy to buy you a drink."

"We are, but Harlan and I have business to discuss while we watch his sister sing. Thanks for the offer. Maybe I can get a raincheck?"

He wanted to smile at her smooth brush off.

"Sure. Anytime." John followed Kevin toward the door.

She smirked when his workers walked out of hearing range. "I hope you don't mind I used you for an excuse."

"Use me anytime." The words slipped out without thinking, and the nicely uncomfortable sensation in his jeans returned.

Her eyes widened for a moment, and her thumb went to her scar again. He made her nervous. He'd take that as a good sign since her impact on him ramped up his pulse. Had she thought about him as much as he'd been consumed with thoughts of last night's kiss?

She canted toward him.

He slipped a hand around her waist and brought her firmly against his hips.

"Harlan—"

His mouth covered her words, tangoed with her tongue, and withdrew to trail kisses from her jaw line to her ear. "I couldn't resist," he whispered.

She nuzzled her cheek against his lips. "Good."

Magpie's voice, grinding out a sixties rock tune, filled the night air. As if she'd joined their conversation, they drew apart ever so slightly. Their hands fell to their sides.

"I guess we should, um…" Phaedra ticked her head toward the bar.

"Yeah, she'll wonder where we are." He didn't want to move out of the moonlight and her lethal space. "Zac is saving seats."

"Oh, saving seats." She shuffled to his side. "Good, sure."

As they strolled toward his sister's music, he touched her back. His fingertips registered her caught breath. *Yes, Dory, Phaedra and me.*

CHAPTER SEVEN

Harlan jumped, disengaged from Nora, and rushed to the landing. "Phaedra?" She stood at the bottom of the stairs. "Hey, come on up."

Nora brushed against his back, her breasts making a distinct impression, as she leaned around him. "Hi, Phaedra. I'm getting the nickel tour. Harlan is a great guide."

"No, um, continue the tour. I see you've had *lunch.* I'll grab some in town and get back to work. Call later. About the house. If you want."

She waved a hand and traipsed out the door.

"I need to update her on my progress. I'll be back in a minute."

He took the steep stairs as fast as he could, catching Phaedra as she slid onto her vehicle seat. "Hey, don't rush off."

"No problem. I didn't know you had company."

He braced hands on knees to come eye to eye with her. "She's not company. She popped in on me while—"

"You didn't know she was coming by today?"

"Well, yeah, she told me when I took her to the store Wednesday night, but—"

"You spent Wednesday night with her?"

"I didn't *spend* the night with her. I ran into her on the street when I was headed to the Little Market. She asked to go along. She told me she wanted to drop by today so I could show her the house."

She shooed him back and closed the door. "You don't have to explain yourself to me."

With his forearms on the window sill, he frowned in at her. "I'm not. I'm telling you why she's here."

"With wine and cheese." She started the engine.

"It's not what you think."

"I don't think anything."

"Phaedra—"

"Really. Stop. Nothing to explain. No big deal. I need to grab some lunch and get back to work. I have a huge order so you might not see me for a while." She gestured toward the house. "If something comes up, you can call." She flashed a quick smile, cranked the steering wheel, and inched from the curb.

He had no choice but to back out of the window or be dragged along with the Jeep. "Yeah, I'll do that. I'll call."

She angled around Nora's car before the last words left his mouth, made a U-turn, and then drove away. Without a wave. Without so much as a glance.

What the hell just happened? There could be no mistaking the jealousy his best friend displayed toward another woman. His reaction came slowly until he felt for sure he looked like an idiot grinning at the now empty street. Whatever the feelings he found himself embroiled in when they were together affected her too. Last night wasn't a fluke.

Shoving his hands into his jean pockets, he pivoted on his boot heel, stepped over the chunks of sidewalk, and ambled toward the house. He strode into the foyer. Thinking of Phaedra as a friend *and* lover expanded his heart…and sent ripples southward. *Whoa, MacKenzie.* How he approached this turn of events needed to be carried out with less aplomb than he normally possessed. Let her take the lead. Phaedra was an independent—

"Oh! There you are." Until she spoke, he hadn't seen Nora inside the foyer closet; he had totally forgotten about her. Her wide eyes held a note of surprise.

"I'm sorry. I had some things to discuss with Phaedra."

Nora's interest in him, in the house, created a mystery. What was or wasn't happening between Phaedra and him posed a bigger mystery. One he'd rather tackle.

"That's okay. I decided I better let you get back to work. I was cleaning up our little mess on the desk. Would you like me to leave any of this?"

"No. I'm good. Thanks, by the way." He held out a hand. "Can I help you with that?"

"I've got it. Unless you'd like to help me finish it tonight?" She lowered her husky voice to a come-hither drawl and cocked a brow that disappeared under her bangs.

"I can't." If he did anything tonight, he'd see Phaedra. His stomach lurched wondering what to say to his lifelong friend.

"Okay then. I'll get out of your way. I'm going to hold you to showing me some more old houses."

"Yeah, sure. When I can fit it in around work." He made a wide gesture with his hand. She could find houses on her own. She could find men who were sure to respond to her flirtations. Yet he couldn't help a modicum of interest from her obvious come on—he wanted to know why—why he intuited something more than simple sexual attraction. People weren't his thing, but this woman drew him in for some reason other than the obvious.

"Surely you don't work on Sundays. Since the houses I'm interested in aren't designated historic, and they're lived in, I could sure use the help of a local to get me in. I promise to be ever so *appreciative*." She cocked a brow, using the come-hither dip of her chin.

When he didn't answer immediately, the telltale eyelash batting eased, and she flashed him a smile. "I'll buy dinner. Or lunch. What do you say?"

The woman was persistent. Despite his resolve, a lingering curiosity persisted. "I suppose I could break loose awhile on Sunday."

"Thank you." With a squeeze to his bicep, she left. "See you then," she called over her shoulder.

As she traversed the veranda, he closed the door behind her and moved to the window. She loaded her wine and bag into the green Cavalier, threw him a wave, and drove away. She wasn't hard on the eyes, but that wasn't the reason he'd relented. Her interest in this house, her story about her book, seemed off. Her flirting didn't seem authentic. And his gut told him he needed to know why.

"Agh." He rubbed the back of his neck. This house with the secrets it hid. The veiled motives of the writer. What he should do about the evolution of his relationship with Phaedra. Confusion, indecision, mixed messages. Was the energy of the house throwing his universe out of kilter? He had no idea what he could do to right it. "Keep on working, MacKenzie."

In the foyer closet, he lifted his pad from the desk, a slight tingle traveling over his fingertips. In more than forty years of experiencing clear feelings from inanimate objects, there had never been a physical manifestation. The reoccurring wave of joy in his gut bumped him. Someone, in some time had enjoyed... *Pleasure*. He took a breath. *Gone*. Shaking his head, he backed toward the door.

Outside the closet, he rounded the corner to the dining room—a room not used often. The baseboards and floor looked fine. In the kitchen, his mind wandered to Phaedra's stories of her time in the house as a child. If he'd known her then, played here with her, he would've tuned into the house, even at the age of two or three. In fact, the vibes would've been clearer as a child. *Children are more open to their inner feelings.* But he hadn't known her, not that he could recall. Until her mother moved them to The Ravine, he had no memory of her. They'd made so many memories after. He gazed out the backdoor window to the J on Spirit Mountain. His gut told him he could make a whole new set of memories with her.

****

Nora clutched the prize in her fist, driving with her left hand and one finger of her clenched right hand. Her heart pattered like she'd hit the lottery. She angled into a parking space at the end of the building which housed the Copper Line Hotel and killed the engine. Beyond the front windshield, the Verde Valley stretched in the distance. Only when she'd stepped out of her car and stood at the railing in front of her bumper did she open her fist. The key's red imprint marred the center of her hand.

Luck had worked in her favor ever since she'd stepped foot in Joshua. First, a room in the hotel of which GG wrote. Then the sexy Harlan MacKenzie working on Lilac End...the not yet occupied house. My God, how much more perfect could it get? How about finding a key to the front door of Lilac End? She laughed out loud, pivoted, and strolled to the hotel entrance.

How convenient Phaedra arrived while she and Harlan flirted. An interruption, but it worked in her favor. From the look on the woman's face and her body language, she guessed they must be dating or something. No matter. She'd continue her pretense of needing to research other houses until she had what she came for at

Lilac End. When she'd asked for some time on Sunday, a flicker of a frown across the handsome construction worker's face told her she might be laying it on a little thick. As gorgeous as he was, he might just be a straight shooter. How…unusual.

She bounced up each step of the hotel stairs to her room. When Harlan chased after the current owner, and Nora found herself alone in the house, she'd done a rapid rummage through the desk drawers, empty except for one tiny drawer where the key lodged between the side and bottom. A swift check to see if the key fit the front door lock and the plan got a whole lot smoother.

She tossed the sack with cheese and crackers on the bed, then set the key and the half-full bottle of wine on the nightstand. She'd need something for dinner while she waited for nightfall this evening. With the room card and a twenty in hand, she made a quick trip to the deli attached to the hotel. She carried the sandwich and potato salad back to her room and stored them in the fridge.

Kicking off her shoes as she collapsed onto the bed, her head hit the mattress. "Life is damn righteous sometimes." The house wasn't rumored to have hidden treasure. No legends surrounding it. *This is good, very good.* If no one had ever gone treasure hunting in the house, then the house still guarded the fortune. Hersey's wife, Lilac, spoke the truth to GG. Lilac Hersey had been a stupid, vengeful woman.

Rolling onto her stomach, she slid the journal off the nightstand to the bed and randomly selected an entry.

April 20, 1924
I've been so bored and so lonely. Lilac had a baby girl. Louise. Not that John has been around to tell me. It's the talk of Joshua. I haven't seen him in almost two weeks. Will he ever come back? Ma hasn't put me on the floor yet, and I'm continuing to receive my portion, so he must still be paying. But I am sooo scared. What if having a baby with her makes him want to give me up? I'll die. I just know I will.

Margaret and I went to Main Street today to get supplies. I prayed I'd run into him. Even if I couldn't speak to him, at least I could see him. But I didn't.

God probably doesn't answer those sorts of prayers for girls like me. Margaret says I should be happy. As long as he keeps paying, I don't have to spread my legs for dirty miners anymore. She's so uncouth! They aren't dirty, anyway. Not really. Well maybe some are. And I won't do it anymore anyway, even if he doesn't come back. There's nothing Ma can do to make me. I have enough money saved to leave this place if I have to. I don't really know where I'd go or what I'd do. That scares me. I could probably get a job in Phoenix as a housekeeper or waitress. Oh, I'm so, so, so unhappy. I don't want to leave. I just want John to come back to me.

She crawled higher on the bed, stacking pillows against the headboard, bringing the journal with her. She never tired of living vicariously through GG. Rearranging into a sitting position, she lifted the bottle of wine off the nightstand she'd shared with Harlan. After pouring a plastic hotel room glass full, she gently thumbed the pages to find the entry where her great grandmother had first visited Lilac End.

May 13, 1924
JOURNAL OF GENEVIEVE JENKINS, TO BE GENEVIEVE HERSEY ONE DAY SOON!!!
This last week has been glorious. Seeing John makes life bearable, if only for brief moments. And then tonight happened, and I can't even express how I feel. I have to try. I have to be able to remember this feeling for years to come, after I'm old and can't remember the me of today.
He'd only just walked in. My face must have given away my mood. I'd been deep in thought about what my future would be like if John hadn't come into my life. I was nearly in tears, scared, and sad to think about it. Holding me, he asked what was wrong. I admitted to him I was afraid he wouldn't love me anymore, and one day he'd stay home with her and the child, and I'd never see him again. That my life

90

and my future would be nothing.

He laughed! He called me his silly, little Genny. And then he scooped me up and carried me down the stairs and out to his car. A couple of the girls sat in the parlor. I thought their eyes might pop out of their heads. I didn't know what to do. I couldn't talk. It's like my heart hurled itself into my throat. He set me in his car and off we went. I kept asking him what are you doing, John? What kind of madness is this? I really thought he might be mad or possessed or something. He said the time had come for me to see my future. I got dizzy and could barely breathe. I couldn't dare to imagine what he meant, but when he parked in front of the grand house, I nearly fainted. Was he going to march me in and parade me in front of his wife?

I practically screamed at him to stop. To leave, take me back to Ma's. What are you doing, I said. He was going to ruin both of us. I shook all over.

Then he told me she was gone. He laughed and grabbed my hands. He kissed my fingertips, but I still shook. He said she'd taken the child to the doctor in Copperdale and wouldn't return until the morning.

After checking the street to see no one was about, he hurried me to the front door, scooped me up, and carried me inside. I wanted to hold on to him and never let go. There was a closet. He set me down and pushed me inside. My knees still wobbled. From a drawer of the desk, he took a sheaf of papers to show me. I couldn't really tell what he wanted me to see. They looked important. I skimmed over them until I saw my name. And then he told me he changed his will. I would be the beneficiary of his estate. Once the words sank in, after he'd repeated it twice, I have to say, I had a fleeting thought about his wife and daughter. I blurted it before thinking. How stupid can I be? I said but what about Lilac and Louise. Yes, so stupid of me!!! What if he'd told me oh you're right. I better leave it all to them. But, thank God, he didn't.

91

He explained his current wife and child would be taken care of and not to worry. That explanation made my heart stop. Oh lord, CURRENT? And then he said he had a very special surprise coming in the next few months, a gift as beautiful as I am. Finally, a rush of excitement made me bounce on my toes. Happiness I've never, ever felt in my whole life. I threw my arms around him, and he lifted me to sit on the desk. He shoved up my skirt and took me right there on the desk, and I loved him back with all of my body and soul.

John Hersey's closet held secrets. A secret door in the floor? The desk? She hadn't had enough time to search, but she would. And she'd find the promised gift. She slid the key from the table, rubbing it between her thumb and forefinger. Having dug it from the drawer, she'd guess Harlan and the woman didn't know the key existed. Now, she wouldn't have to figure out how to break into the house tonight. The closet that doubled as an office had to hold the treasure. Her inheritance. Due her. GG would be avenged. The world would be righted. And she would be rich.

****

Harlan chose a table away from the stage near a window in the Apparition Room. Magpie would be singing tonight, and he needed some dinner anyway. He'd labored over material lists and plans of the house when he'd gotten home. Twice his mind wandered, and he'd considered calling Phaedra. Not sure what he wanted to say, and over the phone, he'd pushed the notion aside and decided not to call her. Tired eyes and hunger forced him to stop work. Phaedra often watched his sister perform on Friday nights, so dinner at the bar seemed like a no-brainer.

The window provided a view of the sidewalk and the corner on Main. The summer sun hung low, partially obscured in purple clouds. The aroma of hamburger sizzling and chili steaming floated from the open kitchen door behind the bar. His stomach growled, and as if she took her cue from the rumble, the waitress appeared with his food.

The Apparition Room, one of two bars in Joshua, added to the flavor of the mining town turned Hippie haven turned tourist destination. The building escaped the four major fires between 1894 and 1898 which destroyed most of the business district. The pressed brass ceiling and cherry wood bar were original. While he ate chili and a side salad, his sister came in with Zac, her someday husband. When they made their way toward the stage without seeing him, he called out, "Magpie." The place hadn't filled yet, so the din hummed low except for the country music playing overhead. She stopped as if she heard him but continued on. "Magpie!" This time she whirled around and waved.

When they reached him, he stood and shook hands with Zac. "Hey, you're in town again."

Magpie shot him a look, but Zac smiled and spoke. "Yep. How are you?"

He ignored her irritation. Didn't take much to get her going. She must've taken the harmless comment as a jab at the couple's living arrangement. He always seemed to say the wrong thing to her. "Great." He kept his tone light, chipper for the lawyer. "Have a seat. You don't go on for a half an hour, do you, Mags?"

"No, I can hang for a minute." She caught the waitress's attention at the next table and waved her over.

"What can I get you, Magpie?" Mary asked.

"A cola with a squeeze of lime."

"Hey, Zac. Good to see you. What can I get for you?"

The waitress had eyes for his sister's fiancé. Magpie kept her head bowed, but Harlan caught the smirk she attempted to hide.

"Nice to see you, Mary. I'll take whatever light beer is on tap tonight."

"You still good, Harlan?" Her gaze flicked to him but back to Zac.

"Yep." He tapped his nearly full bottle of beer.

When she sauntered away, Magpie nudged her fiancé and laughed.

"What? She's an attentive waitress."

"Maybe you two should set the date so the single women in this town quit hitting on you." He tipped his bottle at Zac, then took a drink.

"We have a date in sight," his sister answered. "April."

"Next year?" As soon as he blurted it, he flinched. But damn, why so far off?

Mary appeared with their drinks, more than likely saving him from a reproach from his sister. He finished his chili while the smitten waitress took her time. Magpie's mouth set in a forced smile, and he knew her attitude had everything to do with his slip and not Mary's attention to Zac.

"She's all about having a spring wedding." Zac answered once Mary had served them. "The woman knows what she wants."

The lawyer was a nice guy. From some of their conversations, he knew Zac had pushed for the wedding. His sister might've continued with the status quo if he'd not wanted to marry her. "Seems like you should have a little say in it. Give my sister an inch and she's all about taking charge." He said it with a chuckle, but again Magpie seemed to be looking for a fight. The sliver of hard feelings between them ran as deep as the purported last vein of gold in the mountains of Joshua.

"At least I know how and when to lead, Harlan."

"What the hell, Mags? You always—"

"Whoa." Zac scuffed his knuckles on Harlan's forearm. "It's a joint venture. We're good. Gives us lots of time to plan." Then he put an arm around Magpie. "I'll sit here and visit with your brother. I'll move up front when you're on."

"Okay." She stood, slung her purse over a shoulder, and lifted her cola.

Ah shit. He stood, circumvented the table, and gave her a quick hug. They faced off for a moment, her eyes reminding him of their mother. "Enjoy yourself up there. Hey, uh, you know if Phaedra's coming in tonight?"

This brought the hint of amusement that vanished with her words. "I think so, but listen Harlan, I—"

Zac cleared his throat.

"What?" What did she know about Phaedra that her fiancé interrupted? And why?

"Nothing." She kissed the lawyer and strolled toward the stage.

"It's hard enough understanding women at times, but understanding a sister is near impossible." He took a swig from his bottle and reclaimed his seat.

"I hear you."

"Is there something upsetting Mags tonight? She rarely cuts me any slack, but I seemed to have stepped into it with the wedding date."

"I think she's had the question of why she's putting it off until spring a few too many times."

"Yeah? With Mags and me it's something more. She probably tells you…things. We haven't really gotten along great in years. Our sister, Elidor, called me the other night. We don't see much of her. Too bad I can't find a way to get along with the sister who's here."

"Have you told her that?"

"The subject's never come up. Exactly. She holds a grudge for those years after our mother died. Magpie is a headstrong woman. Hell, she was a headstrong girl. She's always had her feet on the ground, unlike Dory and me. Without Magpie, this family wouldn't have hung together as well as it did after Mom died. And then the whole murdered girlfriend fiasco. Dad was a mess. Dory couldn't get past the voices in her head, and I…well…I didn't give Mags much help."

"You were just a teenager."

"She was younger."

"Have you said any of this to her?"

He finished his beer, and in his head recalled a few past conversations. If you could call their dissonance conversation. With her hackles raised for so many years, any discussion of those times seemed useless. *Her* defenses? He pushed the bowls to the side. Or his. Was he avoiding a truth about himself the same way he avoided any responsibility back then?

"Magpie isn't an impenetrable force, Harlan. If you've never really talked this out, I don't see how either of you know what's going on in the other one's head." He motioned at his bottle. "Want another?"

"No, thanks. I think I'll get a little air before Mags starts singing."

"And I need to get a table closer to the stage."

"Grab that table for four. Let's assume Phaedra will show." He threw a tip on the table. "And thanks, Zac. If I haven't said it before, glad you're joining the family."

He ambled outside onto the sidewalk. A few paces from the entrance, he leaned against the green metal pole of a 1930s streetlight. The moon outshone the electric bulb. Summer nights in Joshua, in the mountains, usually filled him with contentment. Tonight, the chili formed a lump in his stomach. Unfinished business with his sister...the need to put dissonance behind them weighed heavy. But he'd been dealing with that for years. Or not dealing with it.

Right now, how to approach Phaedra's jealousy weighed on him heavier than a miner's lode. His gut told him the direct approach wouldn't work. She'd get defensive and deny it if he mentioned jealousy. Hells bells, as his dad would say. Seems he excelled at bringing out the defensiveness in the women in his life. He strolled around the corner, wasting time, hoping Phaedra would arrive soon. Maybe he wouldn't mention jealousy at all. Stop analyzing and trying to understand her and go with his gut. Dive in and take charge of their feelings. Face her head—

"Are you coming or going?" A hand on his shoulder and Phaedra's voice caught his thoughts and his breath.

"Hells bells, Phae." He spun into her.

She giggled. "You sound just like Frank."

He couldn't help laughing. "Yeah, I don't know where that came from."

Their laughter quieted, and he gazed into crystal blue eyes. "Look, about Nora today—"

"Forget it."

"No, I won't. She hadn't been there long. She asked to take a tour inside the house and promised not to get in my way and then she shows up with wine and cheese and I didn't see any way not to be rude." He rambled, not particularly smooth.

"I had a bad first impression of her, but if you find her—"

"I find her pushy. And I don't know anything about writing a book, but she doesn't seem to know enough about Joshua to write anything."

"Yeah?"

"Yeah. But I'm going to show her around on Sunday. And not because I have any...attraction to her. But I want...need... to know more about her."

"Why?"

"Because." How could he put it into words when he wasn't sure why? "Something seems off...about her interest in the Big Purple House and her claim to be a writer."

She squinted, as if considering his words while her thumb rubbed the scar along her chin. He remembered the day she fell, sliced her chin open on the sharp edge of cement in the ruins they weren't supposed to be playing in, and they all got grounded. The moonlight played in her silver-white hair, loose and long, the ends resting on her rounded breasts. Her ever-present scent of rose oil seemed to waft from the embroidered red flowers on her blouse peeking through the tresses. He stood too close to see her curvy hips, but the image was so imprinted on his memory the total vision filled his head. And how she tasted. The softness, the passion simmering. The warmth of her tongue.

"You're staring." Her low voice teased.

He lifted a strand of her hair, opened his hand, and let the silkiness fall back to her breast. "You seem to have that effect on me. You do the moonlight justice."

"Why…that's poetic."

"You didn't know I had poetry in me?"

"I'm beginning to think there might be lots of things I don't know about you." She angled closer.

He tightened his thighs yet couldn't suppress the effect her nearness caused. "What do you want to know?"

"Oh, are we going to have a tell all?"

"Is there something about you I should know?" His hands found her hips without any forethought decision. Her bottom lip trembled with a hushed gasp. He envisioned drawing her against him, letting her feel what she didn't know about him.

"Hey, boss."

Over her shoulder, two of his employees came toward them. Reluctantly, he drew his hands from her and tucked his fingers into his pockets. "Kevin, John." He nodded.

A brief frown of what he hoped signified disappointment flitted over her brow when she greeted the men. "Hi, Kevin. Long time no see, John."

John came beside her, a grin on his face. "It's good to see you too."

Harlan had the urge to tell him to get out of her space, but bit off the comment. Phaedra might be the only woman in Joshua John hadn't dated.

His employee's body language, a shoulder dipping toward her and feet shuffling closer, were easy to read. "If you're going into the Apparition Room, I'd be happy to buy you a drink."

"We are, but Harlan and I have business to discuss while we watch his sister sing. Thanks for the offer. Maybe I can get a raincheck?"

He wanted to smile at her smooth brush off.

"Sure. Anytime." John followed Kevin toward the door.

She smirked when his workers walked out of hearing range. "I hope you don't mind I used you for an excuse."

"Use me anytime." The words slipped out without thinking, and the nicely uncomfortable sensation in his jeans returned.

Her eyes widened for a moment, and her thumb went to her scar again. He made her nervous. He'd take that as a good sign since her impact on him ramped up his pulse. Had she thought about him as much as he'd been consumed with thoughts of last night's kiss?

She canted toward him.

He slipped a hand around her waist and brought her firmly against his hips.

"Harlan—"

His mouth covered her words, tangoed with her tongue, and withdrew to trail kisses from her jaw line to her ear. "I couldn't resist," he whispered.

She nuzzled her cheek against his lips. "Good."

Magpie's voice, grinding out a sixties rock tune, filled the night air. As if she'd joined their conversation, they drew apart ever so slightly. Their hands fell to their sides.

"I guess we should, um…" Phaedra ticked her head toward the bar.

"Yeah, she'll wonder where we are." He didn't want to move out of the moonlight and her lethal space. "Zac is saving seats."

"Oh, saving seats." She shuffled to his side. "Good, sure."

As they strolled toward his sister's music, he touched her back. His fingertips registered her caught breath. *Yes, Dory, Phaedra and me.*

CHAPTER EIGHT

Nora parked her car in the same spot as the night before, down the street from Lilac End, positioned for a retreat once she'd found what she wanted. Dressed in a black T-shirt, black capris, and gray running shoes, she hoped to blend into the shadows. In the last hour, as the sun fully set, clouds formed. Now, the stars and the bright half-moon peeked in and out of fast-moving black spots across the sky. She grabbed the navy canvas bag containing her supplies from where it sat on the passenger seat.

With a few deep breaths, she waited for a cloud to creep across the moon, then slipped from the car and darted to the sidewalk on the opposite side. As she ran, a light flicked on in an upstairs window of the nearest house. Cursing under her breath, she glanced side to side, and continued forward fifty or sixty yards farther to Lilac End. "Get a grip. You blend into the dark." Breathing came easier. With her bag on her shoulder, she plunged ahead, her calves ready to sprint across the yard to the veranda. Her foot caught. Her ankle turned. She pitched forward, sprawling into the dead grass. Sharp pain shot through her leg.

"Agh!" She slapped one hand over her mouth and clutched her shin with the other. At the point of the pain, moistness met her fingertips. Blood. "Damn it!" she growled into her palm. Rummaging in the bag, she found the cloth tool kit. After dumping the utensils into the canvas tote, she pressed the cloth to her leg. Her heart thumped in her chest and echoed in her ears. She looked toward the nearest house. Satisfied she hadn't brought anyone out from the neighbor's, she removed the cloth and squinted at the cut to see if blood would ooze. None she could see. As she shoved the cloth back into the bag and eased herself to her feet, a throb pulsed through her ankle. While swearing under her breath, she hobbled along the walkway. The cracks in the cement glared at her. She gasped with short, nervous breaths.

Once on the veranda, she picked the gardening gloves out of her bag, slipped them on, and then dug out the house key from the pocket of her capris. Inside, she paused to calm her hammering heart and to let her eyes adjust to the darkness. Limping across the foyer, she entered John Hersey's office and closed the door behind her. In the pitch black, weakness surged through her legs, and shivered her body. "You're in. You're okay." After turning on the overhead light, she plunged her hand inside her bag for the small lantern flashlight. Three clicks of the knob brought the light to high, further lighting the small area.

"Now where the hell is it?" She set the bag against the door and the lantern in the middle of the room. Her great grandmother wrote what was rightfully hers would be sealed in the closet forever. GG had checked the news and magazines, any source that would report such a valuable discovery over the years. Nothing ever showed. Nora's own research confirmed the treasure had never surfaced.

Did the desk hold a clue? Was it bolted to the wall to hide a secret compartment? She needed to move the desk, look behind it, examine all the areas she couldn't see. As she squatted, pain prickled her shin, but she ignored her leg and dug out her screwdriver and hammer. With the screwdriver lined up into the screwhead of one bracket, and with all the strength she could muster, she cranked. But her gloved hand slipped around the plastic handle. She yanked off the glove. Without the impediment of the cloth, she gripped the handle, but all she accomplished was to burn her palm as she twisted. "Agh!" With a huff, she rested a moment, then tapped it with the hammer. Gripping the screwdriver with both hands, she leaned over the bracket and pushed the screwdriver down hard. After several unsuccessful attempts at the decades-old screws, sweat trickled between her breasts and plastered her bangs onto her forehead.

She sat back on her haunches. Her ankle and shin protested with a stab of pain. "Ouch." She rolled onto her butt. The gash in her leg oozed red. Not concerned anyone could hear her, she vented. "Damn it, damn it, damn it!" After stretching the tool kit's cloth holder around her leg and tucking the corner over the edge to secure it, she stood, hammer in hand.

I'll tear apart this whole damn closet if I have to.

As she tapped along the wall above the desk, she found a hollow sounding area. Rearing back, she took a deep breath and then slammed the wall with the hammer. Although expected, the crash startled her. The plaster cracked. Her heart thumped. She hit it again and again, the cacophony thudding in her head. The wall fractured and sent plaster chunks scattering over the desk and floor. "Ah-ha!" She bludgeoned the wall again, expanding the hole. Plaster dust filled the air. A cough erupted. She cleared her throat, pushed her bangs aside, and wiped sweat from her forehead. Working downward, she opened a large gap to the top of the rolltop. She plucked the handheld flashlight out of the canvas tote, swept the bag across the desk, and sent plaster hunks flying to clear the surface. Heedless of the pain in her ankle and leg, she climbed onto the desk, directed the beam into the open wall, and peered downward.

Nothing.

"It has to be here." Shining the light behind the wall in all directions proved fruitless. "What the hell?" She sat on the desk, dangled her feet, and let her shoulders droop heavy with disappointment. "Oh! Maybe…" She raised the flashlight at the ceiling. The surface appeared smooth, no seams. Not likely Lilac Hersey could've opened the ceiling and sealed it back with perfection.

For several minutes, she scanned the walls, vertical and horizontal. Maybe the room had been replastered for some reason. Could Lilac have torn into a wall and then been so skilled at plastering that it wasn't evident where she'd hidden the treasure? She peered at the gaping hole, her eyes inches from the edge of the opening. She didn't know anything about construction, but it didn't appear there were multiple layers in the wall. In fact, it seemed to have been painted only twice with two different colors.

As she slid gingerly off the desk, she snickered at the destruction wreaked upon the wall. Harlan would have to move the desk to fix it. She limped to the wall across from the desk and slammed the hammer into the plaster. Once she'd made a hole big enough for her head and shoulders, she used the flashlight to inspect. She repeated the process on the third wall. With her efforts useless, she whirled and threw the hammer on the floor. Her leg and ankle ached. Her shoulders and arms were heavy with fatigue, soreness setting into her muscles. Plaster dust clogged her nose.

"What closet were you talking about, GG, if not this one?" Hersey's closet-turned-office made sense. He'd fucked her right here on the desk. He'd shown her the revised will and made promises of the priceless gift to come. This is where it should be. "Shit! Shit!" *Stop. Think.* She needed to find the passage again in the journal and reread her great grandmother's description of the hiding place. She couldn't bludgeon every room in the house tonight. If this closet wasn't right, she had to get the target correct. *Regroup.*

Once she'd gathered her tools back into the bag, she extinguished the flashlights and the overhead light. In the foyer, she peeked out the front door, happy the clouds now blocked all light from the sky. On the veranda, she scanned the street and hefted her bag over her shoulder, wincing with the pain of her efforts. After a few minutes, her eyes adjusted to the night. She pulled the front door to but didn't fully close it. Harlan would think he'd forgotten to secure the house and vandals had open entry. She couldn't let him know someone had a key to come and go as they pleased.

Keeping her gaze down, careful of every crack and jagged step, she made her way to her car. She'd have to come back yet again. She'd scour GG's journal for what she'd missed about the hiding place.

She wouldn't leave Joshua without it, no matter what she had to do.

****

Before Harlan climbed out of his truck, Phaedra was out of her Jeep and had her front door unlocked. Whatever reservations she'd had last night must have disappeared with the dawn this morning. They might have kept their hands off each other all evening under the keen watch of his sister, but the playfulness in Phaedra's eyes promised a whole lot of touching to come. She waited in the open doorway and didn't move when he stopped close enough to toy with a strand of hair along her cheek.

"I have pinot grigio. And a couple of red varieties, but you're a dry white kind of guy so I won't suffer you with red tonight." She nodded her head, and he followed her direction, closing the door behind him. "Or I could make us an Irish coffee."

"How about Irish coffee without the coffee?"

"Ha." She bent to open a low door on a small cabinet. "I'll humor you, and we'll have a Jameson's. From the cabinet she lifted the bottle and two tumblers. "You're getting it at room temperature."

"No other way."

When she righted, she flashed a smile. He thought it best to sit on the couch as she stood to avoid getting accused of staring. Which he was doing. Again. But that tiny red rose on the pocket of her jean-covered left butt cheek begged his attention. At least its location called to him.

"Here you go. Promised nightcap." She floated down beside him, one leg tucked under her and inches from connecting with his thigh.

A whiskey wasn't what he thought the promised nightcap would be, but if she needed to slow it down, he could. He didn't want to leave halfway into this again tonight. He clinked her glass. "Here's to—" He stopped himself before he said friends. This was more. *What* he couldn't be sure, but to toss that f-word at her just might break the mood.

"To?" She raised a brow.

"I don't know. What shall we drink to?"

"How about discovery?"

They sipped. The liquor burned on its way down his throat. Discovery made sense on so many levels. The Big Purple House. His family connections to Lilac Lambert. Each other. The latter being uppermost at the moment. And hopefully what she toasted. He rubbed his thumb on the glass, thinking more how she'd feel in his hand.

Canting a fraction toward him, she brought her elbow to the back of the couch, resting her head on her hand. She gazed into his face. He took it as a welcoming movement. Scooting closer, he levered her folded leg so it rested on his thigh. The rise and fall of her breasts, the mesmerizing stare of her blue eyes, and her wet lips sent a spiral of sensations south. With one more sip, he set the glass on the coffee table, took the glass out of her hand, and set it next to his. He couldn't hold back any longer. She'd set the tone as they left Magpie's, and he unraveled waiting for her next nod. When he lifted her onto his lap, she unfolded her leg, settling into the groove between his thighs. A moan erupted.

Her hand slipped from her head and touched the pendant on his chest. "Just like Magpie's."

"Mmm."

"I've never seen you wear—"

When he covered her mouth with his, she slid her arms around his neck and cuddled close against his chest. He ran his hands over her hips and thighs, silently cursing the denim for keeping him at bay. Everything about her, every inch of her that touched him, that he touched, drove him crazy. He deepened the kiss, and she opened up. Offered up, just for him. God, she tasted good. She. Tasted. So. Damn. Good.

When she moved her hands to his shoulders, and one hand migrated to his chest, massaging and rubbing her breasts against him at the same time, his hardness bucked.

Breaking from her lips, he heaved a ragged sigh and then kissed his way to the opening of her shirt. Palming her breasts, he buried his face, bathed his cheeks in his own breath heating off her skin. Her buttons fell away to his touch. He fingered the thin lace downward, exposing swollen nipples she brought to him with a deep breath.

"Harlan?" Her voice floated above him. "Oh. Harlan."

He slid his fingers to the waist of her jeans.

"Harlan?"

He kissed his way back to her mouth. "Yes?"

"Let's move. My bed." Her voice, so husky he hardly recognized it, sent a message, and his groin answered.

He moaned.

"Can you walk?' She tittered.

"I'll manage."

She took his hand, led him along the hall and to the bedroom doorway.

His fingers twined in hers. "Wait, Phae." He spun her to face him. "Are you sure?"

"More than sure." She tugged him forward. Her hair caught the light of the hall lamp. Her hips swayed, the rub of her thighs against each other damn near undid him. At the bed, she pivoted into him, kissed him, her hands on each side of his face. "You shaved."

He was busy unzipping her jeans then shoving his hands inside to cup her bare ass. He pulled her firm against the hard ache contained by the tightness of his jeans. Her words didn't make sense. "What?" The only thing registering was the tantalizing feel of her butt in the palm of his hands.

She chuckled. "You shaved."

His breath caught in two tight gasps as he forced his brain to listen. Drawing his shoulders back, he brought his gaze to meet hers. "What in Hades, if I might quote you, are you talking about?"

Her fingers tickled over his cheeks and chin. "You've had a shadow beard lately. It gave you a hint of the bad boy I haven't *discovered* yet. And you shaved."

In the fog, he remembered her saying something similar a couple of days ago. *Bad* boy? "I can be the bad boy if that's what you need." He yanked her blouse down and off her arms. Unclasped her bra, throwing it across the room. He smothered a laugh at that gesture. He lowered to his knees, taking her jeans and undies with him to her ankles, then giving her a gentle shove onto the bed. Whipping off her sandals then the jeans, he let them fall to the side. "Just what kind of bad are you looking for?"

"You can be your kind of bad, Harlan Muse MacKenzie."

Willing his near bursting erection to behave, he kissed the inside of each of her thighs.

She groaned deep in her throat. "Come to think of it, those whiskers might not have been so comfortable."

****

Nora limped to her room. She keyed the entry card and then once inside dropped everything at her feet. From shin to ankle, she hurt like hell. In fact, she hurt all over. Damn lucky she didn't sprain her ankle. A close inspection of the shin wound showed a shallow gash two inches long with scraped skin all around it. The bleeding had stopped. She'd wash it in the shower. As she hobbled farther into the room, the anxiety to go straight to the journal and skip the shower tempted her, but the pain in her ankle and sting of the wound couldn't be ignored. And she reeked. The stink of sweat and plaster dust and old house smell stuck to her face, hair, and nostrils.

She removed a miniature ice cube tray from the room refrigerator. An opened bottle of wine caught her attention, so she lifted it out too. After a swig straight from the bottle, she hobbled to the bathroom. Using a face towel, she wrapped the ice tray, sat on the toilet, and applied the cold package to her ankle while the shower water got hot. After several more swallows from the bottle, she disrobed and eased into the spray. She soaped head to toe twice and let hot water pound her tired muscles a few minutes longer.

Out of the shower, she wrapped in a robe, and settled onto the bed. She laid the towel-covered ice tray on her ankle, and after more wine, slid GG's journal onto her lap. While relaxing on propped pillows against the headboard, she flipped pages, searching for the entry. One page caught her eye, and although not the entry needed to locate more information about the gift, she chose to reread the passage. One of her favorites. All night stretched before her to find the accounting of the last time GG had seen Hersey. Why not entertain herself with this entry? More wine calmed the earlier angst as she focused on the loopy penmanship of her great grandmother.

> *July 16, 1924*
> *I'm not sure if I'm living a nightmare or a dream. First the nightmare. All day I worried how to tell John. I've missed my period twice. And I felt sick off and on all day long. I'm pregnant!!! There's no doubt. I threw up twice just thinking about what this means. Pregnant!! His promise to me that by the end of summer he would divorce Lilac seemed like a wisp of cloud over Spirit Mountain that blew away. He'd told me once a respectable amount of time passed after the divorce, I'd become his wife and move into the big house. My dreams all seemed lost. I cried for most of the day. I took out the copy of the will he gave me. Real proof of what I meant to him, but would he ever file it? Would my pregnancy change everything? At times I thought, no, he'll be happy I am having his baby. Louise is a sickly child and causes Lilac so much stress she doesn't even share John's bed. The girl is always in Lilac's bed with her. She's a wife in name only. Of course, he must love Louise, but his life is awful. I'M HIS LIFE. But then I didn't feel so sure, not now since I'm pregnant, and I'd cry more. Not long before he was expected, I got myself together. I decided I would tell him, although I*

wasn't sure how.

Then the nightmare grew darker. He didn't say two words when he burst into my room. The sex was fast, and he was unusually rough. When he rolled off, sweating and huffing, my heart ached. I was scared to open my mouth. Something was wrong. And then his words filled the air like icy rain. SHE'S PREGNANT AGAIN.

I couldn't speak. I couldn't breathe. Paralyzed, I couldn't move. Stunned, my future flew from my reach. And angry. He'd slept with her! He'd had sex with her while professing no intimacy existed between them. HE LIED. The son of a bitch lied. He got her pregnant! I wanted him out of my bed. My lungs hurt to breathe. I honestly thought about hitting him.

But then I thought of my baby, our baby. I burst into tears, and the helplessness I felt made me wretched. I was gasping, and he turned his back to me. Anger flooded me again and at least made me quit crying. He was quiet. Time stretched out, and I'd have thought he'd fallen asleep except his breathing was jagged. When I finally got the nerve to tell him to leave my bed, I touched his shoulder. All I got out was John, and he rolled toward me. His face was all twisted. He was crying! IT DOESN'T MATTER, GENNY. That's what he said. He wrapped his arms around me and pulled me close even though I didn't want him to. He buried his face in my hair. I LOVE YOU.

But his words didn't move me. He'd slept with her. And I also had the product of our love. Love? That's what I thought, and without thinking, I blurted out my condition. WILL YOU LOVE ME IF I'M PREGNANT? I hadn't intended on telling him. Not after hearing about Lilac. I figured what good would it do. But I was so, so very angry, and I had to know.

He pulled away. Stared into my face, his own screwed up with all kinds of emotions I couldn't read.

107

My heart went manic. I was sure I'd have a heart attack. My head pounded.

My nightmare spun into a wild tornado when he spoke. He asked if I was really pregnant. But he knew. I could see it in his eyes.

I asked him if he'd leave me.

NO. YOU ARE THE JEWEL OF MY LIFE. AND I HAVE A JEWEL TO GIVE YOU, MY SWEET GENNY, TO PROVE IT TO YOU. I BOUGHT YOU THE CEYLON ROYAL BLUE SAPPHIRE. IT SHOULD ARRIVE VERY SOON.

That's what he said. Was he buying my love? Did he think staying with her, having more children with her, IN HER BED, would mean nothing if I had jewels? That's what I was thinking. I pushed at his chest and even though I didn't want to cry anymore, to look weak and needy, I sobbed. I told him I didn't want his jewels or his money. I hated him. I yelled I HATE YOU. I said it, but I didn't mean it. I hiccup cried and took it back. I told him I only wanted him.

He cuddled me back to him. I tried to push away, but he forced me against him. And then my nightmare vanished like the fog in The Ravine when the sun gets hot. He told me he is mine for now and forever. He said the jewel is a symbol of his love. He said: THE BLUE IS BREATHTAKING LIKE YOUR MOST UNUSUAL AND BEAUTIFUL EYES. WHEN I SAW IT, I KNEW I HAD TO HAVE IT FOR YOU. LIKE I HAVE TO HAVE YOU FOR ME.

I was dizzy. Honestly dizzy. The room spun, and I had to shut my eyes. I buried my face in his chest and tried to make sense of what was happening. All I could think about was his words that I was his forever. When I could finally breathe and not cry, I looked at him and asked him if this was a dream.

IF IT IS, MAY WE NEVER WAKE. I AM OVERJOYED KNOWING YOU CARRY MY CHILD. YOU WILL BE THE MISTRESS OF LILAC END. WE WILL RAISE OUR CHILD THERE.

Nora yawned. This wasn't the passage she needed but she enjoyed it every time she read. Her eyelids drooped. "July. The entry I need is in…" Forcing her eyes wide, she took the last drink from the bottle. "Let's see. June, July, August." She dropped the bottle to the floor. "Late July? Or was it August?" But her lids were too heavy. "Tomorrow, GG. I'll figure it out tomorrow."

CHAPTER NINE

Sunday, Harlan straddled the stool at his drafting table. He sipped coffee and fought to stay focused as he considered the floor plan. This pathetic drawing wouldn't earn him a lowly D in Architecture 101, but the visual rendering was for his eyes only.

Music drifted from the television in the living room. The eclectic selections on the station he chose provided a nice backdrop for working. The quiet neighborhood of Miners' Mile never disturbed him. Tourists didn't venture this low on the mountain. With each line he drew, thoughts of Phaedra crept between the numbers as he scaled the plan. Last night with her provided more than immense physical pleasure. Something happened between them. Something that couldn't be measured in waves of erotic enjoyment.

Their bond of friendship had never waned even in the years of separation. They shared a rare, eternal kind of relationship a person was lucky to have a few times in life. Yet his heart and soul had expanded beyond the love between friends.

And he didn't tell her.

He checked the measurements on his notes and drew the stairs leading to the second floor. "You're a chickenshit, MacKenzie." As if walking a tightrope without a safety net, he feared his words would be akin to a somersault in the air. Would she feel the same and bring him safely back to the rope or scoff and send him off into the void, smashing their friendship when he hit bottom? Roughing out the top floor, he unsuccessfully pushed aside thoughts of how good she felt beneath him, on top of him.

She'd wise-cracked about friends with benefits; praised his delivery of the benefits. Joked about not needing to "wrap his package" since she could no longer have children, and he was a healthy bad boy. How could he get all serious when she was all about the fun? He stopped and stared out the window, tapping his pencil on the table. He jumped from wanting sex to wanting commitment in one night. But when it's right, it's right. There was no need for a long getting-to-know-her period. He'd known her practically all his life, except for a brief decade and a half. Those years apart hadn't diminished their friendship.

He drew his gaze back to his work. She'd dozed off spooned against him, and he'd slipped away and out the door. Would her mood have been more serious on awakening? Who knows? "Yep, chickenshit, MacKenzie." He ran a hand over his bare pecs then scratched his unshaven jawline. Now what?

As he relived the hours with her in his arms, he scanned the drawing. His brow scrunched. What the devil? *Wait. Something looks off—way off.*

He stood from the stool, braced his hands on each side of the paper, and stared. What wasn't he seeing? Every bedroom had a closet except for one. And something was off with his measurements. Why would Hersey put a closet in all the bedrooms except the smallest one? Did the room serve some other purpose? Did it matter? Considering the odd feedback he'd experienced when he stood in the room, yeah, it mattered. Deciding he needed another in-person look, he rolled the plans and secured them with a rubber band.

His cellphone rang. *Dan.*

"Harlan, my man."

"What's up, Danny?"

"My Sunday afternoon date canceled. Want to do something?"

Fingering the rolled plans in his hand, he didn't hesitate to decline. "Eh, wish I could, but I've got some work to do."

"What, *amigo*? On a Sunday?" A television blared in the background.

"No rest for me today."

After a recap of why his date folded, they hung up.

His stomach growled, reminding him he'd worked through lunch. After changing out of baggy lounge pants and into jeans and a blue

Henley, he scooped up the plans. Making a stop in the kitchen, he slapped together a deli beef sandwich, grabbed an apple and a bottle of water, and carried his load to the truck. First, he stopped at the hardware store to have a key made for his foreman. Back on the road, he threaded his way through the typical Sunday tourist traffic in town. As he wolfed the sandwich, he thought about calling Phaedra. She'd said she had to work on her latest order today, so he'd catch her alone. He could give her an update on the house. Tease her about pushing him to work on a Sunday. Then again, he could get this look-see over with and go to her house later. Maybe take her to dinner and back to his place… Spending time with her tonight would make working on Sunday worth it. That sounded like a plan.

He parked in front of the Big Purple House. From the front seat of his truck, he grabbed his water, apple, and drawing and then loped up the walk. At the back of the house, he skirted the yellowed lawn to where it met the rocky incline of the mountain. He lifted a flat, gray rock and carried it to the porch step to hide the key under. On his way to the front again, he passed by the dead apricot tree. Gnarly branches stretched upward as if still hopeful for water and life. Reddish brown streaks on the trunk hinted at what life could look like. He slowed his steps, his attention drawn to the patches of pale green grass by the tree. Shadows? He wasn't much for puzzles of any kind, but he had a fleeting thought of the need to solve one. "Why do I see a hint of green in your otherwise dead lawn?" He groaned. "Now I'm talking to the flora and fauna."

When he put his key to the front lock of the house, the door edged open. *What the hell?* Had he forgotten to lock up when he left yesterday? Not even pull it closed? He surveyed the metal around the keyhole to check for tampering. Didn't look any more scarred than normal. A gentle push and the door creaked open a few inches. "I'm coming in. If you aren't supposed to be in here, you better high tail it out the back before I find you."

After a few minutes, and no response or noise, he entered and was hit with a dusty, plaster smell. The closet stood open, drawing him nearer. Anger ripped through him like a mountain mine collapse when he saw the gaping hole in the wall opposite the door. He flipped on the light switch. "Son of a…" Every wall had ragged-edged holes. Powdery shambles covered the floor.

Vandals? "Ahh, no." He spun on his heel and rushed into the living room. Satisfied nothing had been damaged, he raced from room to room then up the narrow front stairs. No other desecration. Descending the stairs, he wracked his brain for how he could've left the front door unlocked as an open invitation. Back in the closet, he kicked at a chunk of wall sending it across the floor. This would set back any kind of progress this week. With a glance at the desk, he knew what had to be done. He stomped out to his truck for tools.

He hadn't planned on structural work before Annette made her changes, but now he'd have to unbolt the furniture so his men would have full access to the wall. After years of sitting vacant, why would anyone choose now to vandalize the house? Did the impending sale spark interest? Did unusual activity draw attention to the house and inspire some lowlife to get his kicks from defacing the property?

Back inside, he sprayed the bracket screws with lubricant. While the oil worked its magic, he plugged in his electric drill then fitted it with the right sized bit. He huffed, irritation waning. The desk would've been moved anyway to paint the wall. The first two screws came loose by using extra pressure on the drill. The next six took more work with a few muttered obscenities accompanying the drone of the drill.

He piled the screws on the desktop, stored his drill in the case, and rose stretching his back from the crouched position. Gripping the corners on each side of the desk, he tested the maneuverability and tugged the hefty furniture away from the wall. "Why the hell bolt down such heavy furniture anyway?" Some questions would never be answered. A swishing noise and a quiet thump followed his question. Looking under the desk, he found a large manila envelope on the floor which must have been lodged between the desk and the wall.

The flap, secured with a length of twine wrapped around a flat metal clasp on the envelope body, appeared ancient. He unwound the twine. The aroma of aged paper met his nostrils. Smaller white envelopes—*letters?*—were contained inside. He carried his find into the kitchen where the bright sunshine from the windows flooded the cleaner surfaces. Holding the dusty, manila envelope upside down, he dumped five letters onto the kitchen counter. When he touched them to spread them out, warmth tingled his fingertips as if the letters invited him to explore. "All right." They were addressed to Mrs. Lilac Louise Lambert Hersey. The return address on two of the letters read from Mrs. Josephine Biddington. The other three were from Mr. Bradley Biddington, Esq.

The ground trembled beneath his feet. "Biddington?" Lilac Hersey knew the Biddingtons? Could they possibly be related to his mother's mother? For a moment, he stared at the return addresses. His mother's middle name was Lambert. His grandmother's maiden name was Biddington. All the mixed signals and unusual impressions this house gave him…

He rested his forearms on the counter and squinted at each letter, arranging them in order by the post office cancellation date. If a familial tie existed between the Herseys and his Biddington relatives, some plausible explanation might exist for the vibrations he received in this house. With a deep breath, he lifted the first letter from Penelope Biddington postmarked in September of 1924. He slipped out the folded sheets of paper.

> *September 3, 1924*
> *My Dearest Lilac,*
> *I am at once devastated and frightened by the disappearance of John. How utterly heart wrenching for you and poor little Louise. Can you not implore upon the mines to extend the search? You must consider after two weeks with no sign of him that the worst has occurred.*
> *Therein is my devastation for you and for Louise. I'm glad you confided in me that there is something suspicious about his disappearance. I am sorry my first thought was regarding fidelity. But as you stated, the fact he loved you so unequivocally would rule out any attraction to another. A man who shows that kind of dedication and loyalty, especially in a mining town like Joshua, speaks volumes about his character and equal volumes of how much your love held him to you.*
> *But that brings me to how frightened I am for you and for Louise. Since you say you have not ruled out foul play, you have to know you are in grave danger. My God, Lilac, you are as much an owner of the*

mines as John. If he was murdered (I'm so sorry to use that word) for his holdings, in some scheme for the other company to gain control, then you have to know you are in their crosshairs. This sounds like a good reason for women to remain in supportive roles and not dally in a man's world of business. I'm sorry, but I fear for you and have to speak my mind. Had you merely been a beneficiary, you would've received your cash settlement and your life would be a lot less stressful at this point. Now, you're dealing with all matters of business and as a widow.

Toward the end of the month, my brother-in-law, Bradley Biddington, will be in Phoenix. He's a wonderful attorney. I've known him for four years, since I moved from Joshua and married Henry. Not only is he a fine attorney, but he's a trustworthy and moral man. I want you to meet with him. Please. He won't find it troublesome to make the drive to Joshua to see you as a favor to me. You can at least get some good advice. I hardly think any lawyers in Joshua have the experience and knowledge and IMPARTIALITY that Bradley can offer. Without a doubt, he'll help you deal with the crush of what you are going through.

I love you my dear friend. If there is anything I can do, you must ask. I wish you had phone service in Joshua. When is it slated to be installed in your city? I would think with the mining and business, you'd have it by now.

Henry sends his love. Please give Louise a kiss. I hope her various medical issues are under control and not adding further to your stress.

Fondly,
Penelope

Harlan clasped his forehead as if to hold together all his swirling and colliding thoughts. How would Penelope, or better yet, Henry Biddington, fit into his family tree if they were his relatives? Did his mother and grandmother have the middle name Lambert as a tribute to a good family friend, Lilac?

He wanted to read all the letters, but he had to talk to his dad too. His father could know something about his mother's relatives. About the Biddingtons. He plucked his cellphone from his pocket and punched the button for his father.

"Hi, Harlan."

"Hey, Dad, can I come by? I found some letters I want to show to you, but I also wanted to see if you had any old family documents from Mom's side of the family, like birth or death or marriage certificates."

"I think there might be a few things like that in the safety deposit box in Copperdale, but I'm not home."

"Bank isn't open today anyway. When will you be home? Maybe when you read the letters, they'll spark a memory. And first thing in the morning, I can take you to the bank."

"I won't be home until early afternoon tomorrow. I'm in Phoenix. With Annette. She had a stopover here, so I met her."

Annette? That's... "Wonderful. I'm glad you could meet up with her."

"What's this about letters? Is this real important to you, Harlan?"

"They're old letters I found in the Big Purple House. It can wait until tomorrow. Tell Annette hi. Give me a call when you get back."

"Will do on both. Bye."

In spite of wishing he could talk to his dad face to face, to see if he could remember anything at all about his mother's side of the family, hearing Frank was in Phoenix with Annette made him happy. He could take the letters to his sister's, but interrupting her time with Zac wouldn't be cool. She didn't know any more than he did, most likely.

He refolded the first letter, slipped it back into the envelope, and then opened the second. After reading the first paragraph, he stopped. His fingertips warmed where they touched the letter. Anticipation rose from tight stomach muscles to the center of his chest. Without finishing the letter, he tucked it back into the envelope and shuffled all of them into a stack. He wanted to sit, relax, and read them in succession. When he locked the front door, he turned the key harder than needed. He then checked the knob. "Locked."

As he moved off the veranda, he remembered his promise to

Nora. "Ah, hell."

He traversed the sidewalk, carefully stepping over a chunk of cement that caught his eye. The corner stuck out at an angle as if newly displaced. A dark stain formed a line like something had dripped on it, ran a bit, then dried. He puzzled a moment. Blood? Had the vandal upended the cement, maybe tripped and cut his leg? "I hope so. Would serve you right."

In his truck, he dug Nora's card from his wallet and punched the number into his phone. He let it ring at least ten times. She didn't answer, and voice mail didn't click on. As he brought the engine to life, he decided to go to her hotel. Maybe her cell was dead. He needed to beg off on the tour of Joshua he'd said he'd give her today—at least not until he had a couple of hours to read and digest all the letters.

He pulled his truck into the single row of parking next to the Copper Line Hotel. About ten spaces abutted the railing overlooking more of the town below. Standing outside the truck, he surveyed the hill's descent to the area known as Miners' Mile. He could make out the roof of his house before he continued scanning the view into the Verde Valley. He never got tired of being able to see for miles from nearly everywhere in Joshua. The town may have once been known as the "Wickedest Town in the West" but the view was next to spiritual. With a deep breath, he spun on his heel toward the hotel.

When his sandals touched the sidewalk, he tried calling Nora again. Still no answer. Once in the brightly-lit lobby of the hotel, he paused to get his bearings. He hadn't been inside since he was a kid. Although historic, the owners hadn't done much with the building to capitalize. The original tin ceiling and some simple wood-framed doorways remained the only attestations to a time gone. Of course, in the sixties the place had been stripped of the reception desk and any other signs of the hotel it had been in the 1920s. The building had served as a medical clinic and various shops in the 1960s and 1970s. Unattractive fluorescent lights from the era marred the historical ceiling. A new check-in counter held little artistic appeal. Bland brown carpet covered the floors. The clerk nodded as he passed by. Across from check-in, a brightly lit deli advertised fresh hoagies.

He ascended the stairs to the guest rooms on the second floor. This level had been closed during the time of the clinic decades earlier, untouched then, so a few more clues connected the building to another era. The brass and etched glass light fixtures bathed the walls, the color of a red wine stain, in soft light. The cove molding at the junction of the wall and ceiling gave way to carved flowery shapes in the corners. Halfway down the hall, he found room five and knocked. He knocked again, louder.

A lock unclicked. The door opened a few inches. Nora's round, violet eyes sparkled with surprise. "Oh. Harlan."

"I'm sorry to drop by, but I tried to call first."

She opened the door wider, clutching a blue, ankle-length robe around her. "I was probably in the shower." As she backed away, inviting him in, he got the impression she limped. "Please come in."

"I can't stay. I'm in a hurry, actually, to take care of some business. There's been a development with the house. I wanted to postpone your tour around the housing districts."

She shifted her weight from one foot to the other. "Oh." A brief frown crossed her brow. "I'm disappointed of course, but what's the problem with the house?"

"Vandals did some damage last night."

"Oh, no." Her hand went to her mouth in a dramatic gesture. "Did they destroy anything?"

"Walls in the front closet, but they can be fixed."

"They didn't damage that lovely old desk, did they?"

"No, but I did have to move it so the wall behind it can be repaired." He moved back a step, anxious to get on his way.

"Did you find anything else?" She hobbled closer, her eyes wide, searching.

Why did she have to ask so many questions? He supposed curiosity was part of being a writer. Always researching. He could brush her off, but then again, her interest in the Big Purple House seemed off kilter from the start. Why not divulge some of what he suspected and see her reaction? "I found letters from the 1920s to Lilac Hersey."

"Letters." As if disappointed, her body language relaxed. "Well, that's a bit of history, I suppose, but how do they affect the house? Or you?"

"I found out some information about Lilac Hersey." He spewed the coincidental information about the Lambert and Biddington names in rapid succession, not caring to have a conversation but to see if she was caught off guard. Why she would know anything about these people or his family, made no sense. Yet, her fascination with the house led him to believe she possessed knowledge she chose to keep secret.

Her slight smile fell away, and the tip of her chin came level. The hardness in her face he'd seen from day one glared with her silence. An intake of breath came suddenly as if she'd been resuscitated. She blinked several times. "Do you think you're related to Lilac in some way?"

"No idea, but it's a mystery I'd like to solve."

"I bet."

"You're limping. Did you hurt your leg?"

"Silly me. I tripped on the stairs. Bruised my ankle. I'll be fine." She purposely brushed against him to take hold of the doorknob. "I'll get out on my own later. If I see a house I'd like to know more about, perhaps you can help me out."

"Yeah, sure. I'll, uh, give you a call."

"Or I can call your business number if that's okay." She opened the door, gazing upward with a smile. "I looked it up."

"That works. Take care of that ankle."

"Have fun solving your mystery." The click of her door followed her words.

As he descended the stairs, he juggled his keys in his hand. The clerk didn't look up when he passed by and made his way outside. Harlan sat in his truck, sightlessly staring out over the valley. Nora was a puzzle, but he couldn't clearly see why he thought so. She didn't seem too concerned about finding any more houses for her book. And right now, he didn't really care.

He glanced at the stack of letters on the seat and straightened them. His hands warmed at the touch. Technically, they belonged to Phaedra. Her house, her desk, her letters. He pulled his cellphone from his pocket and punched her number while he cranked the truck engine.

"Hi, Harlan. I was just thinking of you."

Her confession sent ripples of pleasure across his chest. "Then maybe you'll let me interrupt your work. I have something to show you. Can I come over?"

"Yeah? Show and tell?"

He laughed. "I'll take that as a yes. And I'll take you out to dinner later too."

"I'm here. Come on."

Within minutes, he parked his truck in her drive, hopped out, and rang her doorbell. She greeted him barefoot, in leggings and a loose blouse that tied on her hip. Without a word, she wrapped her arms around his neck and kissed him.

He backed her into the nook of an entry, knocked the door closed with his foot, and kissed her back.

She squirmed and broke the kiss. "What's sticking me in my back?"

"Letters." His hand holding the envelopes snugged against her. "What I wanted to show you."

"Okay. Then kiss to be continued later." She led the way to the living room. Plopping onto one of two cream-colored loveseats, she tucked one knee under her. "Letters?" She patted the sofa beside her.

Settling close, he clasped the envelopes on his knee. "When I moved the desk so the wall could be repaired—"

"Repaired? I don't remember the walls in the closet needing repair."

"You had vandals last night." He wished he could skip this part of the story—vandals who gained entry by the door he left open.

"Oh no! How much damage?"

"They knocked holes in the walls of the front closet. The office. Made a freaking mess. I had to unclamp the desk from the wall so we can make repairs."

"Did they break windows to get in?"

"No." He huffed. "I was good enough to leave the front door open for them."

"What?"

"Honestly, Phae, this stumps me. I can't imagine not locking up the place. But unless they got in somewhere I'm not seeing and left by the front door, leaving it open, it has to be my fault."

"Weird." She patted his thigh as if in sympathy.

"Yeah. But I can't believe I did that."

"Don't beat yourself up. This house has you rattled, methinks."

He couldn't argue that. "Anyway, when I removed the brackets holding the desk to the floor, these letters, lodged between the desk and the wall, fell loose. They're to Lilac in 1924. Since you own the house, they belong to you."

"Oh, cool." She pointed at the envelopes. "Well? You going to let me look at them?"

He handed her the first one. "I've read this one." He removed the page from the envelope. "I'm stumped, Phae. The name... Go ahead. Read before I talk."

As she read, her forehead furrowed, then she smiled, and then frowned again. When finished, she sighed. "Wow. This is history. The famous disappearing millionaire of Joshua. But the name, Biddington. How does that figure into this puzzle?"

Staring at the rest of the letters in his hand, a trickle of anticipation tripped across his chest. "My grandmother. Monica. Lambert. Biddington."

"Harlan! What does this mean?"

"Something." The heat came again to his fingers clutching the envelopes. "Must mean something. Let's read the rest of the letters."

CHAPTER TEN

Nora lounged on the bed. She never dreamed Harlan would drop by her hotel room if she hadn't talked to him first. She'd avoided his calls, deciding it wiser to nurse her leg until the limp wasn't so noticeable before she saw him again. Not that he could possibly know she was his vandal, but better safe than sorry. Her stomach had dropped to her knees when he'd said he made a discovery after unbolting the desk from the floor. *Letters.* "Big freaking deal."

After last night's disaster, sleeping in helped her recuperate. While eating a deli-delivered breakfast, she watched an old movie. An uncomfortable drive to the Little Market for more wine was followed by a pampering long bath. Her great grandmother's journal on the bedside table seemed to mock her as she moved around her room throughout the day. Why couldn't she decipher from GG's entries in the journal where her fortune was hidden in the house? She had all day to figure it out, and yet she'd not opened the journal once. Earlier, considering keeping her date with Harlan, she'd envisioned seducing him in some wayside location. Sex always took her mind off her problems. But her ankle protested.

She took a healthy swallow of wine. After removing the red wax covering on a round of cheese, she bit off half, chewed, then followed with another drink of wine. This would suffice for an early dinner. She adjusted the pillows propped under her foot as she stretched out on the bed, her back against more pillows on the headboard. At least his discovery had nothing to do with the jewel.

On her phone, she Googled *Ceylon Royal Blue Sapphire* then

skimmed the history. Unearthed in 1908. Purchased by an anonymous man in 1924. She checked periodically to confirm there weren't any new discoveries. No new articles appeared. The few there were declared no sign of its existence since 1924. Today's value would exceed $3,000,000. The hairs on her neck prickled every time she read how rich she would become.

"Well hell." She couldn't avoid the journal any longer. Although she loved reading GG's words, the puzzle of finding the sapphire made her itchy. She scratched her thighs. Reading for pleasure was one thing. Reading for clues, for retention of facts? She rubbed both her arms to ward off the unpleasant skin crawling. "It's in that damned house, and I'm going to find it."

She poured the remainder of the bottle of wine into her glass. "Crap." Swiveling to a sitting position, she rose and checked the hotel refrigerator. The last bottle she'd purchased earlier in the day nestled between a half dozen rounds of cheese. After uncorking the wine and setting it within reaching distance on the nightstand, she took out the ice tray wrapped in a washrag from the freezer.

With the ice tray propped on her elevated ankle, she reclined on the bed. Tonight, she'd go back yet again to the house, but while waiting for nightfall, she'd reread some entries in the diary. What had she missed in the journal? *Pay closer attention this time.* She flipped through pages, choosing a date late in July.

> *July 28· 1924*
> *His child is sickly. I don't wish her ill, but I'm happy when Lilac takes the girl, Louise, to the doctor and is gone for the night. SO HAPPY. I wish she'd take the kid away and never come back. She went to the doctor again today, so John took me to the grand house. He made slow, magic love to me. Or maybe lying in a bed that hasn't had others thrashing around, sweaty and ripe, makes the act magic. This has become OUR bed. We stayed there for hours and talked about our future. He told me he'd pamper me. Buy me beautiful clothes. Our children will want for nothing. And he told me about the jewel again.*

"Crap. They weren't fucking on the desk every time. How did I miss that clue?" She sipped her wine and continued reading.

> *He went on and on about the mining business.*
> *How it's volatile right now. How there is talk of*
> *major setbacks. I didn't really understand any of it,*
> *nor do I particularly care. Of course, he doesn't*
> *know that. Anyway, he said he has plenty of money,*
> *but the jewel is for me. MINE. Something for my*
> *security no matter what the future brings. The jewel*
> *even has a name!! It's called the Ceylon Royal Blue*
> *Sapphire. Ceylon is a country in the Indian Ocean.*
> *When I said I didn't know the Indians had an Ocean,*
> *John laughed for several minutes. I do that. I make*
> *him laugh and enjoy life. She makes him miserable.*
> *Anyway, he kissed me and made love to me again.*

Nora closed her eyes, could almost smell their love making. She visualized the sapphire, a deep glittering blue like GG's eyes…like her own. Wetting her lips, she sighed, her lids fluttering open to read more.

> *Afterwards, he continued his story as if we'd not*
> *taken a break for sex. He told me all about the jewel.*
> *That it's world famous and one of a kind. He should*
> *have it next month. And I'll have it in case of the*
> *worst thing I can ever imagine happening. Which is*
> *not having John. I won't let myself think this. He'll*
> *leave her. One day. Someday, I'll be the most*
> *respectable, envied girl in Joshua.*
> *But he won't leave Lilac until after her baby is*
> *born. I made it clear I'm not happy with that, but he*
> *says it's the way it has to be. I think the jewel is a*
> *promise of his intentions.*

If they were in a bed, then the closet where they hid the jewel must be upstairs. Stairs. Hadn't there been something about hearing Lilac on the stairs?

Nora ate another round of cheese. Finished the wine in her glass, then flipped several pages. "No." Flipped more. "No." Lifted the

new bottle of wine and filled her glass. "Shit, where is the page…"
The first line of an entry jumped out. "This might be it."

> *August 20, 1924*
>
> *Oh my God. Lord in heaven, what have I done?!!*
> *I don't WANT to write this, but I HAVE to because*
> *tomorrow I may be stark raving mad with the*
> *memory!!! If someone should find me throwing*
> *myself against a wall or slicing my wrists, I want*
> *them to discover this confession and to know the*
> *TRUTH. If I'm mad and crazy and senseless, none of*
> *this will matter. But if I am not mad, then I will force*
> *myself to reread about this day from hell OVER AND*
> *OVER so I will always remember to pray for my soul.*
> *Dear God, I pray for my soul.*
>
> *John should not have taken me to the grand house*
> *in the light of day.*

"Blah, blah, blah." She ran her finger down the page.

> *As soon as Lilac left for Copperdale, he fetched*
> *me, and we went to the house. He'd received the*
> *Ceylon Royal Blue Sapphire and was overcome with*
> *excitement.*

"Excitement. Yada, yada." She sipped more wine.

> *We both heard a noise and stopped talking to*
> *listen. But we heard nothing, so we continued,*
> *laughing and talking about wonderful things. Us.*
> *Making love on his desk in his closet the first time.*
> *How we would one day make love in every room of*
> *the house. How we would raise the child, his baby in*
> *my belly. We would raise our child and have plenty*
> *more children. And then we heard the noise again.*
> *There was someone on the stairs. John froze, and in*
> *that moment, we both knew Lilac was there.*
>
> *He jumped off the bed and with his hand across*
> *my mouth, dragged me into the closet and told me to*

be quiet. NO MATTER WHAT!

She skipped paragraphs, squinting blurry eyes. A word here or there registered. "Ah, here."

> *Lilac lay in a fetal position on the floor, still. In the closet, I scooped the sapphire from the floor. OH NO YOU DON'T. She screamed.*
> *I tried to run around her, but she ranted and jerked around wild and crazy. She knocked my knees out from me. She jumped on me and dug her fingernails into my hand. The pain was too much and I let it go.*

"Bitch." She scanned down the page.

> *And the jewel would be entombed in the closet of shame.*

She closed the journal. The closet. Of the bedroom. Which bedroom? She'd tear them all apart. "I just have to wait until dark." After topping off her glass, she peeled another round of cheese, satisfaction settling on her like a cuddly blanket. "In the closet of shame."

She snickered.

****

Harlan slipped the second letter from the envelope. Spreading the page on her knee, which rested on his thigh, he said, "I started this one but stopped." They inclined their heads together and read.

> *October 10, 1924*
> *Dear Lilac,*
> *How absolutely perfect you found Bradley so helpful. I told you, you'd like him. And now I must say something I know I can say to you, dear friend, but would keep to myself if we weren't so close. He is smitten. I could tell it after the two days he spent in Joshua last month. Oh, he wouldn't admit anything at all, but I've not seen him smile so much*

126

in the four years I've known him. And then he makes a second trip, just to "advise" you in more detail?

Oh! How I wish I could talk to you. I tried to read between the lines of your letter after your first meeting with him. It was evident you admired him, found him knowledgeable and professional. But I swear I read something a little more personal in your words. I'm sure you are thinking it's too soon to be considering a man in anyway other than professional. But you can't help it if someone comes along who attracts you. And you probably think your condition is a roadblock to forming a relationship. I can tell you it is not. Not in the case of Bradley at any rate. In fact, I think it's imperative if you do find someone you could care about and someone who cares about you, you must throw caution to the wind and follow your heart. Especially because of your condition.

I doubt Bradley has told you much about himself in the four days you two have been in each other's company. His wife and baby girl were killed in the earthquake of 1906 here in San Francisco. So tragic. Henry tells me Bradley never fully recovered from his loss. He threw himself into his work and is now one of the most respected attorneys in all of California. So, you can see, if he is smiling and has such a lighthearted attitude about him now, it has to be because of you.

Henry is a loyal brother and not one to carry tales, but he says Bradley speaks fondly of you. Henry says you have given his brother something more to live for than work. How did you seduce this man in such a short time?

I'm hoping you have already written me since your second encounter with him last week. I am dying to hear what is going on in your head. I actually pray it is a mutual feeling for you. I'd hate to see Bradley crushed by a lack of reciprocation of your feelings. Your unborn child deserves a man like Bradley.

You and Louise should visit us. We have plenty of room, and the boys would probably spoil Louise to no end. Seeing Bradley at home with family, in a social setting would be a splendid way to test your feelings. Okay, I'm jumping to conclusions, but I have a wonderful feeling about the two of you.

Write me soon!

Penelope

Phaedra sighed and leaned back. "This is like a historical soap opera." She slipped the page from under his fingers and folded it. "Here. Let's read the next one."

He couldn't help but notice the sudden cold when his hand lost contact with the letter. Slipping it into the envelope, he lingered, his thumb pressing the paper into his fingers. The physical heat imparted a sense of familiarity, yet an uneasiness begged him to search beyond the subtleness. His mind wandered over the other sensations he'd experienced in the house.

"Harlan? Are you with me?"

"Sorry. I was…thinking."

"Or something. These might technically be my letters, but they mean more to you. Come on." She scooted closer. "Open the next one."

He read the return address. "This one is from the lawyer."

Phaedra lifted the letter from his hand. "The plot thickens." She spread the paper on her knee and nudged his shoulder with a grin.

October 11, 1924

Dear Lilac,

I was pleased to see you sorting through the legalities of your business with such ease. You might well compliment me on my fine advice, as you did, but I happen to perceive you are a woman with a head for business. I am impressed. Aligning yourself with companies that wish to aggregate and acquire is wise indeed. I should be able to offer a clearer vision of what I foresee for your industry on my next visit.

And now, I am hoping I don't offend by adding a

personal note to you. From our first meeting, I've felt as if we have a bond that exceeds mere acquaintances. I sensed you shared my perception. I've grown quite fond of you in the short time I have known you. If that makes you at all uncomfortable, please express your opinion without fearing for my feelings. I will still be most happy to advise you in a business sense.

I await your reply.
Sincerely,
Bradley Biddington

"Don't you just love the way they wrote back then?" Phaedra's voice held an unfamiliar sing-song tone.

"You mean stiff and proper?"

She elbowed him. "Yeah, I suppose, but it's a little romantic don't you think? I mean not romance romantic but lyrical."

"Hm-mm." Poetic wasn't what he took from this correspondence. The information represented clues, yet he wasn't sure to what. "Let's continue." While he slipped the page back in the envelope, Phaedra opened the next letter.

October 28, 1924
Dear Lilac,
I received your letter today. I am in total agreement with you that now would be the time to liquidate your properties and business. I fear the new year will bring a downturn in coinage metals. As I informed you when last we visited, if the business should be in need of procuring a loan, as a woman, your task will be near impossible to complete. With the climate of the industry, and the obstacles you face as a woman, now is the perfect opportunity for you to sell.

I agree with your choice in enlisting the services of the law firm in Copperdale. My research confirms their reputation is excellent, and they should be able to handle the negotiations and filings.

Although I am pleased you are moving forward

with business, I am more pleased with the last half of your letter. I have read it over and over. Although my heart goes out to you for the process you must endure in having your husband declared dead, it is most wise of you to do so, considering your desire to sell your business without entanglement.

As to your wish in regards to me, I am more than happy to dislodge our business relationship and pursue getting to know you outside of your professional persona. I understand your hesitation in regards to the fact you are with child. In my short time with your sweet Louise, I can say for you to bring another cherub into this world like her only endears me more to you. So please lay your fear aside. I look forward to a visit of a personal nature, and I accept your invitation.

I'll arrive in Joshua on November 15.
Until then,
Fondly,
Bradley

"He's going to marry her." Harlan drummed his fingers on her knee.

"Sounds that way."

"Lilac Hersey becomes a Biddington." Somehow, he could be related to this woman…to the Big Purple House. *Lilac End.* "If I'm related to this branch of Biddingtons, I'm at least related to her by marriage."

"Susie Muse moves to Joshua without knowing she has ties here. How bizarre."

"Yeah, her mother's maiden name was Biddington. But Lilac was a Hersey when she lived in Joshua and all the historical references to her time would be under the name of Hersey. Mom wouldn't have known the connection." But a connection could exist. "Lilac moved to San Francisco. My mother and grandmother were born in San Francisco, so I could possibly be related to the San Francisco Biddingtons." Although nothing in these letters gave him any direct clue to his connection to Lilac, a gnawing in the depths of his core said otherwise.

"Yes, bizarre…" She plucked the next letter from his lap. "Ah, damn, only one left." She wiggled like a little girl excited to open her last birthday present. "Let's read."

He laughed. "I'm glad you're having fun with this."

> *November 21, 1924*
> *My darling Lilac,*
> *I am ecstatic the sale will finalize on December 12, and I will most certainly be there, by your side, to help you sever your ties to Joshua. My heart leapt at your decision to return to San Francisco with me. I was afraid I was rash in suggesting it on my last visit. But, my sweet Lilac, time is precious, and I am loath to set a slow pace in my pursuit of your affection. My happiness is boundless that we might at last enjoy a courtship that will allow me to see you daily. You should not delay the trip any longer than necessary. I want you to have the best medical care for the arrival of your child. Louise will also benefit from the excellent doctors we have in San Francisco.*
> *Yes, I will be patient with you, considering you are navigating the final months of your condition. No, you are not a whale. You are lovely and glowing, and I will treasure every week of courtship with you.*
> *I will be quite miserable until I see you again.*
> *With Love,*
> *Bradley*

"That's that." Harlan stared at the page. Would any of the documents his dad had in the safety deposit box link Lilac or Bradley Biddington to Susie Muse? "Although the letters were behind the desk, I don't think they were purposely hidden. There's nothing in them that could harm anyone's reputation or reveal any *secrets*."

Phaedra lifted the letter. "No. Probably just fell behind the desk and was lost for decades." She scanned it again, and sighed.

"There's that sigh again." He plucked the page from her hand. "I didn't know you were such a romantic." After tucking it in the envelope, he added it to the others on the coffee table.

"Yeah? A girl's got feelings, you know. A mind. More than just a roll in the hay."

He wanted more than a roll in the hay. He kissed her. "More?" Another kiss lasted longer as he drew her onto his lap, bringing her tight against his chest. When he broke the kiss and trailed his lips down her neck, tasting and breathing in her rose scent, his fleeting thought of telling her just how much more he wanted got tangled in what his body wanted.

"Harlan."

Hot breath tickled his ear, and his groin pulsed in response.

Phaedra slapped a hand on his chest and dislodged his mouth from her collarbone. "Harlan."

"Mmm?" He clasped her butt with a hand.

"Feed me." She nipped his bottom lip and leapt off his lap.

"Really? Now?"

"You promised me dinner." She grabbed his hand and pulled him to standing. "We can come back here after and…talk…or whatever."

Whatever. Or talk. They needed to talk. "Okay. How does Rose's sound?"

"Yum. Hot and spicy." She whirled away from him, peeked over her shoulder, and sashayed to the door, an exaggerated swing to her hips giving new meaning to hot and spicy.

This new flirting Phaedra was more than enjoyable, but would he ever get her in a serious moment to broach the other half of his emotions? He caught up with her and wrapped his arm around her waist as they walked to his truck. She bumped his hip and laughed. He really needed to take it a step at a time, but he'd known her for decades. How many more steps did he need to tell her she was way more than a roll in the hay? He couldn't wait for her to make the first move this time. He needed to find that serious side and feel secure in a relationship that went way beyond friendship.

Tonight was the night.

CHAPTER ELEVEN

Phaedra raised her margarita in a toast. Perhaps she could liven up Harlan's mood. The brightly painted Rose's and the lively Mexican music drifting overhead should help. He hadn't spoken on the short ride to the restaurant. Although she preferred his cocky smirk, staring at a brooding Harlan with a shadow beard in a sky-blue Henley did wonders for *her* mood in all the right places. "Here's to the mystery and intrigue of the Big Purple House."

He tipped his chin upward as if asking the heavens for help. "If I must." He clinked her glass.

She licked salt from the rim then sipped. "Hmm. Come on Har, you have to admit the letters added another level of intrigue. Do they help with any of the ambiguity you feel about the place?"

"If there's a chance I'm related to Lilac in some roundabout way, I suppose that could explain the vibrations…and physical reactions…I experience." He dipped a chip in salsa. "Dad will be back tomorrow. We're going to see what's in the safety deposit box."

"What are you expecting to find?"

His margarita got his attention for a few moments. "Maybe something that will explain the name connection. Lambert. Biddington. He's not really sure what papers of Mom's are in there." He crunched on a chip.

The waiter appeared with their dinners. "Chili relleno for the lady." He slid the dish onto the table. "Careful. The plate is hot. And chimichanga for the gentleman. Hot plate. Can I get you anything else?"

"Would you bring me another one of these?" Harlan lifted his half-full glass. "Phaedra?"

That caught her attention. "No thanks." She'd barely made a dent in hers. Since when did he put away a tequila drink so quickly? The letters must be throwing him more than he let on. "Is there anything I can do to help out? Like any research or...I don't know...phone calls or something?" She lifted a bite of relleno, the steam wetting her nose as she blew to cool it. She was crazy busy with the clothing order for the store in Copperdale, but she felt for him. He was rattled, and she wanted to soothe his soul. Maybe doing some grunt work would help.

He spread his napkin in his lap. "Yeah, actually, there is. I thought I might take the letters to the Historical Society tomorrow, but I really need to be with the crew. Wanda is a wealth of information." He cut into his food but pushed it around instead of eating. "Maybe something in the letters will mean something to her. Or she might know some avenue to research."

"I can do that."

"You sure you have time?" He lifted his chin, lips slightly parted. His gaze caressed her face, sending a fire straight to her belly hotter than the relleno.

What is that about?

"More time than you have, if you're going to get the house done before Annette gets back." When she didn't get a rebuttal, his stare seeming to search her soul, she leaned toward him. "Well?"

"What?" He blinked and lifted his drink.

"I expected a smart-mouthed response."

"Sorry, I didn't hear you."

You were looking right at me. "Ha! Catching you at a loss for words is a treat."

He gave her a half-smile and returned to eating.

His mind obviously wandered elsewhere. Harlan appeared to be deeply bothered. She couldn't begin to understand his connection to the past through the house or the letters and how intensely they distracted him.

The waiter brought his second drink as he finished the first. "Thank you."

They ate in silence for a few moments. If they weren't in a

134

restaurant, she'd crawl onto his lap and give him something else to think about. Getting him back between the sheets had been on her mind all day. They'd been friends for enough years that they didn't need to keep a constant conversation alive. They were comfortable with silence, yet her curiosity as to why the correspondence between Lilac and the Biddingtons left him so moody and quiet had her wanting to break the silence. "Are the letters bothering you terribly?"

"No. I have several things on my mind." He stirred the sauce on his plate with his fork tongs.

"Anything I can help with?"

His gaze lifted, intense. Expression serious. "Why didn't you marry either of the girls' fathers?"

The question came so far from left field, she stopped chewing. What in Hades made him think of that? She finished chewing while he peered at her. Frowning, she swallowed the last of her bite, giving thought to his question. "Different reasons." The simple truth to a complicated question.

"Do you have a philosophical opposition to marriage?" He threw the question out, blunt and expressionless, although he cut and stabbed at his burro in a jerky motion.

He acted nervous, covering his edginess by attacking his food.

"I wouldn't call my opposition a philosophy. But I don't see the up side to marriage." Marriage required giving yourself over to a man. Following him around and possibly getting dumped on like her mother.

So, there was more than the mystery behind the letters plaguing him. And apparently, her relationship history must be part of his quandary for him to ask such a question. A question that bothered her. No one except her mother could grill her on her relationship history. Friends accepted her for who she was.

He studied his drink, ran his finger down the curve of the frosted glass. "Have you ever been in love? I mean, you must have, I guess."

Her hand holding her fork jerked, spilling rice over the edge of her plate. She knew her jaw needed propping up. Instead, she took a bite of her rice, but she had trouble swallowing what suddenly clogged her mouth like paste. The banter and jabs they'd engaged in all their lives and the recent sexual repartee between them came easy. This new serious let's-talk-love conversation pushed her comfort zone. "I suppose, Harlan. I have. Why?"

"Curious." He sat back. Seared her with his green gaze. "We've changed. You and I."

Wait. Wait. She had a sudden urge to vault. *We just jumped from friends to lovers.* He was steering into parts unknown. Talking, for Hades' sake, and she'd barely gotten used to the sex part. He could've warned her. She didn't see this coming. *Talking? About them?* This was what the questions about marriage were leading to? *The next step?* There was no finishing her meal now with her stomach in knots. Marriage in general never showed on her horizon. In fact, that sun set years ago without any indication of rising again.

He smiled his damned classic Harlan expression that curled her toes and had her clenching her thighs. Between the Margarita, spicy food, and festive ambiance of Rose's, her head spun enough without Mr. Sexy talking the talk, giving her *that look.*

"Are you okay with us?"

"Of course I am, Harlan. I'm the one, I mean, I kind of started this whole…" She waved her hand between them, knocked over the chips and then the salt shaker as she righted the bowl. Her armpits and the skin on her neck beneath her hair went sweaty. The restaurant was toasty but comfortable until this conversation twisted her insides and heated her comfort zone.

"Yeah, you might've made the first move, but I'd been there, in my head. And it started out just wondering what if we… You know, I like the way you fill out your jeans. Couldn't get my mind off of it." He chuckled then leaned over the table, dropping his voice to a whisper. "Wanted my hands where my mind wandered."

The thought of his hands sent nice ripples low in her belly, and she welcomed the sentiment. Yet there seemed to be more than sexual implications between his words. "After all these years…"

"Yeah." He took a hearty drink of his margarita. Was he looking for courage in the tequila?

A roiling in her stomach from a sudden rush of nerves sloshed the green chili around. He was leading up to something besides their great affair. They'd been having so much fun. Not that she wasn't attracted to him for more than the physical pleasure, but his wounded dove status could cause him to act on feelings he might misinterpret, which would tangle all logic. Although they'd been lifelong friends, and that might give them a jumpstart on a solid romantic relationship, it might also cloud the issue. There were all kinds of love in the world. She needed time to sort out where they were now, where they were going.

She caught herself rubbing the scar on her chin, fisted her hand, and brought it to the table. Marriage wasn't anywhere *near* her expected path of travel. She'd always done fine on her own. Marriage changed people. She didn't want to change. Didn't want *them* to change.

"Tell me again why you've never married."

"What are you asking me, Harlan?" She clenched her jaw.

"Marriage. I'm wondering—"

"I got pregnant with Primrose when Magpie and I were at NAU. Her father wasn't on my happily ever after list. I had to quit school, get a job. We lived together for a time, but I didn't love him. I eventually moved back to Joshua, met Poppy's father." She ground her teeth with her pause. Irritation rankled her mood as her historical recitation continued. "And yes, that time I thought I was in love. I think I already mentioned he wanted to change me. After three years, I'd had enough with the man. Marriage just wasn't part of it." And she really didn't want to discuss the details right now. "Is that what you want to know?" Did he think she possessed some oddball defect because she'd never married?

"Don't get pissed. Maybe I'm coming at this wrong. I'm just curious—"

"I'm not pissed." But she knew her reactions indicated otherwise. She didn't like the third degree. She didn't need him questioning how she led her life.

"Can I get you two anything else?"

She flashed the waiter a forced smile. "No. We're done." She wasn't about to ask Harlan if he wanted anything else. This conversation needed to move out of the restaurant. Or stop altogether.

"Okay. Thanks for coming in." The young man set the bill by Harlan's plate.

She slid her hand to lift it, but Harlan moved faster. "I'll get it. I asked you to dinner, remember?"

"You got lunch last."

He ignored her and stuck cash inside the folder.

They didn't speak as they walked a half block to his truck. He was *so* important to her. Why did he have to bring up marriage? Or her lack of? The engine started. Still they didn't speak. Was he trying to figure out how serious she was about him? Yeah, she was serious. Seriously crazy about him. But this whole friends-to-lovers thing happened so fast, he could blow it all with a giant leap. Especially if he leaped right from sex to marriage without even an I-love-you-let's-live-together phase. There wasn't anyone in either of their lives to crowd the picture. Couldn't they—

"Would you rather I left?"

"What?" They were in her driveway.

"You seem lost to me. I'm afraid I've spoiled the evening. I should leave."

"I guess I was off in my own little world. Didn't realize we were at my cottage already."

"The letters. I left them inside."

"I told you I'd take them to Wanda tomorrow." Her words came out more clipped than she intended.

He gripped the steering wheel, stared straight ahead. "I'm sorry. I have no right to ask you about the girls' fathers."

"Of course you do." She poked his arm. He faced her. A nervous flutter in her stomach scared her. Could they go back to being only friends if he didn't like what she had to say? "I reacted poorly. I thought you were questioning my right to live my life my way. It's happened before. Poppy's father wanted me to be someone I'm not." Leaning over the center console, she wrapped her arms around his shoulders, her palms cupping his neck. The tenseness radiated in hard muscles. "Marriage isn't important to me. Mom managed years alone and then when she got married again, everything changed. I've raised two children on my own. I like my life. But I shouldn't be so touchy. Okay?"

He took a deep breath. Had she lost him? She kissed his cheek. "Is there anything else you want to know about me? Jeez, after so many years, I guess I assumed we knew it all."

He kissed her lips. Relaxing against the seat, he broke the kiss, and his eyes searched her face. "Not at the moment."

She breathed an inner sigh of relief. "You can ask anything anytime from now on. After all, we're friends, the best kind."

A brief frown creased his brow she chose to ignore. They'd crossed the friendship line, and she didn't want to go back.

****

For the third night in a row, Nora parked down the block from Lilac End. "Okay, third time's the charm." Armed with her bag of tools slung over her shoulder, she scanned the street and took on a casual cadence as if out for an evening stroll. She paused in front of the house, once again surveyed her surroundings, then painfully navigated the broken sidewalk to the front door. *Not tripping like an idiot tonight.*

Inside, thinking back to the tour Harlan had provided, she made her way to the stairs with the help of the flashlight and then up to the second floor. Ignoring the ache in her ankle, she entered the master bedroom. Would Hersey have screwed GG in his wife's bed? "God, I hope so."

The closet door gapped open. From the bag, she removed the small battery lantern and a scarf. After tying the scarf around her head to cover her mouth and nose, she turned on the lantern. She set it on the floor just inside the closet. Using the hammer, she tapped the wall facing the door and found a hollow sounding area. "Three million dollars." She gripped the hammer with both hands, juggled it a moment to set the weight comfortably, and slammed into the wall. The slight crack rewarded her effort, infusing her with renewed energy. She battered the wall over and over until a large enough hole gaped to accommodate her shoulders. Goosebumps tingled her arms and neck. Clutching the hand-held flashlight, she maneuvered the upper half of her body into the hole and shone the light in all directions. Nothing.

As she backed out of the hole, pain raked along the underneath of her arm. "Ouch." The ragged edge of plaster left a long red mark on her skin. With the back of her hand, she brushed her bangs to the side, swiping at the sweat on her forehead. Although she hated the cold, winter would've been a better season to take on her treasure hunting.

She faced the next wall, planted her feet, and swung the hammer. With each jarring connection of hammer on wall, the jolt sent a shock wave along her arms, vibrating her shoulders. She lapsed into a rhythm, until the hole reached the desired size. The result was the same. Pushing thoughts of failure from her mind, she methodically punctured all the walls of the closet. Forty-five minutes later, she stood in the mangled enclosure, her heart thrumming and her breathing heavy.

"I guess he wasn't a big enough son of a bitch to roll around naked with her in his wife's bed." She gathered her tools and light and then marched into the second bedroom. Her shoulders throbbed, and the hammer in her hands gained a few pounds. This closet was smaller. "Same number of walls." She gritted her teeth. "Three million dollars." She held the hammer over her head and crashed into the wall. Repeating the same process as in the other closet, she slaughtered the plaster. The only competition with the noise of the hammer was her repeated coughing. But the walls held no treasure.

Sweat dripped from her brow and nose, soaking into the scarf over her mouth. Her lungs burned inside her chest. The muscles ached on the outside of her chest as if she'd been doing pushups. She trudged into the hall to avoid breathing anymore of the plaster dust than necessary and tugged the scarf down around her neck. Bent at the waist, hands on knees, she gasped deep, clean breaths. "I can do this. Two down, two to go." When she straightened, a twinge of protest shot up her back. "A little pain for the gain."

After transferring her tools to the third bedroom, she gulped a bottle of water. She tugged the scarf over her noise and with a mixture of dread and hope, she raised the hammer. Each blow came slower than the one before. She sucked in air. Wiped sweat from her eyes. Her swings took on a side-arm arc with the two-ton hammer. When the hole finally yawned, she shimmied into the cavity. Empty.

Collapsing against the wall, she slid down onto the plaster covered floor. "Shit! Shit! Shit!" Of course the jewel would be hiding in the final bedroom closet. Nothing came easy. "I should've started in there, but noooo, I got all feelie thinking of GG in Lilac's bed." She crossed her arms over her knees and rested her forehead on them. "Maybe more than three million. Last room. I can do this."

She plodded into the fourth room, her head pounding and her eyes burning from blinking through plaster dust. Revolving in a circle, scanning the walls, she wobbled with dizzy confusion. She dropped her tools. Yanked the scarf from her face. Where was the closet? She stumbled around the perimeter of the room as if she expected a door to suddenly appear. The burning in her eyes increased as tears spilled onto her cheeks. "This can't be." She dropped to the floor. Hanging her head, she sucked in air and let the tears fall.

This is the house. The sapphire is missing. It's sealed inside a closet. "Why can't I find—?"

Her head jerked up. GG wrote 'and the jewel will be entombed in the closet of shame.' *The whole damned closet is the tomb.* She snatched the flashlight and stood. Creeping around the room again, she ran the light up and down, side to side. Once upon a time, there was a closet in this room. She tapped. Yes, there were hollow sections on every wall but no evidence of a seam or a different finish. She'd have to tear the entire room apart. Her shoulders drooped and ached as if the weight of the room sat on her back. Fatigue enveloped her, draining her enthusiasm. Maybe she'd get lucky and find it with the first hole. Then again, maybe it would be the last hole. Renewed tears filled her eyes. She wiped her nose on the back of her hand. Her fingers throbbed from gripping the wooden handle and pounding. She rubbed a blister on her left palm. Her legs gave way, and she crumpled onto the floor. A sob shuddered through her. She couldn't quit. But how could she do this?

She needed help. *Harlan.* He'd be able to find the closet. She'd offer him a percentage. She tilted her head left then right to wipe her wet cheeks on the shoulders of her shirt. *Yes, Harlan will help me.* She gathered her tools, pain pulsing with every movement. *Three mil is enough to give away a little and still be rich.* First, she'd seduce him. Sex always softened up a man. She could have a little fun in the process. *Sure.* With a shoulder roll and a self-satisfied nod, she gave herself a boost of confidence. Harlan was a man after all, and men could be coaxed. Downstairs, she left the door unlocked again. When she stepped across the threshold, she glanced around and made a hasty retreat to her car.

In the darkness, she leaned her head back on the headrest. Sex and money were enough to get any man to do what she wanted. After the sex, she'd be able to gauge if he'd partner with her on uncovering the jewel. If he wasn't approachable— *No. Don't even think like that.* She opened her glove box. *But just in case.* Feeling around beneath the papers, she confirmed her gun was at the back of the compartment. "He'll help me, one way or another."

****

Harlan stared into the dark. His thoughts were as stirred as the air circulating from the fan blades clicking overhead. He rolled to his

141

side. The clock blinked back at him. 4:30. His alarm wouldn't go off for another hour and a half. He'd gotten some shut-eye, but a dream woke him, and there was no going back to sleep now. He couldn't remember the dream, but he'd woke unsettled.

He ended the evening last night in Phaedra's bed—not in her heart as he'd hoped. Not that they weren't close—they'd always been close. But he wanted more. The sex, and it was more sex than making love, was good but not as satisfying as it could've been. He'd left, still not knowing where he stood. Then again, he did know. Phaedra wasn't interested in making more of their relationship. He'd botched the conversation at the restaurant horribly. And Magpie worried about *him* hurting *Phaedra?* Fat chance with Phaedra's keep-it-light attitude.

Kicking off the covers, he swung his legs over the side of the bed. He may as well get an early jump on the day. His crew would arrive at the Big Purple House at 7:00. Work would get his mind off his personal life. Unfortunately, this job was tied to his personal life. He scratched the stubble on his cheek. She thought his scruff gave him a bad boy look she found attractive. Maybe he should skip shaving. He stood and stretched. No, attraction wasn't the problem. He was falling in love, but she wasn't. They were the best of friends according to her. A ragged breath didn't help the twinge of pain in his chest.

How could he fix this? He wanted more than a close friend who shared great sex. If he declared his love and an ultimatum? Not only could he lose a love he never had, but he most likely would lose the best friend he cherished. He straightened his bed, thinking of her smile, her laugh, and that funny little "ha." Dragging himself to the shower, he thought of her creativity, her open mind. With the water beating on him, he remembered moments they'd shared over the decades. Toweling off, he contemplated if they could go back to a plutonic friendship. "Hell, no." He *had* to fix this.

In the bedroom, he lifted the sun/moon necklace from the nightstand. Using his fingernail, he pried the photos of Allison and himself out to reveal his mom and dad. In his palm, he carried the photos he'd removed to his dresser. He lifted a small gold-colored box from the top drawer and set it out. Inside were bits and pieces of memories: Garrett's first tooth, the ribbon from Allison's bridal bouquet, a medal he'd received in sixth grade, and various other keepsakes. He gently set his wife's and his tiny photos in a corner of the box, closed it, and settled it back in the drawer. Pieces of the past, never to be forgotten, but cherished as life continued forward. Settling the pendant around his neck settled his mood.

After dressing and brewing a pot of coffee, he stood at the kitchen counter with a cup, toast in the toaster, and his notes on the house. The smell of bread toasting and coffee brewing was comforting. As if the aroma floated in from the past, he touched the pendant and thought of his mom. He had to get through the refurbish, and now repairs, of Phaedra's house. If he could put a freeze on his hoped-for future plans for her and concentrate on the job, he'd tackle why they weren't on the same page later.

He punched a number on his cell. Kevin answered on the first ring.

"Hey, Harlan."

"Hi, Kevin. I left the key under a rock on the back step. It goes to the front door. I'll be there after I make a stop at the B and B to see how Hank is doing." The toast popped. While balancing the phone between his chin and shoulder, he slathered butter.

"Sounds good." The roar of an engine came over the phone. "I'm picking up John and then I'll be there."

"We had a vandal do some damage."

"You're kidding. That's never happened before."

"Nope." He talked around a bite. "Anyway, you'll see it in the front closet. Need to prepare it for a replaster. One more thing I want you to check out while John's working on that. This doesn't have any bearing on the work we have to do, but it's more of a curiosity on my part. One of the bedrooms doesn't have a closet. My measurements of the rooms and the hall look off. Do me a favor and get up in the attic and see if you can see anything."

"Like what?"

"I don't know." He sipped coffee. "Maybe the main framework. I didn't get a chance to check it out. Don't know if the attic is finished or just open beams. But have a look. I saw the access in the ceiling of the master bedroom closet."

"Will do. See you when you get there."

He washed down his last bite of toast with the remainder of the coffee, set the dishes in the sink, and gathered plans and a water bottle. In his truck, his cell rang as he buckled the seatbelt. Not a programmed number. Could be a new job. He put the truck in park and answered.

"Good morning, Harlan."

He recognized the husky voice. "Hi, Nora."

"I hope I'm not calling too early."

"Oh no. It's a work day." *Hint, hint.*

"For all of us." She chuckled. "I'm already at it. Getting some writing done. I've also been doing some heavy thinking, Harlan. I have something I could use your help with that would be mutually beneficial for us."

"What's that?"

"Oh, it's a bit involved so I'd rather talk in person."

His thumb drummed the steering wheel. "I'm on my way to check a job right now." He glanced at the dashboard clock. He needed to get going. Curiosity danced in the background of his thoughts. He needed to know her angle. "Can't you give me a preview?"

"Couldn't you stop by after you check the job? I'll have some coffee ready. Maybe some Danish, if you haven't had breakfast. My room is cozy. Nice way to start your day." She gave a husky laugh.

"Nora, I—"

"Being your own boss must have benefits. Stopping in to see me could be one of them."

He rubbed the back of his neck in an effort to ease the irritation her relentless pursuit had on him. "I just can't."

"Are you at Lilac End? I could come there."

"No, I'm not." *And don't ask if I will be, because I don't need you dropping in today.* "I have a meeting with Phaedra this morning about the Big Purple House." A fabricated meeting with Phaedra seemed a good excuse.

His brush off was met with silence. In fact, for a minute he thought she'd hung up on him.

"Nora? I'm sorry…"

"Phaedra. Sure." Her voice lowered. He imagined her pouting, jealous from her tone. "If you change your mind, I'll be here. Not even bothering to dress today. Just me and my notes lounging in bed. If you want to stop in, I do have a very lucrative proposal. You could be a rich man. Bye, Harlan."

He shifted into reverse, her words spiking his curiosity as he backed out of his driveway. What did this woman want? Him for sure, yet even her approach to that seemed off-kilter. What kind of proposal could she possibly have that would make him rich? Why was she really interested in the house on Lilac Lane? Lots of whats and whys. And he needed to know the answers.

CHAPTER TWELVE

Nora popped three pain pills into her mouth and chugged half a bottle of water. Her temples throbbed. "Damned white wine." She lowered her head to the pillow. "And damn you, Harlan." His help was crucial in finding the sapphire, but he was too consumed with *Phaedra*, apparently. If she could just get him alone for an hour, she could turn his head and convince him to help her.

The thought of tearing apart the last bedroom tonight was torture. She lifted a tube of hand cream from the nightstand. Massaging moisture into her palms brought some relief to the ache from wielding the hammer. Harlan hadn't mentioned the damage she'd done last night, so she assumed he hadn't seen it yet.

She closed her eyes and envisioned the room. Only three of the walls could possibly have once had a closet. *Only three.* She groaned and pulled the covers over her face. If they were built similar to the other three bedrooms, then two of the walls were the best bet. The present ache in her shoulders throbbed with the beat of her heart just thinking about hammering holes into the plaster.

He was on his way to another job…and Phaedra. That woman was getting in the way. A man consumed with another woman was harder to seduce, especially the straight and narrow type like Harlan. What to do? She had to catch him alone, at the end of the day. A little tired, ready for dinner and some down time. All men appreciated a little pleasure after a work day. She would be the one to give him the perfect ending.

She'd sleep awhile and get rid of the headache. Then she'd get some food in her stomach, take a shower, and put on the dress with the low-cut neckline. She'd entice him to go to dinner with her. He'd be seduced by sex and money.

If that didn't work…

She had no choice. Tonight, she'd have what GG was cheated out of, and no one could stop her. Tonight, she'd find the sapphire either with pleasure or with her pistol.

****

Phaedra cursed under her breath. How in Hades did she manage to sew the collar on the jacket backwards? "Because your mind is elsewhere, you ninny." She shoved away from the sewing machine and stomped to the kitchen. After pouring herself the fourth cup of coffee of the morning, she grabbed a Mama Rose pan dulce, shaped like a seashell and perfect for dunking. On bare feet, she padded outside to the back patio to sit at the table. She breathed deep of air fragrant with sweet, late-blooming honeysuckle, and under the flowers' scent a hint of woodsy cedar mingled. The tension in her shoulders relaxed.

Thoughts of Harlan clouded her mind since waking. She dunked the dulce in coffee and ate. Why did he have to go serious on her already? He'd been the cautious one until now. When she'd hesitated to turn their relationship carnal, he'd stepped away, allowing her the time to consider the ramifications. Granted, she didn't have to think on it for long. She craved his touch.

She'd been concerned their friendship would be ruined by crossing the line into a sexual liaison, her worry being if one or the other didn't find the connection enjoyable, walking it back would be awkward. But she found more than enough pleasure, and judging from his reaction, he did too. She hadn't expected the upshot to be a *marriage* conversation. She sipped her coffee. He had to be thinking along very serious lines with the questions he posed last night. Or was he really only curious why she hadn't married?

No. He'd rounded the bend. Already. So soon. She'd answered his questions, but he appeared unsettled. The sex last night was satisfying. Yet not. His body was there; his mind was not. She saw disappointment in his eyes, heard it in his voice.

Did she love him? Yes, yet what kind of love? *I can't imagine you not in my life.* That's what kind of love. The ache in her chest kind of love. A love she'd never experienced before. And yet neither of them had said it.

So why did he have to jump to a marriage discussion?

He'd skipped steps three through ten, at least. They hadn't even professed "never leave me" or "move in with me." She knew he loved her, even without a declaration. If she had given him a different answer about marriage, would he have gotten down on one knee with promises of love? "Not what I need." And not worth the risk of losing what they had.

Brushing crumbs from her jeans, she stood. On her way back into the house she took her last drink of coffee. She had to get Harlan off her brain and finish the jacket before she took the letters to the historical society.

As she opened the back door, her cell chimed from her sewing table. She lengthened her stride, scooped the phone from the table, and read the incoming number. Her chest tightened with a happy flutter. "Speak of the devil." So much for getting thoughts of him tucked aside to work. She breathed deep and touched the answer icon. "Hi, Harlan."

"I wanted to update you." In those few words she heard the strain in his voice.

"What's wrong?"

"We had more vandalism. Serious damage."

"Oh, no."

"Three more closets ripped into."

"Now, that's just weird."

His anger came through loud and clear. He had enough for both of them. She was baffled more than anything else. "They broke in this time?" She wanted to ask if he'd forgotten to lock the door again, but that would be a direct pour of salt in the wound.

A heavy sigh came over the line. "I can't find any evidence. The front door was unlocked when my crew got here." He talked as he walked, evident from his clipped words and breathing. "I made sure I locked it. I double checked. I've walked this house three times, checked every window, and there is no evidence of a break in. It's like we have a ghost."

She snickered, but he didn't join in the laughter. "I gave you my only key. And no one has been in the house for decades."

"Yeah, I know. Picking the lock, I guess. I didn't know deadbolts were so easy to pick. This vandal is slick too, because I can't see that it's been messed with. And I don't understand why they're breaking out walls in the closets."

"They must be looking for something?"

"In the walls?"

"Yeah, well, only thing I can come up with. That or we have a serial closet hater."

That got a slight chuckle which almost resembled merriment. "Looks like I get to play detective…or ghost hunter. I'm spending the night here tonight, and I plan to catch the SOB."

"But there aren't any more closets." She plopped onto the sewing chair.

"No, but if they're looking for something, they might start on cupboards or floors or who knows what. We can't sustain any more damage. Screws with my timeline."

"Did you report it?"

"I didn't yesterday since I thought I'd left the door open, but this is different. I want to put in a few hard hours on this place before I go back into town. I'll stop by the station on my way to Dad's this afternoon. Not sure if my insurance covers this, but having a police report is a good idea, regardless."

"I'm guessing mine will cover it. I hate having you spend the night there. Maybe we can hire Danny or Jennifer if they aren't on duty tonight. Wouldn't hurt to have the law there."

"I doubt we need a cop on site. You're probably right that since we're out of closets, they won't be back. Even if they show again, there's nothing to steal, so it's not like I'll face an armed robber. More than likely, it's kids who need the hell scared out of them."

"Or a ghost who'll scare the hell out of you."

"Hell, yeah. Bring him on."

She lifted the jacket she'd sewn all morning. "I have some work to do on a jacket, and then I'll get to the historical society and talk to Wanda before they close."

"Phaedra?"

Not on the phone, Harlan, please. "Yeah?"

"I'm sorry."

No, please, *don't go there.* Her stomach knotted. "Harlan, don't—"

"About the damage to the house."

"Oh." *That*. She swallowed the rising worry. "Why be sorry? More work for you but not your fault."

"I feel like it is. Like for some reason…"

"What?"

"I don't know. Haven't got that figured out." His crew yammered in the background. "Another thing I can't figure out added to my list." Someone shouted his name. "Let's talk later."

"Sure. Bye." She thumped down her phone on the table. Why did she think his need to talk had a whole lot more to do with her than with the house?

She fingered the red jacket, and her eyes glazed over. Enthusiasm for her work now dulled. They hadn't declared love, but it might be time. If he wanted to talk more, this could be the end or the beginning. He'd have to understand how she wanted to live her life. Yes, she loved him. The way she felt couldn't be anything but love. Yet, her life needed to stay the same. A burning in the pit of her stomach bothered her. Indigestion of the heart.

She might as well run her errand to the historical society. Maybe juicy, ancient gossip would brighten her day. Hopefully, Wanda could provide the distraction.

When she crossed the threshold of the Joshua Historical Society, a pleasant, musky aroma welcomed her. Toward the back of the room, Wanda was ensconced in front of a computer screen, glasses riding low on her nose. The docent twirled her gray ponytail next to her face. In addition to the odor of old paper, the faint smell of incense wafted over Phaedra.

She closed the door behind her. Wanda glanced up, and her face broke out in a wide, toothy grin. "Hi, Phaedra. You must have ESP."

"Oh yeah? Why do you say that?" She joined the woman at the counter.

"I saw one of your blouses at Magpie's shop last week. Yesterday, I found the perfect skirt for it, so I called her to hold it for me. And it's gone! I planned to call you later to see if you had another like it or could whip me up one."

"Well, darn, Wanda. I doubt I have one like it. Right now, I'm busting butt to get an order done for a shop in Copperdale, but give me a note about what you want. I'll get you one after I've finished, probably late next week."

"Great! You didn't come in to see me about my clothing needs, did you?"

"Nope. I'm helping Harlan do some research."

"Oh, good. I am too. In fact, that's just what I was doing." She gestured toward the computer screen. "He's puzzled about his mother's middle name, Lambert, which also happened to be Lilac Hersey's middle name. I'm doing some digging. What's that you have?" She pointed at the envelopes in Phaedra's hand.

"I wanted to show you letters written to Lilac Hersey from a friend and a lawyer with the last name Biddington. Biddington is also Harlan's grandmother's maiden name."

"Oooh, the plot thickens." Wanda clapped her hands like an excited child as she scuttled from behind the computer.

Phaedra chuckled and shared in the excitement. "I know. And these letters are so intriguing."

"Can I have a look?"

"Of course. That's why I'm here." She handed over the letters. "They're in date order."

Phaedra wandered around the room filled with memorabilia and historical documents while Wanda read. Every so often, the woman murmured to herself.

She stopped by a small glass case filled with 1960s paraphernalia. Or at least the signage claimed that era. She'd seen more than one pipe that looked much the same in present day Joshua. A document on top of the cabinet listed city council members in the decades of the sixties and seventies, attributing those citizens with bringing Joshua back from the dead and accomplishing the designation of historical landmark for the city. Frank and Susie MacKenzie held honors with the group.

"I think we can connect some dots." Wanda sounded out of breath.

Phaedra whirled around. "What dots? Those letters mean something to you?"

"Sure do." Her eyes glittered. "My research for Harlan plays right into these letters. I love this stuff. It's like fireworks explode when I make a historical connection relating to Joshua."

****

Harlan knocked on the door as he turned the knob. "Dad?" he called, closing the door behind him.

"Come on in. I'm in the kitchen."

151

He crossed under the arched doorway of the kitchen to see his dad at the counter pouring coffee into a mug. When Harlan founded his remodeling business, he tackled his dad's kitchen as one of his first projects. The varnished oak cabinets and white walls he'd refurbished made it the brightest room in the house. The blue and yellow linoleum on the floor gave way to slatted wood. Before the remodel, the room gave off dark vibes. After his dad's girlfriend was found dead on the floor, he'd avoided spending too much time there. At seventeen, he assumed his discomfort stemmed from the murder. Now he wondered if his clairsentient abilities accounted for those bad feelings. Over the years, he'd finally desensitized to the area. There'd been enough good memories to outweigh the bad.

Frank held up a cup. "Want some coffee?"

"Sure." The remodeled kitchen invited sitting at the table and having a cup of coffee. He took a seat at the table where one fat manila envelope rested.

His father set the cream and the mug of coffee in front of him then sat in a chair to his right. "I stopped in Copperdale on my way home. I brought anything that might be helpful out of the box."

"I appreciate you doing that. Did you and Annette have a good time on her layover?"

"Sure did. We didn't do much. Phoenix is too hot for doing much. We ate out, saw a movie. Just spent time talking." He sipped his coffee. "How's the refurbish going?"

"Backwards. Vandals tore into the walls."

"Hells bells. Why would anyone do that?"

"Your guess is as good as mine. The bigger mystery is how are they getting in. I thought I forgot to lock the door the first time. But I made sure I locked it the next day when I left. Still, they managed to get in."

"Someone must have a key."

"That would make sense, wouldn't it? Except I have the only key. I guess they're picking the deadbolt."

"Did you call the chief?"

"I filed a report with Danny before I came over. They'll go have a look this afternoon. Not sure there's anything they can do. He said they'd dust for fingerprints on doorways. But if it's kids, I doubt fingerprints will be on file." Harlan sipped his coffee. "Might as well look at this stuff." He opened the envelope.

"I brought you marriage, birth, and death certificates."

He flipped through the papers, setting the death certificates aside. "Mom sure liked to keep records, didn't she?" Mentioning her, seeing documents of hers, had him once again missing her.

"Yes, she did. There're other things in the box at the bank too, on the house and business. I need to add one of you kids to the box before long so you can get to all that stuff when I'm gone." His dad said it so matter-of-fact, Harlan took a moment to register his meaning.

"Plenty of time for that." He sorted the birth and marriage certificates into two piles. Flipping through the birth papers, he found his mother's. *Susie Lambert Muse, born October 10, 1944.* "I'd forgotten Mom was older than you. What? Four years?"

"Yep, about that."

"I wonder if her mother's is here." He pushed his coffee mug aside as he spread out the certificates. "Nope." He went back to his mother's certificate. Parents were Monica Lambert Biddington and Jacques Robert Muse. Staring at it for a moment, he tried to imagine the grandmother he never knew. "Too bad she died so young. I don't remember the story, but Mags said she came down with pneumonia in the hospital when she had a baby. Baby died too."

"Sounds familiar."

He fingered through the birth certificates, but his mother's was the oldest. *Damn.* "I sure hoped there would be something old enough to give me more information."

"You mentioned some letters. Did you bring them?"

"No. Phaedra is taking them to Wanda today. You know Wanda—she's a wealth of Joshua history."

"What was in them that you thought I'd know about?"

"Lilac Hersey corresponded with some Biddingtons in San Francisco. From the letters, it sounds like she moved there. Maybe married a Biddington. Thought you might know something about that branch of the family."

His dad's brow furrowed. "Wouldn't that be something." He stared at Susie's birth certificate. "I'm no help. Biddington. The Big Purple House." He glanced up. "Could relate to the reason you're tuning into the place."

"Yeah, my thoughts are running that way." He slid the stack of marriage certificates closer. His mom had saved a copy of both his and Magpie's proof of marriage as well as her own. The oldest certificate was for Monica Biddington and Jacque Muse in January of 1941. *Only sixteen when she married.* "Nothing old enough in the marriage licenses to help." He shuffled the papers together and replaced them in the envelope. "Do you mind if I hold onto these for a while? I want to see if Phaedra finds out anything from Wanda. See if I need to compare any dates or whatever."

"Sure, son. That's fine. You want to stay for dinner? Maggiepie is bringing takeout from the barbecue joint. There's always more than enough to share."

"Thanks, but I've got some things to do." He stood as a knock came at the front door.

"It's me." Magpie's voice rang through the house. She appeared in the kitchen doorway. "I didn't know we were making it a threesome. I would've ordered more." The aroma of barbecue surrounded her as she set two sacks on the table.

"I'm not staying."

"Well, you could. I was kidding. I'm sure there's enough."

"Thanks, but I'm supposed to meet with Phaedra. About the house."

Magpie's brows lifted, and she appeared to be considering saying something.

He interjected before she could start a probable interrogation. "I forgot to tell you guys. Dory called me the other night."

"Is she okay?" Magpie's big sister concern was evident in her tone.

"I know, strange she called me, but she said she couldn't get through to Dad. I suppose she's okay. You know Dory, always a little vague about her life. She says she misses everyone."

"Then she should come home more often." His sister's comment was not a new sentiment.

"I'll give her a call tonight." His dad stood and carried their mugs to the sink. "I talk to her about once a month, so it's time."

"Alrighty then. I'll take off. You two enjoy your barbecue."

Outside, he opened his truck door, but stopped when Magpie hopped down the stairs of the veranda. "Wait up, Harlan."

He propped his butt against the truck seat, half-closing the door and leaned through the open window.

"I haven't talked to you since dinner Saturday night. How're you and Phaedra coming along."

"Coming along?"

"Well, yeah. It's obvious two of the musketeers are starting a new adventure."

Since when did his sister delve into his personal life? And why hadn't she gotten the scoop from Phaedra?

"Surely you've talked to Phaedra since then. You two are nearly joined at the hip."

"I wanted to get your take."

"What's she told you?"

"If you must know, she's being a bit evasive."

"Humph." They hadn't settled anything or come to any kind of understanding. And she hadn't talked to Magpie, wouldn't confide in her best girlfriend? An emptiness settled in the pit of his stomach.

"I got the impression you're being pushy." She crossed her arms on her chest. "Rushing in. Taking charge."

"She said that?" His heart dropped lower in his chest.

"Well, no. I deduced it. Knowing you and all."

Here we go again. "That's pretty judgmental."

She took a sudden interest in her shoes, scuffing her toe against the edge of the driveway. Maybe, for once, she realized her negative attitude about him wouldn't enrich this conversation. Could Magpie be softening?

Now didn't seem like the time, but he remembered Zac's advice about confronting their issues head on. If he was going to be accused of rushing in, he might as well meet her expectations. Magpie wasn't an impenetrable force, or so Zac claimed.

"I might've come on too strong. I might've mentioned marriage."

Her head jerked up. "You asked her to marry you?" Her eyes were as round and gold as a nugget.

"No! Of course not. I asked her why she's never been married."

"Because...?"

He took his turn scuffing a toe and avoided her gaze. "I'm...I'm...she means more to me than what we have right now. I don't know if she—"

"Talk about being a bulldozer. You either avoid a situation or charge ahead without caring what anyone else might be feeling."

His legs tensed as the urge to jump in his truck and leave her in his dust came over him. He took a deep breath, tamping down his anger, pissed at this frequent fissure with his sister. The dissonance between them had to be fixed. He was tired of a non-relationship with her. Besides, he might need a friendly ally in figuring out Phaedra. "Look, Mags, I know you're still holding a grudge for my immaturity in handling Mom's death and Dad's rough years. I know I should've been there for you."

Magpie scanned his face, her lips tightened in a thin line. He'd rarely seen her at a loss for words, but she appeared speechless.

"I know it's taken me decades to realize how much responsibility you shouldered. How little I helped." His eyes burned. He didn't realize confession could melt his core.

His sister's cheeks pinked. Her bottom lip quivered. Why had he taken so long to say the words? How had they functioned with a wall of misunderstandings between them? "You were tough, Mags. I was weak." He swallowed the tears threatening to choke him. Hell, he hadn't cried since his wife died.

He rose from the seat, closed the door behind him, and stood toe to toe with her. "Can we call a truce?" He touched her cheek then lifted the pendant of the necklace she wore around her neck, a duplicate of his. "Mom always said maturity was your middle name."

She didn't speak but wrapped her arms around his shoulders and hugged. When she drew back, her eyes were misty. "She might've said that, but I've not been acting too mature."

He chucked her chin. "You had reason." He could give her that, considering the years her disappointment in him festered, while his silence on the subject only made it worse. His sister was a force to be reckoned with even if she wasn't an impenetrable one. The MacKenzies were lucky to have her.

"I couldn't do what you did back then. You shouldered the pain, the fear, and kept strong for all of us. I guess I've been compensating for my lack of action back then by being pushy, like you say. And instead of telling you how I feel, I chose denial. I'm sorry, Mags."

She sniffed, waved a hand in the air, and decades of animosity vanished into the ether.

"Truce?"

"More than truce." She hugged him. Her face lightened along with the weight on his chest. "Now, what about you and Phaedra?"

"I'm not going to hurt her, Mags. I hope."

"Hey, I'm worried about you. You're my brother."

"And she's your sister-friend."

She smiled. "I like that. But it doesn't trump brother. Have you fallen off the railcar of friendship and into the mine pit of love?"

He burst into laughter then sobered. "It could happen." He kissed her cheek. "Your dinner is getting cold. I just saw Dad peek out the window."

"Okay." She squeezed his arm, turned on her heel, and went back to the house.

Sliding onto his seat, he shut the door then started the truck.

She paused on the steps and waved. "I love you, Harlan." Not waiting for his response, she disappeared into the house.

He sat a moment. *That was easier than I expected it would be.* His breath hitched as he backed out of the drive.

Bumping his way along The Ravine road, he came to Phaedra's bungalow. He slowed. Should he stop in or call first? He had an excuse to stop. She should have some information from Wanda. Hopefully. Should he make another attempt at finding out what she perceived as their future? Or let it ride for now? Be content? *For now?* A light came on in the window at the same time his cell rang. Her name appeared on the screen. He made a sharp turn into her driveway before answering.

"Hi, Phaedra."

"I have lots to tell you. Can you come over?"

I have a few things I'd like to say too. "I'm here." *But how and when are the kickers.*

CHAPTER THIRTEEN

Harlan cut the engine as Phaedra opened her front door. His heart squeezed at the vision of perfection from across the yard of colorful blooms. The curve of her body, from her hand clasping the doorway above her head to her bare feet with lavender polished toenails, sent heat spiraling in his core. The bottom of her frayed jeans tickled her ankles, and the ceiling light inside the entry backlit her silver-white hair. The smile on pink lips and in her crystal blue eyes invited him to step into the scene.

With a sigh, he pocketed his keys and strode the brief walk through a mishmash of flowers and plants.

"Have you added ESP to your bag of mystic tricks?" Phaedra asked.

"I'm not a mystic. I don't think, anyway. Mom held that title."

"You weren't sitting in my drive waiting for me to call?"

"Nope." He stopped in front of her. "Just left my dad's, and you caught me as I came to your house."

"Maybe I'm the mystic since I thought of you as you happened by. When I show you what I found out from Wanda, there'll be mystery enough to keep us guessing."

"Now you're teasing me. What's the story?"

She beckoned him to follow. "You want something to drink?"

"Do you want to go out for dinner?" He didn't want to. He'd botched the subject of his vision for their relationship last time they ate in a restaurant. In the intimacy of the cottage, he could lay bare his feelings easier.

"How do you feel about cold pasta salad and sandwiches?" She gestured toward the sofa as she continued toward the kitchen. "Have a seat."

"Sounds good to me." He stopped by a sofa. "I'm having a coronary here waiting for you to tell me something."

"Ha. Okay, then. Water, tea, or I still have Jameson's."

"Jameson's. I'll switch to tea when you bring out dinner."

While she poured the whiskey, he settled on one of the cream-colored loveseats. "I take it Wanda was helpful."

"You take it right." She set the glasses on the coffee table then picked a sheet of paper from a side table. "I took some notes." She settled beside him, her shoulder brushing his.

He lifted a glass and sipped. Her eyes sparkled like the glitter he'd glued on his grade school drawings. He savored the burn of the whiskey. The hominess of the bungalow combined with her beauty, a good whiskey, and the anticipation of learning more that might connect him to the past of the Big Purple House—*all right.*

"Are you ready?"

"Stop with the big lead-up. Start talking, woman."

"Wanda is amazing. She scoured Joshua records, newspaper articles, and mining records." Phaedra stopped to sip her drink and then set it back on the table. She pulled her legs under her and two-handed the sheet of paper.

Harlan had a notion to rip the paper out of her hands and read it, but she appeared to be having fun making her presentation. He breathed deep to calm the tension she helped to build and sipped his drink.

"Lilac and John Hersey had a child named Louise in April of 1924. And we know John disappeared on or about August 20, 1924. Lilac reported him missing on August 21st. She took over running the mining business." Her voice rose. "That was a *really* big deal back then because *women* didn't run businesses, but all reports showed her quite adept at it." She snickered. "Wanda gets pretty excited about women's rights and accomplishments."

"I've seen her in action. When I stopped in a few days ago, she treated me to some historical data." He patted her knee. "Please, continue."

"Her pregnancy with her second child became evident. Recorded minutes show the board of directors for her husband's company tried to force her out by making a deal out of her obvious incapacity to conduct business. It seems pregnancy renders a woman witless. Apparently, she must have stood her ground for a while, but she sold out in December of 1924." She lowered her notes. "Wanda found that, but we already knew she sold from the letters. And we knew about her pregnancy." She lifted her glass for a sip before continuing. "She possessed brilliant timing. I'm sure the advice from Bradley Biddington, alluded to in the letters, led to her decision." She checked her notes again. "The downturn of mining in Joshua began in January of 1925, but she'd managed to escape with her wealth in December. And we know the big crash came in 1929."

"So, she cashed out and moved. Is Wanda sure she went to San Francisco?"

"A newspaper interview before she left confirmed it. She didn't admit to planning to marry Biddington. She did say she was moving there to live with Penelope Garner Biddington. The Garners had been an influential family in Joshua before migrating to San Francisco.

"At that point in her research, Wanda tried to find more newspaper articles in San Francisco or any mining records pertaining to the sale that might lead somewhere. Nothing panned out. Then…" Phaedra took a breath and squirmed, obviously enjoying getting to this part of her report. "Then…" She took a sip of whiskey. "Then she got the brilliant idea to look at the 1930 census."

As if on the brink of discovering a new vein of gold in an old mine, Harlan's anticipation spiked.

"First, she searched for Lilac Hersey. She couldn't find any Herseys in San Francisco. Next, she searched for Biddingtons. And she hit paydirt. She found a household with Lilac and Bradley Biddington: one child named Louise born in March of 1924 had died in 1929 and another child, Monica Lambert Biddington, born in 1925, age five." She looked up from her notes. "Your grandmother."

His head spun. Dates whirled through his thoughts. "We know Lilac was pregnant when she met Biddington. They must have married shortly before my grandmother was born, giving her his name."

"Yes. Exactly. You're the great grandchild of Lilac and John

Hersey." Phaedra sounded breathless.

He was more than breathless. Instead of being satisfied with this wealth of historical information, he had more questions. He sipped his whiskey. Lilac and the letters. The missing mine baron, John Hersey. The house shrouded in foggy sensations, dark vibrations.

Phaedra sat silently, her fingers tapping on her notes as if becoming impatient for him to speak.

When he'd finally condensed his thoughts into one question, he found his voice. "Why didn't my mother know any of this? Lilac would've been her grandmother. *Everyone* knows who their grandmother is."

Phaedra swished the page of notes. "There's more. Out of curiosity, Wanda checked the 1940 census. Nothing for Lilac and Bradley, but a Monica Lambert Biddington resided with a Sarah and William Biddington."

More dates. More dots to connect. Could he really be the great grandchild of the Herseys? "My grandmother, Monica, married Jacques Muse in 1941. Dad had the marriage license. But no birth certificate for Monica."

"Maybe Lilac and Bradley died. Monica must've moved in with these relatives some time before 1940."

He ran a hand through his hair. How uncanny he'd grown up within a mile of Lilac End, not knowing how he connected to this piece of Joshua's history. "Unfortunately, my grandmother died when my mother was barely two. I suppose Mom didn't have the opportunity to find out the history of her grandparents."

"Harlan, even if Monica had not died so young, Susie probably wouldn't have ever known the true identity of her biological grandfather. Her mom was a Biddington. She would've had no reason to question it."

"We have to assume Lilac raised Monica as a Biddington without ever disclosing she was actually John Hersey's daughter." He settled back against the sofa, his muscles drained as if he'd been in a constant state of tenseness.

"You want another drink?"

"No. Thanks."

"Then I'll get us some dinner. Such as it is."

He jarred as she sprang from the couch. "I should call Magpie."

"Yes, you should," she called from the kitchen.

His sister answered on the second ring. "Hi, Harlan. Long time no see."

Was it his imagination that she sounded friendlier than she had in decades? Or could he finally be at peace with their relationship after admitting his shortcomings? Whatever the case, he smiled. "Hey, Mags. Are you still at Dad's?"

"Yeah, why?"

"Put me on speaker phone and sit down. I have something you'll both want to hear."

****

Through dinner, Phaedra hashed over what could have happened to Lilac and Bradley Biddington with Harlan who seemed at once subdued and analytical about their newfound knowledge. Susie Muse having been robbed of her family history saddened her. "I wonder if Susie might've known more if her mother, Monica, hadn't died so young. Might've known Lilac, even if she didn't know her real grandfather."

"I don't know. It seems to me Lilac must have been dead before Susie was born since she didn't appear in the 1940 census. Bradley Biddington too. Why else would Monica have been living with relatives? Whatever the reasons, Mom didn't know anything about that branch. Her father, Jacque Muse, wasn't around much either. Although who knows how much he'd have known?" He pushed his plate back. "What I'm more embroiled in, is how this affects what I've been experiencing at the house. It's like the house knows I have a connection and has been trying to tell me something."

"Is that even a thing? A house communicating?"

"Maybe in some horror flick." He snorted. "The name for my ability is clairsentience. Basically, I'm intuitive through tactile senses. It's as if the energy of past experiences of humans within the house are left behind. I'm like a human barometer."

"So, you don't know whose energy you're picking up on. It doesn't necessarily have to be as far back as Lilac. Could it be from the hippie era or even when I lived there?"

"No. Don't ask me how I know, but I'm certain it's the original owners. My great grandparents—" His cell rang. He looked at the readout and grimaced. "Nora. Not answering."

"Why not?"

"She wants something."

"Like you." She laughed with the words, but jealousy spiked behind them. The woman was so obvious.

"Yeah, that too, but she made me an offer she thinks I can't refuse."

"Really? What?"

"I'm paraphrasing, but she says she has a proposition for me that will make me rich."

His phone chimed with voice mail and then immediately rang again. He shook his head, hit the ignore icon, and stuck his phone back into his pocket.

"Aren't you the least bit curious?" In spite of her jealousy, her curiosity was piqued.

"I am, but I'm just not in the mood. I could see her before I settle in at the Big Purple House for the night. Don't really want to." He rubbed his jawline. "There's something peculiar about her. The get rich proposition is intriguing, but I don't trust her. And honestly, Phaedra, I'm overwhelmed with this whole family tree unveiling right now. And figuring out who the hell is destroying the house faster than I can fix it up. I'll contact her tomorrow."

From day one Nora's interest in the house as a book subject hadn't felt authentic. "Do you think it's odd how she hangs around you and my house?" Phaedra asked. "You'd think we'd see her out and about more, looking into other houses, getting down the history of the area, or something."

"Yeah, but what do I know about writing a book? Plus," he quirked a brow, "I *am* a pretty hot commodity." He snorted.

"There is that." *There is definitely that.* Yet she didn't trust the woman for reasons unknown. "This sounds a bit crazy, but could she be responsible for the vandalism at the house?"

"Nora?"

She let the name hang in the air. Harlan's brow furrowed as he gazed over her head, lost in thought. She hadn't liked the woman from day one, the bad impression was not due entirely to her flirtatious attitude toward Harlan.

"She was limping last time I saw her." He rubbed his chin. "I think our vandal might have gotten hurt on the broken sidewalk. I saw what looked like blood to me." He finished the tea in his glass.

"What in Hades?" She slapped at his arm. "She could be a crazy stalker or something, trying to get your attention." Although a streak of alarm ran through her, a tinge of excitement lingered. Like watching a car race when the driver loses control and spins off the track. "You're just now telling me this?"

"It just now came to me. But all the damage? She's too..." He opened his palms in a gesture of disbelief.

"Too what? Curvy?"

"Yeah, that's it." He stood with his empty glass and sauntered to the counter to pour more tea. "You want more?"

"No. Should we confront her?" Even if they were wrong about her, Phaedra wouldn't mind tossing out an insult and sending Nora on her way.

"She's not a big woman, so it's hard to imagine her doing so much damage. And why would she want to tear up walls to get my attention? That's a stretch, Phae." He quirked a brow. "Seems like the first day she showed up at the house, she said she saw it driving around. But... She did say something about a book she read. Do you think there's a book out there claiming we have hidden treasures in the homes of Joshua?"

"Who knows? There are more than a few books and stories claiming we have an abundance of ghosts."

"That's truer than hidden treasures." He sat back at the table. "Whatever her angle is, I'll get serious about finding out tomorrow. And if she shows again tonight, I'll nail her."

"You're still intent on spending the night at the house?"

"Yep. I've got my sleeping bag and toothbrush in the truck. Might be fun. Maybe the ghosts of my intuitions will come out and talk to me." A fleeting smile crossed his lips.

Once the smile vanished, his mouth didn't exactly form a frown, but he didn't appear overly happy either as he gazed at her. His shoulders drooped. The Herseys and the house might not be the only things occupying his thoughts. She'd thwarted his attempt at a serious conversation last night. But she wasn't ready for *that* talk. Last night, after the lovemaking, he'd sat for a moment on the side of the bed, while she blabbered on about anything besides them: the house, their kids, her latest clothing order. She didn't ask him to stay the night, and he'd already made his move by sitting up. She didn't want to be a cause of stress for him. Eventually, they'd have to have "the talk." For now, she was perfectly happy to maintain the sexy friendship they shared. An idea came. "I'll go with you."

"Go with me where?"

"To the house. I haven't camped out in ages. I've got a sleeping bag and toothbrush to go. We'll have a camping-in excursion." Maybe the conversation could be broached in the quiet of a haunted house. No distractions. She could explain how much he meant to her and see if he'd opt for the status quo.

"Oh, no."

"Why?"

"If the vandals are up for trouble—"

"You told me it's probably just kids who need the crap scared out of them."

"But I don't know for sure, do I?" He stood and carried his dirty dishes to the sink.

She swiveled in her chair. "All the more reason for you to not be there alone."

He crowded against her to pick up her dishes. The heat of his body gave her the urge to wrap her arms around his hips. She rose, bumping shoulders to get his attention before he could return to the sink. All she could think of was cuddling with him in a sleeping bag while he appeared consumed with the house and his ancestral lineage. *Shame on you, Phaedra.* "I've made up my mind."

He backed away then clanked the plates into the sink. "I don't think it's a good idea."

"Doesn't matter." She closed the distance between them.

"They probably won't even come back again." He turned on the water. "Three nights in a row would be ridiculous."

"Then another good reason for me to be there." She ran a hand down his back while he rinsed the plates. "Keep you from getting bored."

"You're awfully stubborn." He flicked water from his fingers over his shoulder into her face.

"Oh!" Shoving him, she trapped him against the counter then reached around and slapped at the running water.

He whirled away but too late. The water splattered the front of his shirt. He snaked an arm around her, holding her close. "Okay, you can come along, but only because saying no won't do any good."

She wanted to kiss him. In that moment, she wanted to have him at her sink every night. A lifetime of friendship and a lifetime ahead of love. Would love be enough for him? He didn't move to kiss her, so she moved away from him. A topic for a later discussion. "Let me get the kitchen cleaned. Then I'll pack my stuff for an overnighter." She bumped his hip to clear him out of her space. While avoiding the Harlan gaze she caught a glimpse of in her peripheral vision, she finished rinsing and loading the dishwasher.

Whatever they had right now, she wished could take a comfortable course. But what did that mean for them...for her? She'd have to mess with nature and orchestrate the evolution. *Love me, Harlan. Just love me.* Tonight would be as good a night as any other to admit her feelings. *And keep what we have just like this.*

****

Harlan set Phaedra's cloth overnight case, pillow, and sleeping bag on the backseat next to his. She handed him two diet sodas, which he added to his cooler. He couldn't say he didn't appreciate her company for the night, but misgivings plagued his better judgment. And not all his misgivings related to their safety. "When I filed the police report, I let Danny know I'd be spending the night at the house. He's actually on duty tonight. Said he could get there in minutes if I encounter any trouble." Too bad the danger of navigating this relationship couldn't be so easily planned.

"He didn't try to talk you out of lying-in-wait?"

"Only a little. But he's of a mind it's a group of kids from the high school they've caught spray painting some of the ruins. They aren't dangerous, but they need some heavy-handed discipline. This sort of vandalism could lead to more convincing punishment."

"So, he hopes you catch them."

"Hmm, he didn't say that, yet he was thinking it, I bet. But I've changed my mind. I don't think it's teenagers."

"No? Who then?

"It has something to do with the closets." He climbed in, waited for her to buckle up, and then started the engine. "The idea of hidden treasure got me thinking Someone believes there's a treasure to be found in a closet, since they've torn into the walls of all the closets so far."

"Which is one reason I didn't want you to come alone."

He chuckled. "They're treasure hunters, not marauding murderers."

"There's never been even a hint of mystery like a treasure hidden

166

in this house."

"I know, but someone thinks they know something we don't. And with all the messages I've been on the receiving end of in this house, I'm inclined to think they are privy to information we don't have." The house hid something. Protected something. Or someone's secrets. He rubbed his neck, the pulse thumping at his fingertips. His great grandparents walked the rooms, lived out their joys and their sadness there. Could the vibrations, the physical manifestations, the sensual inklings, and dark intuitions be a path to revealing secrets? John Hersey disappeared while living there. A shiver traveled his spine. A fluttery, emptiness took hold of his stomach.

"Earth to Harlan."

"What?"

"Are we going to just sit here and magically transport or are you going to drive us?"

He shot her a grin. "I might be a little distracted." He started the engine, checked the mirror, and backed out of the drive.

"Ha! I guess. Where are we going to camp out?"

"The master bedroom. The crew got all the rooms cleared of the mess, but I had them pay extra attention to the master. Cleaned the floor and walls of dust." The sun dipped behind Spirit Mountain as he made the turn onto Lilac Lane. A nervous patter built deep in his chest. "Plus, from the master there's a good view of the fourth bedroom."

"The room without a closet? Why would they tackle a room if it doesn't have a closet?"

"I think there was a closet at one time. Kevin got in the attic. Looked at the configuration of support beams. Along with my measurements, I'd say there used to be a closet." He parked in front of the house. "And if our treasure hunter really does know something, then maybe they'll destroy that room next. Let's unload, and then I'll park down the block so we don't tip off the vandals we're here."

After grabbing their belongings, and using a flashlight to help light their way, they crossed the sidewalk to the yard. "Be careful, Phae. Just walk in the grass. I need to get a cement contractor out here. I'll have the guys tear out the bad sections tomorrow."

When they reached the door, she asked, "Is it locked?"

He deadpanned her. "You're mean, you know that?"

She laughed. "Couldn't resist. Shall we lock it behind us or leave it open?"

"Lock it. I want to see how they're getting in." He set their supplies inside the door and handed her the flashlight. "Don't turn on any lights. I'll be right back."

The moon and stars in a cloudless sky threw beams of light across the neighborhood. After parking the truck, he jogged back and, once inside, locked the door and then grabbed the two sleeping bags Phaedra had left behind.

Upstairs, he found her standing at the window in the master bedroom overlooking the backyard and Spirit Mountain. Tension needled his shoulder blades. The skylights shone on her profile, her hair catching moonbeams. He wanted to match Phaedra's lighthearted attitude. And he didn't want to. His love had morphed over the last few days into a butterfly of epic proportions. The friend love remained, but a deeper richer creature had taken flight. She didn't want to make the transformation. She preferred the cocoon of the friend-chrysalis. Now what?

"There are things to like about this house. The views out the front and the back are great." She faced him. "But I'm glad I'm selling it. It's too much house for me. And it's kind of lonely high on the hill. The Ravine is so much cozier."

His great grandmother, Lilac Hersey, must have been lonely after John disappeared. Goosebumps rose on his neck and arms. "Okay, that's too weird to think about."

"What? The Ravine being cozy?"

"No. Sorry. I was thinking about the Herseys. My great grandparents. I can't quite get my head around it."

"Maybe you should step in and buy the house. I bet Annette would understand. She could find—"

"No, no. I wouldn't want to live here. The house affects me. The ghosts of my past are strong here. I'm not sure I could stand the barrage of emotions on a daily basis." His sister, Elidor, suddenly came to mind. She'd spent her life running from others' emotions, especially strong in Joshua. A flicker of understanding dawned on him. He'd have to show more compassion for his sister's situation. "Once we're done with the refurbishing, I'd like to do a deep dive into the history of this house and the Herseys. Something went down here, and I'd like to know what."

"So what do we do now?" She strolled close, grabbed a handful of his shirt, and pulled him in for a kiss.

He couldn't resist; he didn't want to. He had no intention of dialing down his feelings. She wasn't seeing anyone else. She'd left their plutonic friendship behind without any coaxing from him. If it took her longer to come around to committing to him, he'd have to be patient. He'd never prided himself on patience. This would be a test he could fail. But tonight—

He broke the kiss.

She moaned.

"I need to lay ground rules before it gets any later."

"Excuse me?"

He laughed. "About if someone shows up."

"Ohhh." She giggled.

"I don't want you involved, no matter what goes down. If we hear so much as a creak, you're to go into the closet, shut the door, and *do not* come out no matter what."

"I'll take my cell with me."

"Do you have our local law on your phone?"

"I do."

"Good." He took hold of her shoulders. "And I'm really serious about this, Phae. You stay in there, call Danny, and *do not* make a peep."

"I know, I know. You want all the glory of busting the case."

"If it's a bunch of teens, and after I scare the holy crap out of them, I'll tell you to come out and scare them some more."

She tilted her head, hit him with a teasing gaze. "And if it's Nora?"

"I'm not into threesomes so—"

She punched his arm. "You're not into anyone else but me." She snugged her hips against him. "Got that?"

"I thought we were…friends." His heart skipped a beat.

"We are."

"I need more friends in my life than just you." *And I need more from you.* His stomach muscles fluttered.

"Not our kind of friendship, you don't. Uh-uh." She kissed him. "Only one friend like me, Har."

He clutched her tighter to him. "I love you." Could he make her understand how much she meant? He covered her lips with his until she broke away.

Gliding her fingers along his face, she smiled, and her crystal blue eyes sparkled. "You want to prove that?" She planted a quick kiss on his mouth. "Maybe warm up those sleeping bags?"

He drew in a long draught of air. "I want to prove it to you every day of our lives, Phae. I want you to know how much you mean to me. Do you?"

"Serious, huh?"

His mouth went dry. "Yeah, I need serious from *you*." He ran his tongue over his lips. "For a bit."

She cupped her hand on his cheek. "You mean the same to me. I love you too, Har."

"Do you? Not friend love. Dinner now and then. Sex at one house or the other. Not—"

"But you'll always be my *friend*." Thumping his chest, she grinned. "We can't lose that. And what's wrong with being together for dinner and sex and hikes and weekends at the Apparition Room with Mags and Zac? What's wrong with what we have?"

"Don't you want more, Phaedra?" He pulled back, frowning at her. The air in the room thinned.

"How could I ask for more? You love me. I love you. The sex is hot." She bumped her hips into him. "Life is great."

His breathing grew labored. Could she be so blind to their future? "Where's the commitment? Where's the long-term plan? Where's the growth?"

"Growth? Long-term?" She spread her palms on his chest. Her brows drew down, crinkling the corner of her eyes with a question. "Don't you think the longer we're together, the longer we love each other, all of those things will happen? We don't need a formal agreement to have a lasting relationship. I can't do more than—"

"What the hell is your hang-up? If you love me—"

A click, a creak, and they froze.

"Shh. Quick." He shoved her away. "In the closet."

CHAPTER FOURTEEN

A ripple traveled across Nora's chest and tightened her stomach muscles when she saw Harlan's truck parked down the block from Lilac End. "Hel-lo, sweet cheeks." Tonight, she'd have help. Maybe mix in a little pleasure with work. She did a U-turn and parked in front of the house. Her ankle still hurt, and since Harlan was already inside, no need to be stealthy and walk as far.

After shutting off the engine, she paused. *Why did he park down the block?* When the answer came, she laughed out loud. *He's waiting for a vandal.* "Only you don't know I'm the one you're waiting for." He must've been too busy setting his trap to answer her earlier calls. "This could be fun." She didn't have the low-cut dress on or any wine to ply him with, but being available in this grand house, just the two of them and the offer of a cool million, should convince him she had a lot more to offer than Phaedra.

She lifted her tool bag and GG's journal from the passenger seat. Her plan had been to call Harlan, again, once inside and lure him to the house. Funny how things came together all on their own. She had the rest all worked out. First, she'd entice him with GG's account of the jewel and a seductive partnership proposal. "If that doesn't work..." She opened the glove box, dug for her gun, and then shoved it in with the tools. She didn't intend on hurting him, but if he needed to be intimidated, she had to be prepared. She'd be long gone before any small-town cop could find her. Besides, she wasn't stealing. The jewel *belonged* to her.

At the door, she tried the doorknob. Locked. As quietly as possible, she inserted the key and turned, but the click echoed in her ears like a crack of thunder. Slipping inside, she pivoted and glanced around. No lights, upstairs or down. *Lying in wait for the big bad vandals.* She stifled a giggle. Barely enough light came in the dining room window to make out the door to the stairwell. A noise above gave her pause. A voice? Steps? Maybe he was on the phone.

She strained her ears, but only silence filled the house.

No lights. No noise. If he was lying in wait, a surprise entrance might not be the best idea. "Harlan? Where are you? It's Nora." She walked to the bottom of the stairs, fairly confident he was upstairs. "It's awfully dark. Can you turn on a light?"

A light came from above, and he appeared at the top of the flight of stairs. "Nora, what are you doing here?"

Hefting the bag over her shoulder and clutching the journal to her chest, she mounted the steps. "I want to talk to you."

****

Although her red hair caught a glint from the ceiling light behind him, Harlan could barely make out the rest of Nora, dressed in black or some other dark color. "How did you get in?" Perhaps the writer was an expert at picking locks. Perhaps the writer wasn't a writer at all.

She didn't answer as she continued to climb with some difficulty. Her leg obviously still bothered her. When she stopped within touching distance at the top on the landing, she flashed him a smile. "I can explain."

"I'm listening." He also trained an ear toward the closet. Phaedra might consider Nora's appearance as benign, but he could get more information out of her without Phaedra's presence.

"Remember I said I have a proposition for you?" She walked her fingertips down his bicep.

He wanted to bat her hand away but crossed his arms over his chest instead. "Nora. How did you get in? And does this proposition have anything to do with you knocking holes in the walls of this house?" Irritation crept between his words, but the fight or flight tension in his body he'd experienced when she'd entered the house now relaxed. The damn woman pushed the limits of his patience.

Her jaw tightened, but the smile returned just as quickly. "What do you say we get a little comfy while I explain?" She peered around him into the master bedroom. "Sleeping bags?"

"I planned to catch my vandal if he—or should I say she—returned."

She sauntered past him. "*Two* sleeping bags?" Her gaze scanned the room.

He joined her. "It's a hard wood floor." It was all he could do to keep a civil tongue.

She lowered her tote. At her chest, she clutched a book with one hand. "I could help you be a lot more comfortable." Extending her arm, she toyed with the buttons on his Henley. "Two bags. Two warm bodies."

The insufferable, single-minded woman must think herself wily, but she possessed about as much foxiness as a rabid coyote. "You were going to explain?"

Her nostrils flared, and her lips pinched as her violet eyes went dark navy. "All right!" She dropped her hand from his shirt and gestured toward his pile of belongings. "Could you at least spread a bag out so we could sit and be somewhat comfortable while we talk?"

No longer coy and flirtatious, the hardness of her personality he'd caught glimpses of over the last couple of days emerged in full force. Keeping tabs of her in his peripheral, he rolled out one of the bags, suddenly not trusting her. He tuned his hearing toward the closet again where Phaedra would hopefully stay put.

Nora hobbled the few steps and lowered onto the bag. She patted beside her. "You should sit."

Complying, he crossed his ankles and collapsed beside her. He didn't wait for her to start talking. "How did you get in, and did you vandalize this house?"

She brought the book to her lap, the fingers of her hand gliding over it. Her gaze lingered on her possession.

"Nora?"

"I have a key, and yes. But I have a purpose, not senseless vandalism." She met his gaze, her eyes still a cold blue and defiant.

"Where did you get a key?"

"I found it. In the desk, in the closet downstairs. John Hersey's office."

"When?" He thought back to her presence inside the house.

"What difference does it make?" She huffed. "When you ran out after Phaedra. So afraid she'd think we were up to something." She touched his knee. "We could've been."

His leg muscles tensed, recoiling. "And you thought it perfectly fine to steal it?"

"I needed it."

"To tear up the house?" He clutched her hand from his knee. "What the hell is your end game here, Nora?"

"I want to find what's mine."

"What are you talking about?"

She didn't answer but dropped her attention to the book in her lap. "This is my great grandmother's journal. My GG. She was John Hersey's mistress and would someday have been his wife. He gave her a jewel that's hidden in this house." She tilted her head, her gaze steely beneath thick red lashes. "I'm willing to give you a share, but you have to find it for me."

"Are you really a writer? Was this whole writing a book a ruse?"

She snickered. "Oh, I might write a book someday, but it won't be about some old houses in this town." Lifting the journal, she spoke, each word punctuated as if she needed to drill her meaning into his head. "I'm the great granddaughter of Genevieve Jenkins. The rightful heir to the Ceylon Royal Blue Sapphire."

"You must be joking." He flung her hand aside. "After decades, you think there's some jewel hidden here. What makes you think—?"

"I don't *think*. I *know*." She searched the journal until she found the sought-after page and then thrust the book at him. "Read this entry."

"Nora—"

"Read!"

He could call Danny and have her in custody. Lock her up for vandalism. Get her shipped out of his life. Instead, he stared at the book. Old. Historical. With her jaw clenched tight, she bore into him with eyes pleading her case. Curiosity won out. He plucked the journal from her fingers. What could it hurt? If his great grandfather had a mistress who kept a journal, maybe he'd learn something new about his missing millionaire ancestor. Would this journal explain his disappearance? Phaedra would love to hear this. He focused on the page and read aloud.

"'August 20, 1924. Oh my God. Lord in heaven, what have I done?!! I don't WANT to write this, but I HAVE to because tomorrow I may be stark raving mad with the memory!! If someone should find me throwing myself against a wall or slicing my wrists, I want them to discover this confession and to know the TRUTH.'"

Sorry, Phae. I can't get in all of the exclamation points and capital letters that would be sure to have you sighing.

"'If I'm mad and crazy and senseless, none of this will matter. But if I am not mad, then I will force myself to reread about this day from hell OVER AND OVER so I will always remember to pray for my soul. Dear God, I pray for my soul.'"

"'John should not have taken me to the grand house in the light of day.'"

Nora stirred beside him and leaned closer, touching her shoulder to his. "This house," she murmured.

Harlan continued. "'He didn't wait for nightfall. As soon as Lilac left for Copperdale, he fetched me, and we went to the house. He'd received the Ceylon Royal Blue Sapphire and was overcome with excitement. First, we made love. Then he gave me the jewel. We made love again. After, he wanted to take me into town, but of course that isn't possible yet. So we dressed to return to Ma's for a dinner celebration.'"

"'We both heard a noise and stopped talking to listen. But we heard nothing, so we continued laughing and talking about wonderful things. Us. Making love on his desk in his closet the first time.'"

Harlan paused, the words slamming into his head. *The closet. The desk.* The sense of intrusion he'd experienced when he first entered the room swirled through his mind. And the tingling. He tucked his elbows against his sides, breathed deep, and continued.

"'How we would one day make love in every room of the house. How we would raise the child, his...baby in...my belly.'"

Harlan's head went light as he stumbled over the words. Another child. This woman carried his great grandfather's—

"Why are you stopping?" Nora nudged him.

He stared at her, his mouth dry. This woman's great grandmother was pregnant with John Hersey's child. He swallowed deeply. Swished his tongue against his teeth to encourage the saliva to replenish and continued.

"'We would raise our child and have plenty more children. And then we heard the noise again. There was someone on the stairs. John froze, and in that moment, we both knew Lilac was there.

"'He jumped off the bed and with his hand across my mouth, dragged me into the closet and told me to be quiet. NO MATTER WHAT!

"'I heard her footsteps. Heard her stop at the doorway. And then she asked what he was doing home. It was the first time I'd heard her voice, and she sounded tinny, screechy.

"'John spoke, and the sound of his steps shuffled on the floor. I guessed he tried to leave the room. He told her he'd forgotten something and to go downstairs to talk. But her voice got louder, like she'd come into the room. She was so close. I was so scared. Her screechy voice demanded an explanation. Then John yelled, asking her why she had that, and to stop and what did she intend.'"

Nora jerked. "What was that?" Her gaze flitted around the room. "I heard something, like a cough or something."

Phaedra. "I didn't hear anything." He cleared his throat, hoping to distract her and dove back into the journal raising the volume of his voice.

"'When the door to the closet jerked open and I saw her with a giant kitchen knife in one hand, I screamed. John jumped in front of me. He demanded she get out. She held the knife over her head, her face an ugly grimace, and she lunged. Oh God, oh God, poor John.'"

Harlan's throat tightened. His dry mouth made it difficult to read, but he wanted Phaedra to stay put and listen. "I need some water." He leaned off the sleeping bag and opened the cooler for a bottle. After a long drink, he wondered if he wanted to know all this journal had to tell. The drama playing out in her great grandmother's words was inexplicably tied to him. His heart pounded in his ears as he refocused on the page and continued reading.

"'Her eyes were scary dark, and glassy. Her nostrils flared with every breath. She bared her teeth. And then she lunged. The knife sank into John's neck. My God I'll never forget the sound of ripping flesh like when I gut the chickens at Ma Betsy's for dinner. He fell against me shoving me farther into the closet. I hit the wall and

176

couldn't move. Why wasn't I moving to protect him? Why didn't I stop her? In horror, I helplessly watched her yank out the knife, flinching as he gasped and gurgled on his blood. In one swift, determined movement, she thrust the knife deep into his chest.'"

"Jesus." Harlan gulped air then took another swallow of water. His lightheadedness wouldn't subside. His stomach knotted. He glanced into the fourth bedroom. She'd murdered him. There. A scuffing noise from the closet where Phaedra hid brought him out of his appalling revelation. He dove back into reading.

"'Why couldn't I stop her? Why couldn't I move or scream or save him? And then he was on the closet floor. And I was beside him. He gasped a sickening gurgle and then fell still. The silence was deafening. The silence of death. I wiped my hand across my cheek and saw blood not tears. Blood. John's blood. I looked down at my dress. John's blood. And finally, I could do something. I screamed. And screamed.

"'She slapped me. Once. Twice. Pulled me out of the closet. Called me a twit and told me to shut up.

"'The real tears finally came. My head throbbed and my chest ached. I thought I might have a heart attack.

"'Lilac stared at John for what seemed forever. Then she picked up my jewel from the bed and threw it at him. Her face ugly. She told me I had to help her get him downstairs and bury him.'"

Harlan's head ballooned with the realization of what the dark sensations and overwhelming feeling of loss meant when he'd descended the same stairway. His head snapped up at the memory, and he visualized his great grandmother and Nora's great grandmother, both pregnant by John Hersey. *Nora is—*

"What? Why are you staring at me?" She frowned. "Just finish. We can help each other. Finish."

He nodded and read, slowly, dizzy with his knowledge, tripping over the words. Then he picked up the pace, making sure to speak loud enough for Phae.

"'I said no over and over, but Lilac slapped me again. She screamed at me to shut my mouth. She said she'd kill me too if she didn't need me. We had only about twenty minutes or so before dark. I cried so hard. But she said if I didn't help, she'd run from the house screaming for the neighbors. She'd say she saw me murder him because he wouldn't leave her, his wife. I had blood all over me, and no one would take a slut's word against the respectable wife of John Hersey. She'd let them hang me for his murder.

"'Her words struck me dumb. She was right. No one would believe me. I went numb. I stopped thinking. Stopped feeling.

"'We wrapped him in several sheets and buried him in the backyard. We scrubbed the closet floor but couldn't get all of the stain off. She said awful things while we worked. Things like how I planned to fornicate with her husband in every room of the house, like when he had me on his desk in his closet. She'd overheard our conversation. She cheapened what we had. I wanted to slap her. Stab her with the knife.

"'Just as we finished, the little girl in her crib in another room cried out. Lilac froze. The child's crying grew louder. Lilac trembled, fell to the floor, and sobbed.

"'I went to the bathroom and washed as good as I could. At least I got my face and hands clean, my hair in place, and did the best I could with the blood on my dress. I had on dark gray so the blood didn't stand out too much. Lilac and the child cried and cried. I didn't think she'd notice, so I went back into the room to get the sapphire. Lilac lay in a fetal position on the floor, still. In the closet, I scooped the sapphire from the floor. OH NO YOU DON'T. She screamed.

"'I tried to run around her, but she ranted and jerked around wild and crazy. She knocked my knees out from me. She jumped on me and dug her fingernails into my hand. The pain was too much and I let it go. I screamed back at her that the jewel was mine!! John gave it to me!!!

"'She told me she didn't want my slut gift. And she said I couldn't have it either. She threw it back into the closet. She said I deserved a lifetime of torture. John would be entombed in her ground where I would never see him again. And the jewel would be entombed in the closet of shame. Then she ordered me to get out or she might decide to kill me too.

"'Now as I look back on it, I'm sure John thought she meant to kill me. He tried to protect me. I don't know how I found my way back to Ma Betsy's. I've been here crying for hours. I don't know what to do. I don't know if the sun will rise tomorrow.'"

Harlan couldn't take his gaze off the page as if hypnotized by the slanting scroll of Nora's ancestor. His great grandmother and Nora's great grandmother buried his great grandfather. The idea looped around in his head until his vision blurred. The faint patch of green grass in the back yard that he'd thought the shadows played on his imagination? Another message this house sent him?

"Will you?" Nora's question came as if from the top of the mountain, drifting on the breeze. "Harlan!"

He shook his head coming out of his shocked meandering with a deep breath. "You think the sapphire is still in this house?"

"GG followed the news of jewels and rare finds all of her life. The jewel never surfaced. She wrote in this journal until she died. The sapphire is here." She pointed across the hall to the fourth bedroom. "And I think it's in there."

"What did you intend to do tonight? Tear up every wall in the bedroom?"

"If I had to, but I hoped you'd help." She leaned against him. "I called you earlier but you didn't answer. I intended to call you again. After I got here. Like I said, we can be partners. And here we are. Luck plopped you into my path once again." She tickled fingers down his chest.

He stopped her hand before it reached his belt.

She snickered. "I'll share with you, Harlan. The sapphire is worth millions." She rubbed her breast into his arm. "I'd be ever so grateful."

He drew back. "You want me to tear up another room? I highly doubt Lilac Hersey would've left such wealth behind."

"Didn't you digest anything you read? GG's journal proved it." Flared nostrils and a pinched mouth telegraphed her anger. "She did, and you *will* help me!"

A scuffing noise came from the closet. Nora jerked, her hand going into her bag. "I know I heard something this time."

Concern flitted across his mind. *What's in the bag?*

The closet door burst open, and Phaedra shot out, gasping. "S-sorry. I couldn't take it any longer." She bent and then righted taking a deep breath. "Claustrophobia. And besides, this crazy lady isn't doing any more damage tonight."

"You!" Nora leapt to her feet as her hand came out of her bag with a gun.

Harlan scrambled to stand with leg muscles tightening. "What the hell?" His heart thumped.

Nora jumped out of his reach and leveled the weapon at Phaedra. "You always show up at the wrong time."

"Whoa. Nora." Extending his hands in a gesture to calm, he swallowed against the fingers of fear strangling his voice. "I didn't say I wouldn't help." His words sounded amazingly tranquil in spite of the surreal scene.

"Two sleeping bags because the floor is hard? You *lied*. And you had her in the closet spying on me. In the closet!"

"I didn't expect you, Nora." He lowered his voice and took a half-step toward her. "I thought it could be dangerous vandals."

"Get back!" She waved the gun in his direction. "Go! Stand next to her. All offers are off the table. You're stupid, Harlan. You could've had me and millions."

She couldn't be crazy enough to shoot them. He didn't move, his mind running scenarios of leaping, going for her legs. First shoving Phaedra aside and then charging her. Grabbing Phaedra, hitting the floor, and then—

"Move!" Her hand tightened on the handle of the pistol.

"Okay. Okay." He moved backwards, not taking his gaze off the gun.

"Listen." Phaedra spoke. "Nora—"

"Shut up, bitch." She zeroed her aim on Phaedra's chest.

Phaedra's face hardened, her arms clasped together at her waist.

Nora lasered her glare on him. "I was more than happy to share with you. I've offered you numerous times to align with me. You've done nothing but lead me on."

"I didn't mean to." The pulse in his temple pounded. He had to talk her down.

"While the artsy-fartsy curvy-bitch kept you distracted. She wants what I have. She's not getting the jewel."

"You've read it all wrong." He again considered rushing her and immediately dismissed the idea. She could easily get a shot off, most likely hitting Phaedra before he could overcome her. "*She* didn't know about any jewel. *We* didn't know."

"It's mine, and I'm going to have it. Both of you turn around."

"Nora, please let me help you." His chest tightened as if imprisoning his flailing heart. He forced a smile. "Phae doesn't need any jewels or money. Let her go so we can get to work finding the sapphire."

"Oh, really? You're so transparent, Harlan." Her sneer hardened. "Now, turn around!"

With a glance at Phaedra, he nodded, and they turned. A crack assaulted his ears, a gut-wrenching sound, as Phaedra collapsed beside him.

Harlan fell to his knees. Nora had hit her over the head with the gun. Blood seeped through her white hair at the back of her head. He didn't know whether to try to help her or attack Nora. Rage quivered his muscles. Concern roiled his stomach. He clenched his fists, ready to fight, when cold steel poked the back of his neck.

"Get up. Close the closet door."

"Are you freaking crazy?" He jerked around to face the madwoman sending her retreating several steps.

"I might be. Let's not find out." She moved farther back, the gun steady and pointing at his face. "Close her in the closet and get up slowly. I'm tired of knocking out walls, but I can do it by myself if I have to. Would you prefer to join her in the closet with a hole in you? Or maybe I should shoot Miss Artsy-Fartsy first." Her gun wavered between them. "By the time anyone found you, you'd be dead."

"Nora, please. She's bleeding. You could've killed her." Icy fingers clutched at his core.

"But I didn't, did I? Felt good to whack her though."

"She needs medical attention."

"Then you better hurry." The once pretty mouth held an ugly sneer. "The longer you stall, the more blood she loses."

In an instant, he gauged if he could lunge at her legs and escape a bullet in his head. But if he could, Phaedra lay directly behind him. Nora could shoot her just as easily. Better to knock holes in walls until he found a chance to knock out the so-called writer. He raised his hands in defeat. "All right. But I'm getting the sleeping bag to lay her on." Not waiting for a response from the crazy woman, he snatched the bag from the floor and spread it in the closet.

As gently as possible, he lifted Phaedra, settling her into the closet. His stomach threatened to spew its contents. He bunched the material against the gash in her head. Could the knock and the amount of blood lost be fatal? He felt her pulse. Strong. He breathed easier. Wiped sweaty palms on his legs. Touched her cheek. Rising on shaky legs, he moved back from the doorway and closed her inside.

A slight crook of her mouth and a lifted brow gave Nora a self-satisfied expression. "Pick up my bag. I'll follow you to door number four. A guaranteed prize." She sniggered at her reference to an old game show.

As he crossed the threshold into the fourth bedroom, the dark enveloped him. He halted. The bag slipped from his hand and sent an echoing clunk through the room. Even when Nora switched on the overhead light, the room remained in a smoky haze. His breathing grew heavy, reminding him of unfulfilled desires. He sucked in air. The word desire might have come to mind, but he wasn't enjoying these sensations.

"Pick a wall, any wall, and get to work. Hammer's in the bag. Get out a flashlight and set it in front of me."

He bent on one knee to riffle through the tote. "I've got better tools in my truck. How about I get something to make this job go quicker."

"How about you suck it up and use my hammer. If I can punch holes in walls with it, a big, strong hunk like you can manage."

He kept his ear trained toward the master bedroom as he lifted a flashlight and a hammer from the tote. He set the flashlight at her feet, gripped the hammer, and then stood. Had Phaedra called the cops before she'd abandoned the closet? Knowing the intruder was Nora and not some gang of vandals, had she assumed no need for police intervention? Would she wake and call for help now?

"What are you thinking about? Get started."

"I'm considering the best wall to attack first." His grip on the hammer slipped in his sweaty palm. He couldn't be sure his anxiety came from the gun pointed at his head or the clairsentient emotions the room washed over him. With a deep breath, he approached a wall. "If the designer of this house followed the same pattern as in the other bedrooms, then I'm guessing this is the most likely spot."

He tapped across the wall, side to side and top to bottom. A three-foot-wide area sounded hollow. He considered stalling, hoping Danny would barrel in with backup. But more important, Phaedra needed medical attention. If he could find the jewel, would Nora take it and leave? Or would the crazed, phony writer shoot them both before fleeing? The weight of the hammer in his hand grew heavier. A hammer to her head could put an end to this nightmare. If he got the chance—"

"Sling the damn hammer. My trigger finger is itching."

He increased his grip on the handle. *Get close enough, bitch, and you'll wish you'd done this on your own.*

He went at the wall like a miner on a new vein of gold. Bits of plaster pinged off his squinted eyes and cheeks. Billowing dust swirled up his nose. As if releasing pent-up emotions and mind-ghosts, each crack of contact lessened the dark desire encasing him. Soon, a hole the size of his head punctured the wall. Panting, he paused to wipe his face and grab a breath of dusty air, but a glance at Nora, and chills tripped along his spine. Her smile wide, she licked her lips repeatedly—like a hungry wolf tunnel visioned on its prey.

A creak on the landing. Danny? A scuffling noise from the master bedroom. Phaedra waking? He darted another glance at Nora, but she appeared to be so enthralled in his progress she hadn't noticed. He smacked the wall again to mask the sounds.

"That's big enough. Get back. I want to look." Poised to move forward, she paused, darting a glance from the flashlight in one hand and her gun in the other. He could see the wheels spinning in her head. She had to be assessing the outcome. If she chose to stick her head in the hole, with her back to him, he wouldn't hesitate to use the hammer on her.

He gripped the would-be weapon tighter and flinched when another subtle creak came from the hall. He cleared his throat to cover.

She zeroed in on the hammer in his hand. "Put the hammer on the floor and kick it to me." When he complied, she stooped, gun still on him, and shoved the flashlight across the floor. "You look."

He lifted the flashlight and fake coughed for added cover noise. "You don't have to keep a gun on me, Nora." He spoke louder than needed. *Are you listening, Danny?* "I'll help you. I'm helping you right now."

"Shut up, Harlan. You blew it. The sapphire is all mine." She waved the gun toward the wall. "See if it's in there."

He flicked on the flashlight, dared to show his back to her, and stuck his head and one arm into the hole. Shining the light side to side, he surmised the area had definitely been a closet. Pointing the beam downward and inching the light along the floor, he passed over a lump and scattered papers, but quickly set the beam back on the find. Dust covered the floor and disguised what could possibly be...

"Well—?"

"Hands up!" A male voice shouted.

"Nooo!" Nora screeched.

A gunshot rang out.

Someone screamed.

Harlan lurched, hitting his head. Swearing, he hit the floor crawling toward the door. He darted a glance over his shoulder. Trousered legs, Nora on the floor screaming. No Phaedra. He stood. Danny grappled with cursing Nora while Jennifer cuffed her. *Where the hell was Phaedra?*

Staggering out the door, he tripped over her legs. "Oh, God, no."

CHAPTER FIFTEEN

Phaedra awoke to a soft touch on her cheek. She tried to open her eyes. Her eyelids were heavy, thick, and wouldn't respond. Another feather-like stroke on her cheek. With effort, she managed to peek through her lashes on half-opened eyes. Harlan's face floated over her.

"Hi, Phae. Don't wake up unless you want to. I'll be here. I'm not going anywhere."

"Hmm." Her tongue stuck to the roof of her mouth. "Thirsty."

He held a cup of ice chips to her lips. Her right arm wouldn't move to take the cup from him. *Strange.* He lifted her head, and she lapped in chucks of soft ice. Nodding she was done, she chewed as he gently let her back to the pillow. *So good.* She licked her lips to moisten them.

She didn't like the darkness of the room. "I want to."

"What?" He bent close to her.

"Be awake." Although she could now see Harlan clearly, the darkened room surrounded him. The outline of a television high on a wall. A small whiteboard a few feet over hung lower. No paintings. A vinyl chair behind him. Drab surroundings reminded her of a black and white photo. "Am I...in the hospital? Copperdale?" The drawn curtains revealed light around the edges. Streetlights or sun?

"Yep."

"Could you...open...curtains? Feel closed in."

After parting the dark green black out material a few inches, he came back beside the bed and took her hand. "Better?"

She couldn't grip his fingers. *So weak.* "Mmm. Ambulance ride. Crazy writer…hit me?" A dull ached throbbed at her temples.

"She did. I'm so sorry." He let go of her fingers and ran his hand up and down her left arm.

"I couldn't stay…in the closet. Like you said. Before she hit me. And then…the closet again." She strained her memory around the ache. A nightmare of impressions she couldn't understand flashed half-frame images in her head.

"You got out of the closet at about the same time Danny and Jennifer came to our rescue. You must have called them. Nora shot you."

"My arm?"

"Yeah. I think she aimed at Danny as he stormed in. I'm not really sure. It happened fast. Unfortunately, you managed to get into the hallway at the same time as he did. She missed Danny and shot you. It's not a bad wound. The bullet went through, and the doctor said you'll heal just fine. The blow to the head has been more of a concern to them." He bent and kissed her cheek. "How does your head feel?"

"Hurts." *And heavy. Hit with a sledgehammer.*

"When she shot you, you fell and might've hit your head again."

"And the crazy lady?"

"She's in jail."

The door swooshed open. "Oh good, our patient's awake." A short, round woman in pink scrubs appeared at her side. She set a pitcher of water on the bedside table. "How's the head?"

"Aches." Talking made it worse.

"Thought it would. This might help." She produced a packet from her pocket. "It's all you can have for now. We need to watch you for at least twenty-four hours before we can give you anything stronger." She poured water into a glass, then raised the head of the bed.

Harlan moved to slip a hand under her head, but she stopped him with a frown. "I'm okay." Every movement deepened the throb in her temples. The nurse held the water to her lips as she swallowed the two pills.

"Thank you."

"You're welcome, hon. Just rest easy. Let me know if you feel nauseous or have severe pain or dizziness. Anything at all that concerns you, okay?" She glanced at Harlan. "You look like you could use some sleep."

"I'm fine."

Phaedra peered at Harlan. Now that the nurse mentioned it, he didn't look too good. Dark circles. Creases deep around his mouth.

"You should go home and sleep." The nurse pointed a pudgy finger at him. "Come back later. We'll take good care of her."

"Thanks. I will soon."

She closed the door when she left.

"How long have...I been here?" She searched the walls for a clock without moving her head. "What time is it?" The fog lessened.

"It's a little after six."

"In the morning?"

He nodded.

"You've been here all night?" Now she understood why he looked dead on his feet.

"Of course."

She breathed deeply. How sweet of him. "What in Hades are you still doing here?" She wanted to sound gruffer, but she still hung on the edge of drowsiness.

He took her hand between his. "What do you think I've been doing? I let you come with me to stake out the house. I got you knocked out and shot. I had to see you awake and talking sensibly."

"You didn't *let* me do anything." Fully awake, she got her voice back. "Go home, Harlan." His red-rimmed eyes attested to his zombie state. "No, wait. You shouldn't drive in your state."

"I'm not. I rode with you in the ambulance. Mags should be here shortly. I'll hitch a ride back with her."

She stared into his face. A cozy, contentment enveloped her. "You two are the best friends a girl can have. I love you both so much." The gratitude she found in herself for having them in her life soothed her in spite of her physical pain.

He let go of her hand and stood straighter, creating some distance between them.

She wanted to grab and kiss him, but weakness permeated her body—and the expression on his face. Disappointment? She didn't mean to say he was *only* a friend. He was so much more. Last night she might've been able to explain. *Tomorrow, Har. I can't talk that much now.*

"Mags called Primrose and Poppy. They'll be here later today."

"They didn't need to come. Not like I'm dying." But she smiled at the news.

"I'm sure your girls don't see it that way."

"She didn't call my mother, did she?"

"She didn't have her number, and Poppy told her not to call her anyway. Primrose agreed. They said with your mom's age and all— she didn't need to be worried—unless your condition grew serious."

"Good girls." She closed her eyes. Thoughts of being closed in the closet drifted through her mind. No matter how many times she'd reassured herself, the dark got heavier, and the walls drew closer. When the fingers of dread crept around her neck so her breathing got difficult, she had to pop out. The second time, she didn't even remember getting out. The first time... *The journal.* The words read aloud. The murder. She startled at the memory. Her eyes flashed wide. Her arm pinched from the abrupt movement. "Oh!"

"What?" He leaned over her. "Are you okay?"

"Yes, can't move fast. The journal. What you read. The sapphire. The murder. Did you find it?"

"I think so, but I don't know for sure yet. I'd just stuck my head in the hole I'd knocked in the wall when all hell broke loose." He dragged the side chair closer to the bed and sat. "I found the hidden closet for sure. There were papers and something next to them, but with all the dust, I can't be sure."

"You have to go back. No, wait. You need sleep. Can your crew—?"

"No. I've already moved them to another job for the day." He rubbed his eyes. "I don't want anyone in there but me." He touched the bed but drew back before his fingers reached her arm. "It'll be fine until I get back."

"What you read—from the journal—I could hear most of it, but I was beginning to hyperventilate so I'm not sure I understood. Did I dream you and Nora are—?"

The door opened. "Oh, my God, Phaedra." Magpie rushed in. "Look at you! Are you okay? How do you feel?" Loosened, corkscrew tresses from the mass of curly, brown hair knotted at the back of her head bounced around her face and on her neck. "I mean, I know you're okay, but are you?"

"They tell me I will be. I've got some pain, but not bad."

"What a nightmare." She patted her leg beneath the green waffle weave blanket.

"That's the half of it. We were just talking about the evil lady who put me in here."

"*Sacrebleu!* Can you believe her? She won't be getting any invitations to family gatherings."

"Then she is your cousin?" Her gaze went to Harlan. He now leaned back in the chair and appeared to be drifting off. She nodded toward him. "Mags, you need to get him home."

"You don't want me to stay awhile?" Her friend's brows pinched together over caramel-colored eyes. "He can snooze in the chair."

"Thanks for offering. I love you for it, but I think I need to sleep some more. No need for you to watch *two* sleeping people. I'll call you when I wake."

"Okay." She shuffled between the chair and the bed, jarring Harlan's knee in the process, and planted a kiss on her cheek.

Harlan stood. "I'll get back to the house after I take a nap."

"I'm not worried about it."

He had grey shadows under his eyes. His hair was mussed like he'd just climbed out of bed. She'd like to scoot over and let him stretch out beside her.

Magpie eased toward the door.

"Got to earn my fee." He patted her hand.

"Pfft."

A swift grin came and went. "You rest."

"Call me when you're up to it, Phae." Magpie flashed her a smile. Before the door closed, she had a thought. "Hey, wait. Harlan."

"Yeah?" He stuck his head in the doorway.

"Whatever you find—it's yours."

"It's in your house."

"The house originally belonged to your family. If there's something in the closet, it belongs in your family. I mean it. No arguments."

He stared, a pensive slant to his brow. "We'll see." He nodded then shut the door.

Left alone, she didn't want to sleep regardless of what she told Magpie. She was too spent to visit, but too awake to sleep. She found herself stalled in her emotions. What she'd just gone through would upend anyone, but her near death experience—not technically correct, but still—gave her the notion she should rethink her values. Magpie might say the universe was trying to tell her something.

She closed her eyes. *Listen to the universe.* Until tonight, she'd been happy with all facets of her life. Her work made her a great living and provided a creative outlet. She had two wonderful daughters and the benefit of her mom still alive. Although not close to her half-brother, they had a good relationship. She loved her cottage and The Ravine neighborhood. Her friends—lifelong. As close as family. But... *Harlan.* Harlan wasn't just family anymore. She wished she could go back to the last conversation with him. She gulped a ragged breath. Couldn't get enough air in her lungs. He'd confessed his love. But loving him back wasn't enough. Would they have resolved their differences if Nora hadn't interrupted them, before the world blew up? When she'd opened her eyes and saw him hovering above her, she knew she needed him with her *every* time she opened her eyes. He had to believe that. He had to love her forever. Love had to be enough.

****

Harlan slumped onto the passenger seat of Magpie's car. His head lolled on the headrest and his eyes drifted shut. Phaedra's blue eyes stared up, her hair covered in blood. He jerked awake.

"Sorry. I didn't mean to startle you." His sister shifted the gear lever into park. "You're home."

He rubbed a hand over his eyes and face then scrubbed through his hair. "Man, sorry I wasn't company on the ride back. You're probably tired too."

"Not like you. Go get some more sleep."

"I need to get over to the Big Purple House." His declaration rang hollow. Exhaustion ruled his body and mind in spite of his curiosity.

"Whatever is in the closet has been there for decades. It isn't going anywhere."

"Yeah, you're right. A little sleep first. Check on Phaedra..." He let his words trail off with his thoughts. He'd been so scared of losing her last night. Physically. But with their conversation not finished, he might have lost her anyway. "What a night."

"I can't imagine." She patted his shoulder. "But you and Phaedra are okay." She left it at that but quirked a brow as if she'd asked a question.

He needed to talk. "If we hadn't been interrupted by Nora... I

190

don't know, Mags." He took a deep breath, wishing his sister had the answer to unlocking Phaedra. "I told her I loved her."

"She loves you."

"I know. In her way."

"What does that mean?"

"I'm not overly convinced her love for me is more than friendship. We didn't get that far before Nora busted in." He rubbed his eyes and yawned. "She calls me a friend but says she loves me. She's not looking for commitment. I don't want to be loved like a friend. Even a special friend."

"She loves you, Har. You mean more to her than a friend."

"She told you?" Hope swelled his chest.

"Not in so many words."

The balloon popped. "Ah, so you're now a mystic like Mom."

She tittered. "Only when it comes to Phaedra." Turning serious, she patted his arm. "Does it have to be marriage?"

He shrugged, considering the alternative. "I've always thought that's the natural progression. Relationship. Marriage. If you want to spend your life with someone, you take the final step."

"You are old-fashioned, aren't you?" She laughed.

He chuckled with her. "Maybe."

"I'll bet part of what you love about Phaedra is her inner creative fire. She's nontraditional. Doesn't live inside the box."

"Yeah, that's for sure. And of course it's part of why I love her. That's what makes her Phaedra."

"On the surface, marriage is traditional. Expected. I don't think she likes doing the expected. She's capable, attractive, financially self-sufficient, and doesn't need to prove her worthiness with a wedding ring on her finger."

His face heated. "Of course not. That's—"

"Over the years, she's done pretty darn well without a guy."

"Damn it, Mags, I'm not saying she hasn't." He shuffled his feet on the floorboard. "I'm not trying to complete her."

"Then what can marriage offer her you can't give with just your love?"

He put his head in his hands. Marriage was his hang up, not Phaedra's. He wanted to love her and be loved.

"'All you need is love.' Someone famous said that. Go sleep on it. The chief will be calling you before long, you know. I doubt you took time for a statement last night."

"No. Danny said to go into the station today."

"I'm still having trouble wrapping my mind around being related to the demon author."

"There's a story to tell you. How about we meet at Dad's tonight, and I'll relate the whole mess."

"Sounds like a plan."

He dragged himself from the car on weary legs and trudged along his walk, throwing a wave as his sister pulled away.

Peeling out of his shirt and pants, he left his clothes in a pile on the floor. He folded back the quilt and slipped under the sheet, rolled to his stomach, and closed his eyes. Visions of Phaedra sprawled on the floor, blood in her hair and spreading down her arm and across her chest haunted the dark behind his lids. He thought he'd lost her. All the emotions of that moment seized him. The air thinned. His heart galloped. His stomach roiled. Anger. Fear. He buried his face in his pillow. *I never want to lose her.*

She was distant at the hospital. Avoided his touch. Called him her friend, yet she might blame him for her condition. Hell concussed and shot. He could totally understand if she questioned their relationship beyond friendship. And after their argument last night?

His sister claimed Phaedra loved him for more than the friends they'd always been. He needed total commitment. He wanted her in a way she wasn't willing to give. He wanted her as his wife.

Would she think about what he'd said before Nora came in? She knew his feelings, knew he loved her. Would she consider his point of view? Maybe she needed time. *Give her space. Let her come back to me.* He had to try something. While she healed her body, maybe her mind would reconsider.

****

By the time Harlan had a bite to eat and went to the station to give Chief Kellogg his statement, the sun hung low in the sky. He'd called the hospital, asking for the on-duty nurse rather than Phaedra's room. She wouldn't give him any information. Unless Phaedra gave permission. She hadn't listed him as a family member or as a contact. His stomach folded on itself. Could this be his fear come to fruition—he'd lost a friend and a love he never had?

He punched Magpie's button on his phone. "Hey, Mags. How's

Phaedra? Are you able to call and find out?"

"I talked to her not an hour ago. The girls are there, and she's being released tomorrow."

His chest pinched. "Okay. Good. I'm headed to the Big Purple House."

"Are you okay? You sound funny."

"No, fine. I'll see you later at Dad's."

In a fog, he drove to the Big Purple House, parked along the curb and cut the engine. He rubbed his eyes, but the burning behind his eyelids wouldn't cease. With a long, low sigh he exited the truck. "Don't give up yet, MacKenzie." He'd vowed only a few hours ago to give her time. *She'll relax with her daughters and heal. Give her time.*

Instead of going in the house, he followed the veranda around to the back. At the bottom of the stairs, he meandered to the faint green grass under the dead apricot tree. He removed his ball cap, snapped it against his leg, and shoved a hand into his pocket.

"John Carl Hersey." *Great Grandfather.* "I think it's time you rested in peace." He'd arrange for the remains to be moved to the Joshua cemetery before Annette moved in. Squatting for a moment, no words came to mind. Wanda would have information on the man. Maybe photos. "I'll see what I can find out, sir." He flipped his cap on, stood, and climbed the steps.

When he entered the Big Purple House, Lilac End, the inside seemed somehow brighter. With a deep breath and the sense he was putting himself and the house through a test, he used the main stairwell at the back to ascend to the second floor. Had solving the mystery chased away the tragic notions? He climbed slowly, inviting whatever vibrations remained to assault him. Instead of the dark and overpowering cloud of loss he'd experienced before, he noticed the smooth railing, the rich color of mahogany. The wooden steps slightly worn in the middle. He'd sand and refinish them, bringing the wood back to the original beauty. Imagining Annette, maybe even his father, enjoying the refurbished stairwell brought him peace.

In the fourth bedroom, he stood a moment. Other than an anxious bent to get to the closet contents, he didn't intuit gloomy sentiments. "Satisfied, huh?" He shook his head. Talking to the house again. Once he covered his mouth and nose with a face mask, he battered at the wall with a small sledgehammer until he could step into the closet. He turned on the lantern flashlight and set it inside. He stooped, picked up the papers, and brushed dust from the chunk on the floor. What he saw sent a lump to his throat. Even dirty, and in low light, the brilliance of the blue jewel was evident. "I'll be damned."

He stood, papers in one hand and jewel in the other. He carried them into the master bedroom and then sat on the sleeping bag where he'd read about the murder and the sapphire. Staring at the rock in his hand made his head spin. He blinked to settle his focus. After hitting the papers against his knee to clear them of dust, he skimmed the paragraphs. John Hersey had intended on leaving the bulk of his wealth to Genevieve Jenkins, providing for his first family too. But the will was never filed. No marks of legality. He rubbed the jewel against his jeans, bringing the full color to light. "Wow." Now what? As if searching for the answer, he scanned the room. No voices in *his* head.

His gaze fell on the journal.

He flipped through the pages until he came to August 20, 1924. He reread the entry. The murder. After finding the sapphire, the passage was even more thought provoking on the second read. He turned the page to the next entry.

September 5, 1924

It's been two weeks. The rumors are crazy. Some say John must be lost in the mines. Others say, he ran off with millions belonging to the other owners. Ma says he paid for me through the end of the month. I have to go back in the crib come October. I won't be here.

My grief has finally subsided, and I'm angry. I decided this morning, Lilac couldn't control my life, so I waited until after dark then climbed the hill to visit the murderess. I offered her proof that he intended on divorcing her and marrying me. At first, she acted as if she didn't believe me, until I held the will in front of her. She screamed and yelled at me, calling me all sorts of ugly names. I threatened to go to the authorities and tell them how she murdered him unless she gave me the sapphire. She has no proof I was even in her house that day. I burned my bloodied clothes.

We argued back and forth. In her ramblings, she confessed to having found the other copy of the will and destroyed it. My having a copy did nothing to sway her. Demanding the jewel back proved fruitless. I think she'd rather I tell the police she murdered her husband than give up the sapphire. John's promise to me. I can't understand the workings of her mad mind. In the end, we struck a deal. Instead of giving me the sapphire, she agreed to provide for me for the rest of my life. She said the filthy stone, the testament to John's evil ways, would never see the light of day. I made her write down she owed me money for unspecified goods, and her promissory note to pay me. In exchange, she also wanted my copy of the will. It scared me to give it to her, but knowing the location of the body gave me leverage. If she ever thought to double cross me, I'd go to the police, even if I ended up in jail too. And if she ever sold my jewel, I'd know. A stone like the Ceylon Royal Blue Sapphire would make the news. I'll be an avid watcher.

In three days, she will deposit the first 6-month payment in my bank account. After that, I will receive a monthly payment until the day I die. As soon as I confirm the money is there, I'll be headed for San Bernadino, CA and my new life. I have a cousin there who said she'd help me find a place to live. I want to get settled long before my baby is due…John's baby.

Some of the same ancestral blood in his veins flowed through Nora's body. Her soul and his soul shared relatives, a heritage. He stared at the pages while fingering the pendant hanging around his neck. "Wish you were here, Mom. I know you'd help me make sense of this. Put it in perspective."

As he thumbed through the smattering of entries at the back of the journal, a photograph fell from between the pages. The cloudy black and white of a woman from decades ago bore a striking resemblance to Nora. He gulped. Genevieve Jenkins. Nora's GG. He turned to the last entry of the journal. What had the young woman become by the end of her life? With a glance at the photo, he then focused on the scrolly writing from March 16, 1988.

I've been deep in thought today about my life. How different it could've been had John lived. Somewhere in this world, my daughter has a half-sister. My granddaughter and great granddaughter have cousins. I'm not sure I'd want my precious girls to know any of them...the lineage of a murderess.

My monthly payment stopped two weeks ago. I found Lilac's obit. Yet it no longer matters. My health is waning, and I no longer need her money.

The Ceylon Royal Blue Sapphire remains hidden.

John's daughter, his granddaughter, and great granddaughter live on, never to know who they are or where they came from. They will outlive me. I'm close behind Lilac.

Do you suppose Lilac and I will meet in hell? I believed John to be a good man, but his intentions for Lilac may have landed him on the wrong side of the afterlife. Perhaps he's been waiting for us all these years.

Harlan closed the journal. If a way existed to right the wrongs committed on so many levels, then finding a path to fixing at least some of them fell to him. He knew what he had to do.

****

Phaedra sat on the sofa in her living room while in the kitchen her daughters bumped each other making dinner. Now fully recovered, she left them to cooking one last meal before they left for their homes in Las Vegas and Tucson in the morning. Having them with her for the past three weeks had been a godsend. The repartee as they cooked dinner tonight fell somewhere between sisterly banter and bickering.

"French fries again?" Poppy sounded exasperated.

"It's a vegetable." Primrose said. "Get over it. And you don't have to eat any."

"I don't know how you stay so thin."

"Aha, that's what it is. Jealousy."

A pan banged. Probably Poppy. "Are you saying I'm fat?"

"Don't be stupid. You're anything but fat. You're curvy. Like Mom. But you always did hate how I stayed thin and ate what I wanted."

"What I'd hate is to see your arteries."

"They're skinny too."

Phaedra pushed to the edge of the sofa. "Are you girls actually making dinner or just talking about it?"

Laughter filled the air. "Come and get it," Primrose called.

Poppy rushed into the room. "You need help?"

"Stop already. I'm totally healed. And I'm not old yet, so save your concern for another couple of decades." Once she'd felt better, they'd shared laughs and enjoyed each other. But she was ready to get back to her life and have her own space to herself.

In the kitchen, Phaedra settled on the chair at one end of the table, a daughter on each side. Primrose, the older by three years, scooped a heap of fries onto her plate. Her long brown hair was twisted into a messy knot at the back of her head. She resembled her father with her chestnut eyes and height, a good four inches taller than her sister and her. He'd been tall and handsome. There was no mistaking who her father was with her dark arched brows, straight nose, and full lips.

"Pass me some fries, Prim." She gave her other daughter a don't-you-dare-complain face.

"Here, Mom." Poppy lifted the bowl of salad. "I didn't put any kale in it."

Phaedra chuckled. "It still looks pretty green, but I'll have some." After salad and meatloaf covered her plate, she glanced at each of her daughters. "I'm really glad you came, but you didn't have to. I'm sure you'll both be happy to get home tomorrow."

"Of course we had to." Primrose spoke around a fry. "I needed a break from Las Vegas, lights, and taking food orders from tourists anyway. Ugh. Waiting on you has been a vacation."

Poppy patted her hand. "Mom, we've had a great time taking care of you. And since I didn't have any summer classes, it worked out great. I left Howard to do some wedding planning. Less work for me when I get there."

Her youngest was altar-bound after college graduation. Another year. Or was it two? In addition to school, she worked in some lab doing something Phaedra couldn't understand. As a waitress in a high-end casino restaurant, her oldest probably made more money than both of them together, and she'd lived with a nice guy for the last couple of years.

"How's the love life, Mom?" Primrose waved a fork in the air.

"Prim!" Poppy protested.

She made a squinch-face at her sister and continued. "I overheard part of a conversation with Magpie. Apparently, you and Harlan are an item?"

Phaedra pushed meatloaf around her plate. "I don't know if we are or not, actually. Surely you eavesdropped enough to know that." She quirked a brow and chortled at the feigned innocence on her daughter's face.

"What's the problem? Did I hear the M word?"

"Yeah, you probably did."

"Oh, Mom." Poppy clapped her hands. "He's perfect for you."

In all ways but one. "It's not that simple."

Primrose smirked at her sister then shot Phaedra a closed mouth grin. Her oldest daughter had the same view of marriage as she did. "Is it a deal breaker for Harlan? Why is it so important to him?"

"Because *most* people want to make that commitment, Prim. If he loves Mom, then he wants to present as a couple, show the world they're as one."

"Oh, God, Poppy, you are so corny. I've never married. Mom's never married. It isn't a necessary evil we all have to endure."

"Evil? You are so—"

"Come on, girls." She thumped the table. "No arguing on your last night here." She glanced at each of them. Poppy might have her fair complexion, blonde hair, and blue eyes, but Primrose shared personality traits with her.

"Corky and I have lived under the same roof for two years. We're just as committed to each other as any married couple. You don't need the document to be a couple." Primrose jutted her chin toward Phaedra. "You can maintain individualism and still be in love and happy. Right, Mom?"

Had she presented these sentiments to her daughter as a girl so plainly that she now mimicked her thoughts? Or had she led by example?

"Oh, hell, Prim. You're full of it. A woman can maintain her individualism and still be married, still stand up for a committed relationship that isn't dissolvable at the drop of a hat. Why on earth would publicly declaring your love forever take away from a woman? It only adds to her." Poppy leveled Phaedra with the same icy blue eyes she saw in the mirror every day. "You taught us to be strong women. I have no doubt my impending marriage won't change me in the least, but my life will be enriched."

Primrose's jaw tightened, but she stayed silent.

Her daughters watched her, malcontent stirring within her. Her legs jittered as if she needed to do a walk around and think. "You know Harlan." They nodded and smiled. Both girls had crushes on him way back. "He's important to me. But I haven't seen him since the night the crazy lady shot me." The angry words from the night still hung over her like a thunderhead encasing the highest peak in the mountains. "We haven't been able to talk, other than a few words on the phone. I do know he loves me."

"Do you love him?" Poppy asked.

"Yes. But how do we work it out? I'm just not sure yet."

"Oh, Mom." Primrose linked fingers with her.

"Don't you two worry. I'll figure it out." His distancing bothered her. If he loved her, what did his absence in her life for the last three weeks mean? She needed to see him. Tomorrow. After the girls left. If she could just find a good dose of persuasiveness. For him or herself? Hearing both sides of the argument from her daughters made her wonder.

CHAPTER SIXTEEN

Three weeks had gone by since Harlan had seen Phaedra. He paced the parlor of the Big Purple House. A cool breeze, fresh, warm, and fragrant, swirled through the rooms from the windows he opened on both floors. The chandelier overhead tinkled a happy sound. The polished and inviting fireplace promised gregarious gatherings in the winter months. The gloomy cloud engulfing the house blew away when he discovered the history, his history, of the house. The refurbish was well on its way to completion. Two rooms to paint and a final cleanup remained before Annette assumed ownership. He shared in the joy of the house for the future.

Now, here for a meeting at Phaedra's request, he longed to see her and yet nervous as hell about what he *would* see—in her eyes, in her attitude. They'd spoken only twice since she'd gotten home from the hospital. When she'd called him and her face lit the screen, his stomach did a somersault, yet each time the impersonal, mundane house talk left him deeply disappointed and unsatisfied. Her girls were still there watching over her when last they spoke. She was practically back to normal. Apparently, normal described their friend-relationship. He kept his promise to himself to give her space. He wanted her to make the move. Did she miss him? His heart beat high in his chest. Would they finish the scene that started upstairs the night of the shooting? The disagreement unsettled between them. Anxiety twisted his core. Had the last words he'd said to her, mixed with his declaration of love, mean anything? What more could he say? She either felt what he did, or she didn't. She'd known him forever. He had nothing left to win her over.

Busy with the house and sorting out the financial windfall from the Ceylon Royal Blue Sapphire kept him busy. With Zac's help, he secured a buyer and the legalities of the expeditious sale continued. The authentication and appraisal finalized yesterday. Disposition of the soon-to-be windfall taxed his accounting abilities, but Zac came through again with a trustworthy financial professional.

He'd taken every opportunity to distract himself from thoughts of Phaedra. An old friend from his years in Phoenix called with an invite to a Diamondbacks baseball game. He spent the day down in the valley, but as he returned to the mountain in the evening, the 'Welcome to Joshua' sign left him with a hollow spot inside. Keeping his Saturday morning racquetball ritual with Danny helped to get out his nervous energy, but sitting with Zac at the Apparition Room Saturday nights when Magpie sang increased his loneliness. Phaedra would normally have been with them.

At night, lying in bed, he couldn't stop his mind from wandering with thoughts of her. Lonely. Sad. Impatient, waiting for her to come to him. Night after night. Rehashing. Commitment. Marriage. He'd analyzed himself. Through the evolving friendship with Phaedra, overcoming the challenges the house presented, and the renewed relationship with Magpie, he sensed personal growth he'd not experienced in decades. And then he tore apart his values. In the end, he'd restructured his principles. The thought of losing her raked his nerves raw. If she would love him, he was prepared to accept her on her terms. He just needed her love.

Today, the call came that had his emotions on overload. He checked the time on his phone. He hadn't eaten lunch. The coffee from hours ago soured his gut as the minutes ticked away. She said she needed to see him. *Needed.* Her tone serious. The lump that formed still stuck in his throat. He didn't ask why. He wanted to *see* her. When he offered to go to her cottage, she said no. At the house. Not exactly neutral territory, but not an atmosphere of intimacy either. Was it going to be like this? He rubbed the tense muscles in his neck. She might want to do a walk-through, a closeout of his work. Not what he hoped...unless she wanted a let's-be-friends talk. He'd prefer a closeout over that.

At the sound of a car engine shutting off, his heart stuttered, and he stopped his pacing. He opened the front door. The sun, barely a whisper above Spirit Mountain, threw orange rays over her white hair and glowing skin. She wore a deep lilac-colored dress that flounced around her ankles as she navigated the steps and walkway. He couldn't remember seeing her in a dress, and the clinging fabric mesmerized him. First hugging one hip, then plastered onto her legs and breasts with the next gust of wind, a moment later whipping up to reveal shapely calves. His desire flogged him as the breeze caressed her. Her feet appeared bare until she moved close enough for him to discern the strappy tan sandals. His legs weakened from the ache of needing her.

"Little windy today." She brushed hair away from her face as she ascended the veranda steps.

Why did it seem like centuries since he'd looked into those crystal blue eyes?

Her shiny pink lips pursed, and she paused, one hand on a hip. "You're staring, again, Harlan." Her throaty chuckle teased the tightness in his groin.

"I was thinking about your dress. I can't remember you wearing dresses much. And lilac?"

"Actually, it's called periwinkle. I needed a change today. Any complaints?" She sauntered close. Her rose oil scent filled his head.

"None whatsoever."

She brushed by him.

Her flirtatious actions, her sway as she passed, and her scent fired every nerve in his body. What the hell was she up to? He followed her and shut the door behind him.

She strolled into the parlor. "This looks fantastic." Her path took her to the fireplace. "Ah. So pretty." She twirled, her dress shimmying around her body. "And the sidewalk looks great out front. The roof too. What more is there to do?"

"Painting the dining room and kitchen. Some cleanup outside." His great grandfather's remains had been moved to the cemetery in town. "We're about done. Annette is due in next week. But then I guess you know that."

"Uh-huh." She doubled back and peeked into the entry closet. "I talked to her about the desk. She's thrilled to keep it."

He followed close behind, wanting to breathe her in while he could. "Did Poppy and Primrose go home?" What he wanted to say had nothing to do with her daughters. *Do you love me, Phae?*

"They left this morning."

"I bet that left you feeling lonely." He could relate. If she thought of him as only a friend, he'd be lonely forever, even with her around.

"Yes, I always miss them after a visit. But they were like mother hens and beginning to drive me crazy." She laughed. "And I have some things I'd like to...do...without my daughters hovering." She slipped her hand into his. "Let's see how the upstairs looks."

He trailed behind her, holding onto her fingers. She glanced over her shoulder halfway up and smiled. Mischievous. What the hell? She led him into the master bedroom. When she turned into him, she slipped her other arm around his neck. "I've missed you, Harlan. Why didn't you come to see me?"

He'd missed this. Would it ever be more? "Working my butt off to finish the house."

"Is that all?" What did she want to hear? His throat went dry. He could out last her. She had to be the one to start the dialogue. How she perceived what they meant to each other. Finish the conversation they'd started three weeks ago in this same room.

"I've had a lot to do with the sapphire appraisal and sale. Kept me busy. Still working through getting accounts set up. Researching how to fund scholarships."

"And you're really giving a chunk to Nora?"

"She needs help. She's family. We share a great grandfather. Zac is helping me, or rather set me up with a lawyer who can help *her*. And she can get some psychiatric help. Maybe live out her life a happier person."

"You're something else." She brushed a kiss across his lips.

"I hope you're okay with that. Nora swore the gun went off accidentally. She thought she had the safety on, never intending to hurt anyone, just intimidate." He brushed hair from her cheek and willed himself to quit looking at the mouth he wanted to kiss. "Of course, she did conk you on the head."

"Yes. There is that. But if you can forgive her, so can I. She had no reason to shoot me, so I'm going with the accident angle. After reading the journal, I'm of the opinion she became obsessed. She's a weak natured sort. I think she wanted to set things right for her great grandmother."

He snorted. "I think she wanted to get rich, but you can take the romantic angle."

"You could've delivered the journal to me yourself instead of sending your sister." She fingered the hair at the back of his neck.

His resolve to stay neutral melted, and he slipped his hands around to encircle her waist. He wanted her—God he wanted her—but worry crowded his pleasure. What was she feeling toward him? *Say you love me, Phaedra. Beyond friendship.* "I knew you'd enjoy reading it before we gave it back to Nora. And Mags said she was going to visit you." The buttery-soft fabric of her dress did nothing to conceal the curves and heat of her body. His chest tightened with shallow breaths. "Like I said, busy trying to get this place done."

"Is that all?" She dragged the all out.

"I knew you had your daughters to keep you company. Figured you needed some recoup time." Speech grew difficult. "What more could there be?"

"Seeing me. You haven't missed me?"

"Hell, yes, I've missed you." Like the wind blew him off his feet, he didn't touch the ground when she kissed him. He'd missed her lips, the way her body melded against his, how her butt filled his hands, and her breasts crushed into his chest. But there was more. He needed more.

When she broke the kiss, he moaned.

"You're thinking too much, Harlan."

He drew back.

"Yeah, and don't deny it." They'd known each other so long she could sense unspoken words. "I can practically hear the wheels squeaking in your head."

"You saying my thought processes are rusty?"

"Ha! But wait." Backing away from him, she stopped in front of the closet. She opened the door and tugged out a box.

"What the heck is that?"

"I dropped it here yesterday when you were gone. I told Kevin to put it in this closet. I told him it was some of the new owner's things." She giggled. "But it's not." Bending, she lifted the flaps and pulled out two sleeping bags.

"Looks like you have a plan." His groin told his head to shut up and go with the flow.

She whipped off the elastic around the rolls, unzipped the zippers, and stacked the opened bags. "We didn't get to finish our last night here, together."

His heart pumped all the blood south. He smiled.

"Oh, my, there's the Harlan gaze." She reached behind her, and the sound of a zipper filled the quiet. "I can't resist that look, you know." The dress slipped off her shoulders and breasts, floated down, skimming past her hips, and gathered like a cloud around her feet. The remaining thin lace hardly qualified as undies.

Oh hell. Yes, this. But… They needed to finish the discussion that spawned angry words last time they met. He could give in, but he had to hear her say—

"Stop. Thinking." She stepped out of the cloud. Wrapped her arms around him. She pulled his shirt over his head.

When her fingers lingered, unfastening his pants, he followed orders. All thoughts gave way to sensations.

****

Only a half-moon lit the room when he rolled to his side and wrapped her in his arms. "That was—"

"Yes, it was." She kissed his chest.

"You appear to be fully healed."

"Good as new."

"Did you see enough of the house? Are you going to sign off on it as satisfactory?" He teased a finger around her lips. Hugging her tighter with his other arm, he decided he could pull the sleeping bag over them and spend the night. He didn't want to move.

"Not until the last bit of work is done. No gimme."

"Then what are you doing here?"

She canted away. Squinted into his eyes. "I told you. We needed to finish what we began before your crazy relative shot me." A half-smile tickled the corner of her mouth. "And I wanted to seduce a rich man. Never had a rich man."

"You harlot." He chuckled. "Was it worth it?"

"Oh, definitely worth it, but I have to say, the wealth doesn't seem to have affected your sexual prowess. Thank the universe."

He shifted his shoulders and rose on one elbow so he could look into her face. Always the light-hearted Phaedra. Could he draw out her serious side without spoiling this incredible, sensual moment. But it was only a moment. He needed a lifetime.

"What?" She batted long lashes.

"Nothing. I just wanted to see you better." Joy threatened to burst his chest. If only all his tomorrows could be as perfect as this point in time.

"And?"

"And nothing. Still the same beautiful Phaedra I've known forever. Or so it seems."

She rolled away and sat. Lifting her panties and bra from the pile of clothes, she stood. "I think it's been forever. Maybe a past life too." She stepped into the thin lace undies and then slipped into the equally thin lace bra.

The balloon of joy deflated. This would be the routine. This would be their affair. For how long? "Forever friends?"

"Of course." She winked as she shimmied into her dress.

A knot cinched tighter in his stomach. He rose to get dressed. If he asked her if this was all there was, would even this much evaporate?

"Do you like where you live in Miners' Mile?" The zip of her dress mirrored a closure to something larger.

"It's okay." Mundane conversation. He tensed.

"You always liked The Ravine, didn't you?"

"Yes, but when I needed a home for Garrett and me, when we moved back, I had two choices. Nothing in The Ravine."

"You like my cottage, don't you?"

"Yes, I like your cottage. Why? Are you having second thoughts about selling this place?"

"No. It's sold. A done deal. Why would you think that?'

"Well, what's with the house talk? Miners' Mile or The Ravine. My house or your cottage. Sounds like you're thinking about houses."

She set her hands on her hips, tilted her head, and frowned. "You're out of sorts all of a sudden."

"No. It's not all of a sudden." He zipped his jeans. "We have the best sex ever—no, we make great love. I made love to you, Phae, and then you hop up and talk about where's the best place to live. What are we doing here?" So much for letting her control the direction. Breath caught in his chest as if the uncertainty interrupted an exhale. He could hold back only so long.

"What in Hades, Harlan? We weren't done? I didn't know you weren't ready to talk." She reached behind her and unzipped her dress halfway. "Did you want more? I didn't mean to—"

"Phaedra! What the hell?"

She burst out laughing.

"What's so damned funny?" His neck and ears burned hot.

"I'm sorry. You really are in a serious mood. Really. Sorry. I'm teasing." She waved a hand through the air. "But the house part was me trying to talk about us." She rubbed the scar on her chin.

He cooled with her rambling and her obvious case of nerves. "Us?"

"Yeah, us." She plopped onto the rumpled sleeping bags and patted next to her.

His heart lurched. He lowered on shaky legs.

"I've missed you horribly over the last three weeks. When I'd smell the coffee brewing in the mornings, I'd picture you at the kitchen counter. Not my daughter. After dinner, I'd imagine you on the patio with me having a glass of wine, not Poppy. I sound like a horrible mother. I love them and enjoyed them immensely, but I missed you and what could be."

"What *could* be, Phae?" He scooted sideways to face her. "Good friends? Forever friends?"

"Of course. Always and forever. I don't want this..." she gestured to the sleeping bags, "to get in the way."

He rolled his shoulders, tried to bring his breathing to a steady rhythm.

"That's why I asked about your house and my cottage. I love my little cottage, and you could improve upon it. We could be very comfortable there."

The dim light from the half-moon shining in the window held her in a spotlight. He leaned closer, staring into her eyes with cautious hope. "You're asking me to move in with you?"

"It would be just plain stupid to have two houses."

"It would?"

"You're making this really difficult."

"*How* am I making *what* difficult? You're making this difficult for me. Sounds like you want a roommate. A live-in..." He rubbed his eyes with the heels of his hands.

"I've thought about us a lot over the last three weeks, Har. Actually, I probably thought about myself more. When you asked me why I've never been married, I gave you the chronology of how I ended up alone. But the truth of it is I never *wanted* to get married. I didn't need a piece of paper with the power to change people. I don't need marriage to prove my love. And that piece of paper, the tradition, locks you up. The idea is claustrophobic to me." She gestured to the closet. "Just like I experienced in there."

He took her hand, kissed her knuckles. "We don't need to get married, Phae. I've also done a lot of thinking. If I have your love, the long-haul kind of love, I don't need a written guarantee."

She chuckled.

He continued. "Things are good between us. I like the idea of living in one house. We can figure out where later. But the most important part of this whole thing is the us part. With or without marriage, all I ask is for you to love me as much as I love you. And to trust me, Phae. Can you do that?"

"I've been afraid of risking our relationship, of losing the best guy friend a lady can have. You're willing to give up marriage for me?" She slid onto his lap and wrapped her arms around his neck. Her kiss was short, gentle. She added two more on top of the one.

His whole body thrummed with joy.

"So, shall we live in the cottage? Or do you plan on buying one of the mansions since you've got more money? I can understand. I guess."

"House talk again. No, I don't give a damn about a bigger house. That's not the point, Phae. I love you. And—"

She laughed. "I love you more. Like a friend, like the best sex toy in the world, and like a forever live-in, soul mate, partner. And I promise to always love you more than you love me and trust you. I do trust you, Har." She kissed him hard and fast. "Will you marry me, Harlan Muse MacKenzie?"

"What?" He must have heard her wrong. "I go a little senseless when you kiss me, but I thought you said…or maybe—"

"You heard me. If I'm going to do *all* that other stuff like trust and love, I might as well get the guarantee you mentioned."

"Ah, well, you better read the fine print. Most guarantees are limited."

She dug her fingers into his sides, tickling him.

"Ah!" He whipped sideways, kissed her as he pushed her back onto the sleeping bags. "There will be no tickling in this marriage."

"Oh yes, there will be. I'm not dumping decades of the way we were. Friends and lovers. Husband and wife." She shook her head and gazed upward. "What in Hades am I doing?"

He slipped her dress off her shoulders. "Exactly what you should. I love you, Phae." He kissed her. "Friends and lovers. Husband and wife."

A NOTE FROM THE AUTHOR

Although I've lived in other places, my heart resides in the west. Born and raised in Arizona, I have a love for the rural and small-town atmosphere from the southern desert to the northern high country. Legends of miners in the mountains of southern and central Arizona have always fascinated me.

Another fascination is the era of the 1960s. Although most might conjure the hippie settlements of California and Oregon, Arizona had its own hippie communities.

With The MacKenzie Chronicles, I took my interest of legendary mining communities and the 60s subculture to create stories centered around the MacKenzies who live in the contemporary and purportedly haunted city of Joshua, Arizona—1800s mining town turned ghost town turned hippie community turned tourist town.

I hope you enjoy reading The MacKenzie Chronicles as much as I enjoy writing them.

ABOUT THE AUTHOR

Brenda Whiteside is the author of suspenseful, action-adventure stories with a touch of romance. Mostly. After living in six states and two countries—so far—she and her husband have decided they are gypsies at heart, splitting their time between Central Arizona and the RV life. They share their home with a rescue dog named Amigo. While FDW is fishing, Brenda writes.

Visit Brenda at https://www.brendawhiteside.com
FaceBook: https://www.facebook.com/BrendaWhitesideAuthor
Twitter: https://twitter.com/brendawhitesid2
She blogs and has guests: https://brendawhiteside.blogspot.com/

Join the Quarterly Newsletter Group to stay up to date on Brenda's writing life and to be eligible for quarterly and year-end gifts that only members of QNG receive. Visit Brenda's Webpage to join.

Books by Brenda Whiteside
Sleeping with the Lights On
The Morning After
Amanda in the Summer
Post-War Dreams
The Love and Murder Series
       The Art of Love and Murder
       Southwest of Love and Murder
       A Legacy of Love and Murder
       The Power of Love and Murder
       The Deep Well of Love and Murder
The MacKenzie Chronicles
       Secrets of the Ravine
       Mystery on Spirit Mountain

Audiobooks by Brenda Whiteside
Sleeping with the Lights On
The Love and Murder Series
       The Art of Love and Murder
       Southwest of Love and Murder
       A Legacy of Love and Murder
       The Power of Love and Murder
       The Deep Well of Love and Murder

Made in the USA
Columbia, SC
08 October 2021